This book is dedicated to my father, Vytautas Valasinavicius.
I miss him every single day.

MADMAN ACROSS THE WATER:

THE CURSE AWAKENS

BY CAROLINE ANGEL

CHAPTER ONE

The truck pulled up to the edge of the woods, a grassed parking area surrounded by bollards, a loose chain hanging between each pole, and litter bins dotted here and there. While it wasn't as nice as the other side of the woods, where the park was located, there were still some picnic tables and a small amenities block that housed a unisex bathroom and a drinking faucet. The town planners had thought it a great place for hikers to park and walk through the magnificent soaring trees; a place to rest after a long walk, or just take in the view of the town, the lake, and the rolling hills behind the forest.

It was a little-used area, the forest not being a very popular destination for hikers, though no one ever discussed why. For a little while there had been a steady stream of visitors after the 'unsolved' murders five years ago, the curious and daring venturing into the dark, dry woods to feel the eerie atmosphere, and imagine the terror and horror that had unfolded for those taken and killed.

The novelty wore off after a while, and though a few people still made their way into the forest, time had dulled the memories of folks. The strangeness seemed surreal and nothing more than overactive imaginations now.

Today the stories were mostly told around a campfire, or at children's sleepovers, and the details were embellished and muddied. The fear and caution about the woods died down, and the locals largely ignored the pine forest. That is, most of the locals. Some had a great deal of interest in these woods. A great deal indeed.

The people in the parking area today were not locals, and they had not heard any of the creepy stories about the woods. All they wanted to do was get their job done and get out of there.

The three burly men from Crosspine Timber and Sawmill clambered out of the truck, all dressed in high visibility safety gear, donning their helmets as they climbed out.

"Joe, grab the shit from the back, okay? Mark and me can see which trees'll give us a good sample."

"Yeah, yeah, yeah, I always get the menial labor jobs," Joe joked as he opened the door on the back of the truck. As the other two men walked over to the woods, he hawked a great wad of spit at his feet and hefted out a large toolbox, groaning as he carried it over to his workmates.

"You want the chainsaws, Gary?"

"Yup, we need to take some samples of a few of the trees, make sure they're consistent. We can drill some holes and take some bigger chunks of others. Maybe even cut a couple down, take a few pictures."

"This is the best plantation I've seen in a long while," marveled Joe as he walked over to the trees. "Must've been planted ages ago, look how thick the trunks are!"

"Weird that they're so thick when they're planted so close together, but yeah, looks like we'll have a few months' work here. Patrick will be jacking off all over the place when he sees this." Gary laughed at his own joke and opened the toolbox, taking out a core sample drill. He snapped a battery unit onto it and walked up to the closest tree as Mark grabbed the sample bags and a sharpie to label them. The three men walked into the woods, the path leading them out of the warm summer sun into the dark, cold forest.

"Fuck me, it's like you turned on the air conditioner! This is freezing! Jesus Christ!"

"Fuck, you complain a lot, Joe," Mark rubbed his arms. "It is cold, though. No light gets in here, no warmth, then."

"You two guys shut up and help me here. Mark, get some pictures. You grabbed the camera, didn't you?"

"Whoops no, I'll just get it." Mark handed the sample bags to Joe as he ran back to the car.

Gary shook his head and walked up to the closest tree. "Maybe get a flashlight too, it's really dark in here," he called to Mark as he chose the first tree to take a sample from. He got down on one knee in front of the tree and held the core drill against it, pulling the trigger. The cordless drill buzzed and whined, and Gary leant his weight behind to help bore a hole into the sturdy trunk.

It was a struggle, but eventually the blade caught, and he started to drill, the effort making his arms ache. He stopped the drill and tabbed the reverse switch, withdrawing the sample and dropping it into the bag Joe was holding. Joe took a yellow plastic tag and tore it in half; one half went into the sample bag and the other was hammered into the tree. Gary continued to take a few samples from different trees as Joe tagged them, while Mark worked with the camera, the flash illuminating the darkness as he took multiple pictures.

"Okay, I think that'll do for samples, let's cut one down and take some cross sections." Gary turned and looked at the trees on either side of the path. "There's no room to drop one in here, and I am over this cold. Let's take one from the perimeter, they're all the same anyway."

"Yeah, they are." Mark was scrolling through the pictures he had taken, checking he had all that he needed. "They are all *exactly* the same, from what I got here. Even the branches are the same."

"Who cares? That's for the tech guys to worry about. I'll get the grapples, who's turn is it to cut?"

"Yours, you jerk," Mark laughed. "I'm always getting stuck cutting, and these trees are like fucking iron. Your turn to rip one up."

Joe donned heavy gloves and safety glasses before putting on his protective earmuffs, his colleagues doing the same. He lifted the heavy chainsaw and set to felling one of the trees. As Mark had predicted, the tree was hard, the bark resisting the saw as it barely put a mark into the enormous trunk. Joe let the saw drop and looked at Gary, shrugging and pointing to the small marks he had made. Gary nodded and walked to the truck, taking out an even larger chainsaw. He gave it a few pulls to start it and the roar echoed through the forest, the silence broken by the loud, abrasive noise.

Joe stepped back as Gary attacked the tree, the larger saw finally catching and tearing into the timber. He leaned into the saw, the slow progress and the heavy saw tiring him quickly. He handed it over to Joe, who got a little further, before letting Mark have a go.

It took over an hour, but they finally heard the crack as the huge tree shifted and started to fall. The men were very experienced and they set the fall of the tree perfectly, allowing it to crash down into the clearing, right alongside the parking lot.

"That's one motherfucker of a tree there, guys." Joe wiped his forehead with the back of his sleeve. "If they're all like that it's going to take a marathon to cut down the whole bloody forest."

"Not our problem." Gary shook his arms before lifting the chainsaw. "Let's grab a few slices, then we can head back for lunch. I tell you; we should get a bonus for this sucker. I've never seen such hard wood on a pine tree!"

"Might be a special variety. Maybe you'll get to name it or something," Mark smiled.

Gary laughed at the thought. "The Garypine. Hah, I like it," he joked as he put his earmuffs back on before pulling the starter cord, the roar of the chainsaw again assaulting the calm summer day. From atop a hill nearby, overlooking the parking lot and the men cutting the trees, a woman sat astride her painted horse, her long hair braided down her back. The early summer breeze lifted her horse's mane and tail, making them look like a picture postcard of Americana. She lifted her binoculars to her eyes and watched the men, a twisted mass of anger and fear combining and rolling in her stomach. She watched as the men took slices of the mighty pine they had felled, their chainsaw assaulting her ears even though she was so far away. She watched as they packed it all up and drove off, leaving the canopy of the tree crushed and broken on the ground, a massive wounded body of a once majestic, living thing, now laid out in a grotesque display of waste.

She picked up her reins and turned the horse to home, galloping off through the tall grass as the winds whipped about her.

CHAPTER TWO

The morning was clear, a crisp and cold dew adorning the neatly cut grass with a halo of bright shining diamonds, as the early morning birds put throat to song to herald in the first day of summer. Along the edge of the lake, water irises were starting to bloom, the impossibly vibrant purples and blues reflecting on the mirrored surface of the still water. The lake was very long, it swung around one side of the town, a park and a school bordering one side, and a tall stand of woods on the other. Here and there brightly colored butterflies flitted amongst the last of the late spring flowers, and the deep melody of a bullfrog broke the stillness of the early quiet.

The sun glinted on the lake as a gentle circle of ripples broke the perfect surface, dragonflies touching down before immediately taking off again, barely missing the hungry mouths of the fish awaiting their next meal. From across the water, out of the densely cold and dark woods, a soft, white fog drifted onto the grass, then touched the surface of the water. It was a strange, low-lying mist which coated the ground as it rolled and swirled, waves breaking like those of the sea against the beach. It slid out across the water and covered the lake, and as it moved all the wildlife that were singing and chirping fell silent, each frog, each bird, each insect silencing their morning joy as the cold fog washed over and around them.

The mist covered the entire lake, rolling right up to the manicured gardens of the park, before it stopped, still and silent, as if it waited for something. No one saw the mist, no one was around in the breaking dawn to see the strange white fog as it started to withdraw, pulling back from whence it came, softly, silently, disappearing back in the woods.

The morning song of the birds and insects resumed, and the lake returned to its brilliant beauty, ready for the day of kayakers and picnickers to grace its presence.

CHAPTER THREE

The woods were about the best he'd ever seen. He hadn't seen more than some pictures taken a few hundred yards into the woods, the drone flyover footage, and what was in front of him here, in the clearing, but so far, they were phenomenal. In all the years he'd worked for Crosspine Timber and Sawmill, Patrick Halls had never come across such a pristine crop of naturally growing pines. This forest would make his company, and himself, a very large amount of money. Patrick smiled to himself, and subconsciously patted the hip pocket of his designer rip-off pants, where his bill fold was kept. Yes, a very large amount indeed.

"What do you think? Would your company be interested?" Albert White, the works and civic planning manager for the local Campbelltown government asked. Albert was sweating despite the coolness in the shadows of the great trees, his shirt was tightly buttoned, his clip-on tie high on his throat. He was a large man, very large, his balding head and rolls of chins presented a very unattractive, and sweaty, visage.

Patrick tried to hide his smile before he turned to the rather obese man, he didn't want to appear too eager. If he had to pay more than his original quote to get the rights to log this forest, then it would impact his profit margin. And Patrick was all about the profit margin.

"Seems okay, so far. I mean, I'll have to look inside the woods, and we'll have to do a few feasibility tests, but it seems okay."

"Awesome! It's rather cold in there, do you have a jacket?" Albert reached into his car and pulled out his heavy parka. "Trust me on this one."

Patrick shook his head. "I don't really feel the cold, and we have no need to be in there very long. I'll be fine, this cardigan is an angora mix, it's really quite warm."

"Well, you were warned!" Albert laughed as he handed Patrick a flashlight. "It's also very dark in there. The trees are so closely grown that the canopy pretty much cuts out all light."

Patrick accepted the flashlight and followed Albert into the forest. He expected his senses to be hit with the usual scents of a forest, the dampness, the rich loamy aroma of mosses and rotting leaves, the sharp acrid scents of animal excrements and guano, the fresh sting of pine needles, of bark, of soils, of so many wonderful, tantalizing aromas.

He was mildly surprised that there were none of these scents. The path, mostly clear, just sprinkled with rusty colored pine needles here and there, was dry, and weed free. The scrubby, twisted undergrowth that grew off each side of the path was sparse and looked unhealthy. Patrick couldn't decide if he'd ever seen these plants before but didn't really care other than to be pleased that the clearing of logs wouldn't be hampered by a mass of useless shrubs. And by the sound of silence in the forest, no protected or endangered species.

Patrick frowned a little. The forest was eerily silent, there was no sound of anything other than the footfalls of the two men. Outside of the woods there were a cacophony of birds singing, brightly colored butterflies, beetles chirping and buzzing, and the azure rainbow gloss of dragonflies from the nearby lake.

Inside the woods it was as dark and silent as a mausoleum.

The trees were enormous, their trunks wide and straight, their branches lifting high into the air, into the closely knitted canopy that blocked out all light bar a few errant beams here and there, shining down like spotlights hung from the high dark ceiling of the forest.

Eerily quiet, and, as Albert had advised, unusually dark, Patrick found his flashlight handy as he leaned in to look at the tree trunk and structure of many of the towering pines.

"You're sure this wasn't planted intentionally? The trees are almost in perfectly straight rows, like a plantation."

Albert shook his head. "We have no idea where it came from, the woods have been here since Campbelltown was just a little frontier settlement. It never gets any bigger either, the trees don't self-seed, or germinate, or even throw out suckers."

"Pines don't usually throw suckers," Patrick noted. "Though I just realized I don't see any pinecones, either. Odd. I'm not even sure what species of pine these are, but they look to be very healthy, and surprisingly large, considering how close together they are. That's very unusual. Anyway, I think I've seen all I need to see from this side. I'd like to take a look at a few other parts of the woods, just to make sure that the quality is consistent, and then we can get down to brass tacks."

Albert smiled. He was nearing retirement, and the sale of the timber in these woods would make him a hefty bonus, come settlement time. And then, of course, the developers would be ready to move in. If this side of the lake was forest free and ready for some infrastructure, Albert could quite likely profit from a second bonus when the city sold off the land.

Today was shaping up to be a very good day, indeed.

"You weren't wrong about it being cold in here," remarked Patrick as he pulled his thin cardigan tighter around himself. "I swear the temperature has dropped the further we walked in."

"I did warn you, though I have to agree, it's much colder than when we first started in." Albert rubbed his hands together then shoved them into his parka pockets, the flashlight stowed in his back pants pocket. "I didn't notice the fog before, either. Strange, isn't it?"

Patrick looked down at the soft white fog. It *was* strange, the way it flowed and ebbed around his shoes. It couldn't be more than a couple of inches deep, and it was flowing like water. He hadn't noticed it at all until Albert had said something, but he was sure it wasn't there before. "Do you get this kind of fog often?"

Albert shrugged. "I'm not from Campbelltown, I commute to the office from the next town over. Truth be told, I've never been in the woods before, only ever driven around the outskirts."

Patrick stamped his feet, making the fog swirl and dance around his ankles. "Damn stuff is making my feet freeze!"

"Let's head out and have a look at the other side, then I'll take you back to the office for a hot coffee, get the chills out of your bones."

Patrick nodded. "Think that's a good idea, though it'll probably take a bit more than coffee to do that!"

Albert laughed and led the way back towards the forest edge. The fog had completely covered the path, but it wasn't hard to see the way. The trees surrounding the path were close together, some so close that it was nearly impossible to pass through, so he followed the gap in the trees that could only have been a path. The temperature seemed to be dropping, and Patrick could see his breath in a white cloud as he walked. He regretted not grabbing a jacket before entering the forest, he was near frozen to the bone. He could no longer feel his feet, the strange fog that was covering them was like a river of ice, and the cold was quite literally seeping into his bones.

They walked briskly, the two men, the plumes of white mist flowing from their mouths as they hurried to the edge of the forest and the warmth of the early summer sunshine.

"We seem to be walking for a long time, Albert, are you sure we're going the right way?"

Albert stopped and turned around, his face flushed with the cold, his brow knitted in confusion. "There's only one way to go. The path we came in on didn't have any other paths that led off, there were no forks, or other trails. We have to be going the right way. Hey, don't think I'm crazy or anything, but is the fog, um, glowing?"

Patrick screwed up his face, his shaggy eyebrows raised in disbelief. "No, I don't think so. Are you sure this is the right path? You said you've never been in these woods before. I'm thinking you got us both lost, my friend."

Albert scratched the top of his bald pate. "No, no, I'm sure we are going the right way. Pretty sure, I mean, there's no other way to go, is there?" He looked back down at the fog, and he was certain that it glowed, very softly, like there was a nightlight on the path.

Shrugging, he turned back and continued on his way. Patrick noted with much distaste that the freezing cold fog had risen dramatically and was now swirling around his thighs. He walked faster, his arms hugging himself as he struggled to keep warm. He didn't want to tell Albert, but he noticed the strange glow in the fog, it *was* illuminated, just a little.

"Well, I think we are definitely headed the right way, I can hear music, just faintly. Can you hear it?" Albert increased the pace, the woods had started to make him feel very uneasy, the darkness, the silence, and the weird, cold fog was like nothing he had ever seen before. He was sure they hadn't walked this far in, and they had meandered along the path, whereas now they were practically running. They should be at the clearing by now, they should be standing in the warm sun, not freezing their toes to icicles in these dark and creepy woods.

"I think I hear something, yeah, I think you're right!" Patrick was right on Albert's heels, desperate to be out of this weird place. "The fog is getting thicker, and colder, my nuts are sucked up so high I think they're inside my pelvis."

Albert would have laughed if he could still feel his lips, but the cold and the strange fog had stolen his humor. The music was still faint, it was just a touch of some half heard, almost melodic tune that he couldn't quite make out.

"It's strange, Albert, I swear it's music, but the more I try and listen the harder it is to figure it out. I gotta tell you, this place is really starting to freak me out. Can you see the clearing yet?"

Albert turned his head to answer as something caught his foot and he fell, crashing in a heap into the fog. His hands were clenched tightly in his pockets and afforded no softening to his fall. Landing hard, Albert jarred his chin on the ground, biting his teeth into his tongue. He gasped, breathing in the frigid air as it burned his lungs and throat; it had to be below zero. He rolled onto his back and struggled to sit up, his knees stinging, his pants torn, and blood from his mouth dripping down his chin.

He lifted his arms up, thinking Patrick hadn't helped him to his feet as he probably couldn't see him.

When no helping hand appeared, Albert heaved his heavy frame up, gasping for breath in the frigid fog, his face and hands feeling the sharp sting of the ice-cold air. His head spun for a moment and he bent at the waist, his hands on his lower thighs as he took a couple of breaths to steady the spots dancing in front of his eyes. Bent like this, his face was completely covered with fog, and he needed to straighten, or he wouldn't be able to breathe any more, the cold making it too hard to inhale.

Fingers and feet numb, he kept his eyes closed for a moment to soothe himself. "You could've leant me a hand, Patrick." When there came no answer, he looked to see why Patrick was not responding, only to find that there was no sign of him. He turned, slowly, but could not see Patrick anywhere. He was sure the man had not gone past him, the path was fairly narrow, and Albert had splayed across most of it. In the thick fog, there was no way that Patrick could have stepped over him without at least bumping some part of him.

"Patrick?" Albert's voice was hesitant, worried, and very confused. "Dude? Where are you?" The mild alarm he had been feeling when the fog appeared was now turning into a full-blown panic. "Patrick? *PATRICK*!" He tried yelling louder, but there was no answer, just the soft echo of his words as they bounced off the trees and returned to him in a hollow parody of his own voice.

He stepped around a bit, feeling with his foot in case Patrick had also fallen, but couldn't feel anything around him. He couldn't find what had caught his foot to spill him onto the path, the path felt flat and even, just as it had when they first walked into these creepy woods.

The music seemed a little louder, and Albert was torn between looking for the timber company man or hoofing it out of there and calling for help.

The fog was getting higher, he could actually see it rolling towards him, looking like a foamy wave at the beach. He'd never seen fog like this before, not ever, and now, standing here on his own, the music all around him, but still too distant to make it out, he felt fear start to grow in his belly.

"Patrick?" Albert's voice was thin, frightened, and high pitched. "Are you there?" Remembering the flashlight in his back pocket, Albert pulled it out and shone it around. The glow from the fog wasn't enough to illuminate the woods, and Albert thought perhaps it was darker now than before. His heart was starting to beat faster, and despite the cold he could feel a prickly sweat break out under his arms and along his spine.

His light caught something in the distance, further down the path. At first, he thought it was just another tree trunk, but a second glance made him unsure. Had it moved? Was it moving? "PATRICK!" Albert squinted and leaned forward, trying to see if the man was coming towards him or walking away, back into the woods. "Patrick, c'mon, man, you're going the wrong way!"

Albert lifted the flashlight higher; he had lost sight of the movement. Taking a hesitant step forward he shone the light side to side, trying to pick up the movement again.

There.

He could see something.

"Patrick?"

The movement was definitely someone walking, someone coming towards him.

Someone, but not Patrick.

The flashlight wasn't revealing much, but what Albert could see was enough to make him feel dizzy again. This was someone tall, someone very tall. Too tall.

"*What the fuck*..." They had to be about ten feet tall, he thought. Ten feet tall, and thin, like a stick insect. A fucking *big* stick insect.

Albert started to walk backwards, the fear that had begun to twist in his belly was now a knife, slicing his insides, spreading the horror throughout his entire being. The thing was getting closer, and Albert could see that it was no man.

Impossibly tall, the fog that was lapping at Albert's chest didn't even cover the tall man's knees. The knees that lifted too high when he walked, the thin, black clad knees that lifted as high as Albert stood. It had arms, long, winding, waving arms, that seemed far too long for even a thing that big.

Too scared to turn his back on it, Albert started to shuffle backwards faster, an almost half jogging trot as he tried to get away from the thing's advance. The tall man-thing was gaining on him, it was fast, the giant steps covering much more ground than Albert's shuffle.

Realizing he would soon be overtaken, Albert turned to run but his feet got tangled together and again, he fell.

This time he managed to catch himself with his hands, breaking his fall, saving his face. His knees took the brunt of his weight and again he took several layers of skin off but he didn't stop to notice. Within a moment he was up, running as fast as he could, running as fast as his obese frame would allow, not looking back, not stopping, not thinking, just running.

His heart was pounding in his ears and he couldn't catch his breath, but he didn't stop. He couldn't hear anything behind him, he couldn't hear the music, he couldn't hear the steps of the thing, the pounding of his ears drowning out everything but the rushing pulse of his struggling heart.

Before him, impossibly close but still so far, he could see the opening of the woods, the soft glow of the summer sun a tantalizing beacon of hope. Somehow, he managed to find an extra burst of speed, and he ran, ran with all his might, ran with every fiber of his being, just as a long, white hand reached to grab him.

Gasping, he broke the edge of the woods and fell forward and down, bouncing away from the grasp of the thing that reached for him as he rolled and tumbled onto the grass. All around him it was warm and sunny; no fog, no creepy music, no thing that chased him. His head felt like it would burst, his heart pounding so hard that he was sure it was tearing in two, but he was free of the woods.

"Hey, hey buddy, are you okay?" A voice, a man's voice, called out to him, but bright pulsating lights appeared in front of Albert's eyes, and his ears were ringing. His chest was hurting, it was agonizing, and he couldn't look up to see who spoke, couldn't answer around his dry tongue, couldn't warn them of the thing coming for them from the woods.

Hands grabbed him, somehow, he was rolled onto his back, hands touching him, loosening his collar, asking him if he was okay as the dancing spots grew dark and became nothing but dark, nothing but emptiness, nothing at all.

Just nothing.

CHAPTER FOUR

"Boss, you gotta see this shit. It's going to kill me, I tell you." Mike shook his head. "Seriously, why do I have to break in the new guys?"

Wallis took a sip from his cold coffee and winked at his blonde-haired deputy. "I figured these boys needed to see middle-aged white privilege at its best."

"I'm not middle-aged, boss, that would be more like you. And I'm hip with the new kids, jive with the lingo, W.T.F and L.O.L. out loud."

"Sir, that shows you are absolutely not down with the lingo." A bright-eyed young deputy walked into the office carrying two take away coffee cups. "Here's your latte. And we don't buy into that white privileged stuff. People are people, Jacob and I are just normal guys like you three."

"A lot more handsome than us guys, I have to say," Shirl was laughing. "Anyway, we're lucky to have you, even if Mike gets all worked up about you doing things differently. He never went to college and don't understand the computer anyway."

"Well Jacob has offered to teach you how to use it a few times now." Shirl accepted the second coffee from Aaron. "Thanks for this, Mike gave you guys the money, right?"

"No, the Sheriff did," answered Jacob as he walked in, a paper tray of coffees in his hand and a bag of donuts in the other. "Alicia sent these, too. Says to say hi to Alex."

Wallis sat his cold coffee back on the desk and accepted the hot takeout cup from the young deputy.

"Despite Mike's bitching, we're all very glad to have you two here. Though why anyone would want to come to this town from the big smoke is beyond me."

"The girls are prettier here," laughed Aaron.

"And they like to see two black dudes in uniform, it's a nice break from all the middle-aged white men," Jacob added as everyone laughed.

"Not middle-aged," muttered Mike as he reached for a ringing telephone. "Deputy Taggert speaking."

"Anyway, Alicia can say hi to Alex herself. He's going to stop by the diner before he gets here, he needs to drop his sister off for her shift. I'm sure she'll be waiting out the front for him to pull up."

"Boss," Mike had one hand over the mouthpiece of the phone.

"She's a pretty little thing, that Alicia. Really got the hots for your boy, Sheriff!" Aaron smiled.

"Boss," Mike called again, a little more insistent.

"She can keep her eyes elsewhere; he needs to be on time this afternoon so I can take my brother to his appointment." Wallis took another sip of his coffee, grimacing as he burned his tongue.

"Well, she may be pretty, but she doesn't hold a candle to that daughter of yours, sir," Jacob teased. "I think one of us needs to ask her out."

"She's not legal, boys. And don't forget, I carry a gun!" Wallis frowned at his handsome young deputies. "Besides, she's got her eyes set on going to college in a big city and won't let the wandering eyes of any small-town jerks distract her."

"*BOSS!*" Mike yelled, his hand still covering the phone. "You really need to take this call."

"What is it, Mike? Can't you handle it?" Wallis strode over and took the phone. "Sheriff Wallis speaking."

23

"What's going on, Mike?" Shirl asked, his voice in a whisper.

"Something happened at the woods. Local laws guy collapsed, heart attack they think."

"So why does the boss have to know?"

Mike looked grim. "Guy from a timber company is missing. And something else. Before the laws guy passed out, he muttered something about a thing in the woods. A tall, thin, scary thing."

Shirl's face lost all color and he sat down with a thump. "It's gotta be a mistake. He probably hallucinated, or something."

"What about the missing guy, Shirl? Missing in the woods?" Mike ran a hand through his close-cropped hair. "I'm telling you man, the guy at the hospital sounded freaked."

"You know it's gotta be a mistake, you know that."

The two younger detectives exchanged glances as they waited for Wallis to be finished with the call. They were confused, and curious as to what the older deputies were talking about.

The Sheriff hung up the phone and looked at the grim expressions of Shirl and Mike. "Nothing conclusive on what happened, but we need to search for the timber company guy. Aaron, Jacob, you two boys go and check out the council offices and get me some details on who this timber guy is, and who Albert White is. Mike, Shirl, saddle up, you need to go check the woods and see what exactly happened."

"Is it back, boss?" Shirl asked.

"Excuse me, but is *what* back? Is there something we should know?" Jacob asked.

Wallis glared at the young deputies. "You should know that I told you to go and see who this timber company guy is. We need to know who exactly we're looking for. Anything else relevant pops up and I'll let you know. And tell Michelle on your way out, so she knows where you are. Get her to give Alex and Ayden a call, see if they can come in early."

All the men sprang into action, the two younger men leaving by the front door, stopping at the reception desk as instructed.

Mike and Shirl followed Wallis into the car park, the Sheriff waving them towards the squad car before speaking again.

"Listen up, guys, we don't know exactly what's happened here, okay? Just go and see what's going on, see if there really is anyone missing. The paramedic I spoke to said the sick guy was babbling, so they couldn't be certain, but there were two cars at the woods, and only one man came out."

"It can't be back, can it, boss? We killed that thing, I mean, it disappeared, there was nothing left!" Shirl looked at Wallis, his face still pale.

"Colin died because of that, your nephew, so many others, but we got it, didn't we? It's been five years, more'n five years, and nothing till now?" Mike put a hand on Shirl's shoulder. "Wouldn't it have been back before now if it was still alive?"

Wallis took off his cap and ran a hand through his thinning hair. "Well, you'd think so, but honestly, guys, I'm hoping this is all just a very sick man hallucinating as he was having a heart attack." He slapped the roof of the squad car and headed back inside, his stomach in knots. *Was it back? Was the nightmare just beginning again?* He felt that he would have known if it was. Or if he didn't then his kids, or brother, would have felt something.

They hadn't said anything, so Wallis hoped that it was just a guy hallucinating, his mind taking him to the scary campfire stories from his childhood.

With all his being, he hoped that was all it was.

CHAPTER FIVE

Harriet drummed her fingers on her desk. This class was taking forever, or at least it seemed that way. She was a junior at Campbeltown High, and a good student. Not sporty like her brother, she was more academic, and usually enjoyed most classes.

Just not this one.

The substitute teacher was about as interesting as the wads of gum stuck to the underside of her desk, and it was all she could do not to yawn, again. She shifted restlessly in her seat, and could hear the shuffle of other feet, the sighs and murmurs behind her indicating her classmates were just as bored as she was.

How this guy ever thought his career as a teacher was something that was suited to him was beyond her comprehension, clearly, he didn't enjoy his work, and his droning monotone made sure that no one in the entire class enjoyed it, either.

Stifling another yawn, she surreptitiously slipped her cell phone from her pocket and checked the time. Jeez, another fifteen minutes before she could escape this ridiculous man, and the wasted class time. She yawned, this time making no effort to hide it, and sighed. She was worn out before she even got to work, it seemed like this was going to be a very long-assed day.

"Well, class, that is the end of my summary," the teacher droned. "As you have all been very well-behaved students, I'm going to let you out to lunch early. Please be quiet as you leave, so as not to disturb any other students still in their classes."

Harry felt like cheering, this was the best news of the day. A long lunch, and no more Mr. Substitute.

"Did you bring your own lunch?" Veronika, her best friend, asked as they shouldered their bags and headed to their lockers.

Harriet smiled at the red-haired girl. "Absolutely! I can't eat that cafeteria food, not even if my life depended on it, Ronni."

"Cool beans! Let's go stake our claim at the best table, my girl, and await our audience!" Ronni laughed.

Harriet stowed her bag, grabbed her lunch from her locker, and waited while Ronni did the same. The day was bright and sunny, a beautiful summer's day and the girls headed to the prime table in the outside area. As juniors, they were the undisputed users of the main tables, though they were not always first to grab the best table, the one with the view to the Junior boys' locker rooms.

It was here that Harry, Ronni, and their friends would discuss the end of this year at school, the dances, the boys going in and out of the locker rooms, fashion, TV, and social media. Everything that was important to girls their age.

Harry dropped her lunch bag, and as she bent down to grab it her head spun. She stood, grabbing the handrail on the side to steady herself. She felt dizzy, and her stomach was rolling. The weird feeling had come over her suddenly. She started to sweat yet she was suddenly cold, and a greasy foul taste was on her tongue.

"Hey, babe, you okay?" Ronni touched Harry on the shoulder. "You're sweating like a footballer after a game!"

Harry looked at her and tried to focus her eyes. Ronni was saying something else, but it didn't make sense. And she was moving, strangely, like she was swaying.

"What?" Harry tried to shake her head to clear it, but it just made her feel even dizzier.

Ronni spoke again, but to Harry it seemed as if she were under water, the words sounded hollow and muffled, and everything was out of focus. She tried to wipe her forehead, but her hand wouldn't do what she was asking it to.

"I don't understand you," Harry's words were slurred, her tongue felt too big for her mouth. She could tell Ronni looked frightened, but she didn't understand why. Right now, she didn't really understand anything.

Ronni grabbed her and Harry's head rolled back on her shoulders before she collapsed in a heap, her lunch bag again falling to the ground. The last thing she heard was Ronni screaming for help before everything went black.

CHAPTER SIX

"Hey Dad." Alex was much taller than his father, his blonde curls cropped into a sedate style in keeping with his position as deputy. His uniform was crisply ironed, and he wore it well. Many a girl hoped to catch the young man's eye, his handsome, chiseled features were everything the young women in the town desired.

"Thanks for coming in so early, I know you had plans today." Wallis stood up from his desk. "Did Michelle fill you in?"

"A bit, she said some guy had a heart attack at the woods, and that there may be a second guy, but no one is sure what the story is?"

"That's the gist of it, yeah. Think one man has wandered off in the woods and needs a little help finding his way out. Shirl and Mike have gone to suss out the situation. I've got to get your uncle to his appointment, I didn't want to leave the station with only Michelle to look after things."

"I haven't told Harry I can't give her a lift; I was hoping that I'd get a chance to slip out by then, or maybe you can take her after Uncle Simon's appointment?"

Wallis shrugged. "We should be able to work it out. Say, Alex, I gotta ask, and I know this is a weird question, but have you been feeling anything, I don't know how to put this, um, maybe off, or strange?"

Alex looked at his father, his face alight with a smile. "What? How do you mean?"

"Sit down son, let me tell you a bit more about the guy that's missing."

Alex's face lost its smile, a serious, worried expression taking its place. Wallis filled him in on what the paramedic had reported, watching his son's face the whole time, looking for some recognition, or awareness, of what was happening.

"I get why you asked me if I was feeling anything," Alex shook his head. "But no, I don't feel anything is off. Seriously, do you think this guy saw something?"

"I'm hoping that he's just had a cheeseburger high, or something, an LSD flashback or whatever. But I had to ask. I figured if there was any chance the thing was back, you or Ayden would be the first to feel something."

Alex chewed his bottom lip as he thought about it. "It's not us who'd feel it, I mean, not necessarily. Harry was the one that had the main part in that whole freak show, dad. I reckon she's the one you need to talk to."

Wallis sighed. "I didn't want to bring it up with her if I could avoid it. You remember her nightmares, and how long it took her to get over it. I just don't want to have to say anything unless I'm one hundred percent certain."

"Let's hope it doesn't come to that, then. Ayden will be in at five, I can ask him if anything's up, if you want."

"Only if he doesn't tell Harriet."

The intercom on Wallis' desk buzzed, interrupting the two men. Wallis leaned over and pressed a button.

"What's up, Michelle?"

"It's the school, Sam. They just rang an ambulance for Harry, she's collapsed. They said for you to go straight to the hospital."

The Sheriff looked up at his son. "Do you know if they called her mother?"

"Yes, Sam, they tried, but they couldn't get hold of her. I said you'd come straight away."

31

"Go dad, I'll hold down the fort. Let me know how she is."

Wallis grabbed his keys from the rack on the wall. "Keep trying Lisa, and let Ayden know as well, but tell him to come to work, not the hospital. I'll let you know if you two are needed there once I see what's going on."

Alex walked his father to his car. "It's happening again, isn't it? Why else would Harry collapse?"

Sam took his son by the shoulders and looked him straight in the eye. "We don't know that, Alex. It could be anything. Let's just see what everyone reports back with, and then we can figure out what to do from there." He turned and unlocked his car. "I'll call past and grab Simon on the way to the hospital; I don't want him getting all worked up if he has to miss his appointment."

CHAPTER SEVEN

"Hey, Ronni, are you okay?" Callie ran to the red-haired girl's side as the ambulance pulled out of the school gate. "Why wouldn't they let you go with her?"

Ronni brushed the tears from her cheeks and turned to her friend. "Family only. They didn't even listen when I said we were practically sisters. OMG, Callie, they just told me to go away!"

Several more girls ran over, the call of drama much stronger than the call of friendship. They wanted to be in the spotlight, wanted to show that they cared, that they were there to support someone when the eyes of the whole school were focused on them.

Callie turned to the girls, all members of the very elite, very bitchy clique of the most popular girls. Normally they wouldn't even look at Ronni, Harry and Callie, unless the girls had taken the prime position at the lunch tables. That was the only time the three girls fell under the radar of these prima donnas, unless it was to deride them on their clothing or hair choices.

"Ronni! Baby we are here for you! OMG, you must be traumatized. I know I would be!"

A chorus of 'me too' and 'OMGs' had Ronni looking from face to face, her tears drying on her cheeks. Like all mildly unpopular teens, she had always wanted to be friends with the cool kids, to be a part of the group of girls that everyone, especially the boys, looked up to.

"It's terrible! They wouldn't let me in the ambulance with her, and we are practically sisters!" Callie could see the girls looking her up and down, assessing if she was worthy of their attention. She was so glad she had worn her finest ensemble; it was perfectly on point. She grabbed Ronni's arm and hooked it through her own. "We can't believe they'd do that; I mean, she *is* practically her sister!"

"I know, right?" Talia, the leader of the group, tossed her latest on-vogue haircut and batted her eyelashes. "So, tell me, I hear she's pregnant, that's why she collapsed, am I right? Is she preggers?"

"Pregnant?" Ronni gasped. Harry was her best friend, and not once had she even mentioned having a boyfriend, let alone sleeping with anybody!

"I knew it! Wow, so who's the lucky boy? You have to tell us! But we have to get to class, so meet us after school, we'll walk home together, and you can spill the beans on everything! This is so exciting! Oh, you can come too, Cassie."

"Thanks, I will! Oh, and it's Callie."

"Sure, see you guys later!" Talia crooned as she spun on her heels, her posse following close behind.

"Can you believe that?" Ronni asked, still shocked over the pregnancy allegation.

"I know! OMG, Ronni, we are going to be walking home with Talia's bunch! I *cannot* believe it. I'm gonna die. Like, literally die."

"Get a grip, Callie. Harry is our best friend."

"Yeah, a friend who didn't even tell us she was dating anyone, let alone that she was pregnant. Does that sound like a good friend to you? We got one more year at this school, and I'd rather be hanging with the popular girls than someone who isn't even honest with us!"

Ronni frowned. "But Harry is our friend."

"I'm not saying not to be friends with her, Ronni, I am saying that we get a chance to hang with the *in* crowd, for a change. And, if they like us enough, we can stay in their group, and even bring Harry over. C'mon, tell me you didn't always dream about this?"

"Well, okay, let's just meet them after school and see what happens from there. But Callie, I don't know if Harry is preggers or not."

Callie squealed with delight, her own happiness pushing any concern for Harry completely out of her mind. She couldn't concentrate on the rest of the day, and skipped final period, dragging Ronni with her to spend the time in the girl's room, fixing their make-up and making sure their hair was perfect. They didn't want to appear too eager, but also were worried about missing the other girls, so they hurried to the gate as soon as school ended, happy to see that Talia and her girls were waiting there for them.

"Hiya Ronni and Cassie, glad you made it!" Brianna smiled; her teeth covered in colored braces that matched the bright bands that were scattered throughout her dreadlocks. With a Japanese mother and an African American father, she had dark, almond-shaped eyes, and clear, beautiful skin. Brianna was the new grade-school teacher's little sister, and new to the high school. Her whole family had moved to Campbelltown when her brother accepted the transfer, with Brianna quickly finding that her city fashion and exotic looks sealed her place as one of the more popular girls in the school.

"Wouldn't miss this, and it's Callie."

"Sure." Brianna rolled her eyes, then turned and looked at Talia. "Should we go through the park?"

Talia tossed her head, knowing everyone could admire her brand-new copper highlights that made her brunette hair shine. "I hooked a packet of smokes out of my dad's car, so duh, of course we're going through the park!"

She led her crew out the gate and immediately headed towards the park, but instead of taking the picturesque route that traversed the gardens and manicured lawns, she chose the path that led to the back of the school, and the woods that lines the edge of the lake and this side of town. Callie was terrified of the woods, she had grown up on stories of horror and fog, tall scary men and a waft of distant music, and her older sisters had known some of the boys that disappeared five years ago. She knew Harry was involved somehow, but it was the one thing their friend had never shared with them. Well, that and being pregnant!

Once they were out of sight of the school grounds Talia pulled a packet of Slims from her designer backpack and lit one up, handing the pack and the lighter to Brianna to share around. Callie had never tried smoking before and was a bit scared of coughing and making herself look stupid. Ronni just politely declined, along with a couple of the other girls, and so Callie didn't feel so bad when she did the same.

"What's wrong, you scared?" Charlie, another of the in group, asked.

"My mom is a bloodhound, if Callie or I have any smoke on us she'll make our lives hell. Callie's waiting at my house till her mom knocks off, so she can't risk it," Ronni replied.

"Yeah, mine's like that, too," Brianna took a practiced lungful of the acrid smoke and blew it out in an exaggerated mouthful. "But she ain't coming home till after I have a chance to shower and brush my teeth, so I'm good."

"Now spill it, girls," Talia didn't draw back on her cigarette, she seemed a lot less practiced than some others in the group. "Who knocked up miss goody two shoes Sheriff's daughter?"

Ronni made eye contact with Callie, who mouthed the words *fake it* to her. Ronni shook her head, and Callie shrugged.

"She never said anything to us. I'm like, you know, totally blindsided. I had no idea!" Callie winked at Ronni.

"Really? You have no idea who she was hanging around with?" Talia turned and pointed at Ronni. "I bet she tells you everything."

"I thought she did," Ronni ran a hand through her hair. "Maybe it turns out she likes to keep some secrets. I mean, she didn't say she was sick, or anything. Though she did say she was putting on some weight."

Callie was grinning, and winked at Ronni, giving her approval. "Yes, OMG, she did say that. And she eats like a pig, I mean, she eats more than her brother, and he's like huge, all muscle and really tall!"

Everyone giggled, some of the girls blushing.

"She has the hottest brothers! Can you imagine having those two as your family! I bet you just drool the whole time you hang out with her, am I right?" Brianna feigned a swoon, her hand on her forehead in a theatrical style.

"Don't you start, girlfriend. You got the absolute hottest brother living right in your house, and his best friend is even better!"

"That's not just his best friend, that's his *boyfriend*, girl."

"I don't care, they're still hot!" Talia stubbed out her cigarette on the path as she laughed. "Let's cut through the woods, I wanna get home and shower before my mom gets back from whatever appointment she has on a Tuesday. Hey, why don't you two come hang out with me and Brianna?"

Ronni frowned. "I don't like the woods," she spoke hesitantly, not wanting to elicit the disapproval of her newfound friends.

"But we'd really like to hang with you girls, so I guess you'll just have to suck it up this once!" Callie's enthusiasm was infectious, and Ronni nodded.

"Okay, sure, I guess if we're all together we'll be fine, right?"

"You a scaredy baby, miss Veronika?" Talia teased.

"When it comes to the woods, I am a bit, yeah. Just coz, you know, my sister Sabrina went to school with Shane and the others. You remember." Ronni spoke quietly, but all the girls heard her, and they fell silent for a moment.

"I don't get it." Brianna looked at Talia. "Who is Shane, and what happened to him?"

"Some creep was grabbing and murdering people in the woods nearly five years ago, and Shane was one of them. But the Sheriff killed him, or caught him, or something. Anyway, he's gone. Well, that was then, and this is now, and we are all together! So, safety in numbers, and all that, am I right?"

"Not me!" Harper, one of the girls said. "Kiely, Laura and I are this way, so we'll catch you guys tomorrow."

The three girls air-kissed and fake hugged everyone before heading off on a path that skirted the woods and led around to a housing estate, leaving the six remaining girls to head off into the woods. Talia handed around her cigarettes again, but only she and Brianna took one.

The girls stopped at the edge of the woods and pulled their sweaters out of their bags; despite the warm day they all knew that the woods were cold and chatted happily as they pulled their designer clothes on.

They continued to laugh and talk, marveling over what boys they found interesting, who was crushing on who, what to wear to the summer dance and who they would let take them. Ronni had let her concerns fall away and she was enjoying the company of these girls. Callie had been right; she was having fun with these girls and was even imagining that she could become a part of their group.

Callie had left her side to walk with one of the other girls, their arms linked together as they laughed and talked, only dropping arms on the narrower parts of the path, then linking up again when the path widened to allow them to walk abreast. The cold air in the woods seemed to be more frigid than normal, Ronni noticed she could see her breath as she spoke and pulled her sweater close around herself.

Brianna and Talia were leading the girls, with Talia turned around to walk backwards and chat, Brianna holding her hand to steer her as she walked. The girls were enjoying the traverse home, the cold, while not a pleasant thing, was easily forgotten with their bright banter.

"Can you hear that?" Brianna glanced behind her to check with the other girls. "I hear music, I think. Can anyone else hear it?"

"Nah, but it's probably just someone else taking a shortcut through the woods and playing some tunes." Talia fished another cigarette out of her pocket and lit up. "You want another smoke, Bri?"

"You're going to throw up if you smoke any more Tals. I can hear something, you guys. I hope it's not some creepy pervert guy. I mean, who listens to music without headphones?"

"Old people!" Callie laughed, and this made everyone giggle. "Boomer with a boombox!"

Ronnie had heard the stories and she knew what the soft wisp of half heard music meant. She felt her heart beat a little faster and wanted to turn around. She wanted to turn and run the other way until she was out of the forest.

Even so, she knew if she did that, she would be the laughingstock of the school, and never ever be invited back into the popular girl's group again. She chewed her lip with worry and tried to laugh at the right places in the conversations but wasn't really listening to anything anyone said. Instead she was straining to hear the music that Brianna had reported.

Someone tapped her on the back of the head and she nearly screamed. Her reaction made everyone laugh, and Ronni felt her face start to grow hot with embarrassment.

"Earth to Ronni!" Phillipa grabbed her from behind in a hug. "You nearly peed your pants!"

"Ah, yeah, you got me. I was miles away, I guess."

"What the fuck is that?" One of the girls stopped and pointed at the ground in front of her. "Do you see this shit?"

The girls crowded forwards, as best as the narrow path would allow, to see what Brianna was pointing at. Moving slowly, swirling and rolling like a living thing and softly glowing, a low-lying wave of fog flowed towards the girls.

"Hey, I don't want to come across as a flake or anything, but I think we should head back the way we came. You know, just to be sure." Ronni took a step backwards, wanting to avoid the fog.

"Defo coming across as a flake!" Talia shook her head to toss her hair around, forgetting that her highlights wouldn't be shining in the dark of the woods. "It's just a little fog. I'm not surprised, it's beyond freezing in here, of course there's fog!"

Callie withdrew her arm from the other girl's and moved back with Ronni. She grabbed her friend by the hand and turned to her. "We need to get out of here. We need to get out now. You guys know what happens with the music and the fog."

"I don't know what happens," Brianna said. "But I am freezing, and wanna get outta these woods. The quickest way is straight ahead, fog or no fog."

"Yeah, Bri is right, if we just hoof it this way a bit, we'll be out of here quicker than if we turn back."

Ronni was stepping backwards, her hand squeezing Callie's tighter and tighter. "If we go forward, we could see it."

"See what?" Brianna asked, turning to face the two girls.

"You know, *it*," Callie stepped backwards. "Um, like, thanks for the invite to yours and all, but Ronni and me are going back. Anyone else wanna come?"

"You guys seriously should be on your knees thanking us for including you, not running back to school like a couple of dweebs. Like, seriously?" Brianna tossed her dreadlocks behind her shoulders. "I mean, *seriously?*"

"I can hear it now," Shena, one of the other girls, said. "I can hear the music."

Ronni turned to run, pulling Callie with her. Shena broke rank and ran with them, as Talia yelled something incomprehensible after the feeling trio.

Harper was looking up the path, towards the rolling fog. "You guys see something up there, through the trees?"

Brianna turned to Harper. "No, I do not see anything, coz I am pissed! How dare they run off on us? What are they, kindergarten kids scared of the big bad wolf or something? I mean, OMG, these woods are right on town. It's not like there are wild creatures living here!"

41

"I can see something," Harper was slowly backing up. "Something is definitely there."

Brianna turned to look where Harper was pointing.

"What? *What* is definitely there?"

"I see it too," Talia had lost all her bravado, her voice small and childish. "I can see something coming towards us."

Harper pushed past the girls and ran in the same direction as Ronni and the others. "Rude much? She nearly knocked me over!" Brianna brushed at her clothes. "Bitch."

Talia grabbed Brianna's arm and tried to pull her along with her to follow Harper.

"Girl, what *are* you doing?" Brianna snatched her arm back. "You catch the crazies from those other girls?"

Talia was fast walking backwards, her face contorted in fear. She tried to grab Brianna again but the girl pulled her arm away. "Shit, Tals, are you crazy?"

Talia turned and ran, leaving her friend behind. Brianna threw up her hands in confusion. "What is wrong with all of you?" she cried, before shouldering up her backpack and turning to continue on her way. She was looking down, the cold fog had now reached her and was swirling around her ankles. She put her hand down to swirl it around in the thick, weird, milky white mist, before snatching her hand back, the cold biting right through to her bones. "Damn," she muttered, before something in her peripheral vision caught her attention.

She looked up, and gasped.

Something was walking towards her, something tall, and thin, and terrifying.

She felt her bladder release as she stood there in shock, the mist growing and swirling up to her waist now, as the thing got closer.

Much closer.

Brianna screamed.

Talia stumbled when she heard a piercing, fearful scream from behind her, but she managed to keep her feet, somehow, and continued running. She threw her backpack off and ran, her legs pumping, breath in short, frigid gasps. Despite the dark she could just see the outline of Harper in front of her before a bend hid her friend from view.

Glancing down she saw the fog had caught up to her and was racing ahead. She had never seen fog move that fast, never seen fog like this before. Her mind was racing, a mix of fear, adrenaline, and sheer panic was forcing her thoughts into strange places. She wasn't going to think about the scream, she wasn't going to think about the fog, and she wasn't going to think about the thing that she half saw closing in on them.

She heard footsteps behind her, thumping, widely gapped sounds of clumps muffled by the fog, and she bit back a scream as she pushed herself faster, harder, her heart fluttering in fear as she kept pushing herself as fast as she could possibly run, and then pushed some more.

When she felt the cold, bone-like fingers circle her waist and lift her up, legs still flailing, she did scream.

She screamed with every bit of her being.

She screamed until the hand squeezed her so hard that she couldn't draw breath to scream, she couldn't breathe at all.

Blackness overcame her as the hand lifted her higher.

Harper fell.

She had twisted her head back when the scream split the air, and somehow tangled her feet, hitting the ground hard. She split her lip and grazed her hands, the sting making her gasp in pain. She tried to get to her feet and for a moment her jarred, grazed knees refused to obey.

She heard the steps get closer and jumped forward, adrenaline giving her the extra push that her knees couldn't. She took only one step when she felt something grab her, something wrap around her middle and lift her into the air. She looked down, her feet hanging, and saw what looked like long, bony white fingers that encircled her waist.

Harper reached down and touched the fingers, her brain refusing to comprehend what she was seeing, what was happening to her. She tried to pull the fingers off her waist, but they were like iron, cold, hard, and unmoving. They were holding her tight, too tight and she couldn't breathe. Twisting her head, she tried to get a look at what was holding her. A blank white face met her gaze, and Harper threw up, vomiting all over herself. The thing dropped her then and she hit the ground hard, rolling off to the side of the path. Winded and shocked, she watched the thing move off down the path as everything faded to black.

Ronni broke through the edge of the trees with a desperate cry, she was clear of the frightening woods but didn't stop, she ran like the thing was still following her, she ran with a speed and stamina that only fear could produce. Callie was hot on her heels, her relief as she broke the woods causing her to fall to the ground, and she burst into tears at the sight of green grass and sunlight. She rolled onto her back and sat up just in time to see Shena broach the edge of the woods, her face breaking from fear to relief. Callie watched as something snaked out, something long, something black, an arm, but impossibly long, with a white hand that grabbed Shena by the head and yanked her back into the woods.

Callie screamed.

She screamed and screamed and didn't stop even when people rushed from the school to help her, she didn't stop when the school nurse arrived, she just screamed and pointed to the woods.

CHAPTER EIGHT

"Hurry up, Simon!" Sheriff Wallis called through his squad car window. His brother was fussing with the front door lock, taking way too long, so Wallis tapped the horn to hurry him up.

He knew that his brother was finding it hard to cope with just one arm, but hopefully his appointment today would see the cast removed and his life would get a bit easier.

"Sorry! I thought I was ready, but I forgot my hospital appointment book," Simon explained as he opened the passenger door. "Why the hurry? We're very early."

"Harry collapsed at school; they've taken her to the hospital. I only stopped to get you as I'm practically passing the front door. But hurry up and pass me the seat belt so I can buckle you in, man!"

Simon did as requested, but his face had paled, and he chewed his bottom lip with worry. The brothers did not speak during the short trip to the hospital, both caught up in their own thoughts and worries.

As they pulled up Simon put his hand out to Wallis. "Give me the keys, I'll lock the car and get myself inside. You hurry on and see how the girl is."

Sam hesitated a moment, then handed over the keys. "You okay to see the doctors on your own?"

"I can, and I will. Go."

He watched his brother run into the hospital and took a few steadying breaths. He had been living with his brother and nephew since he broke his arm, but rarely went outside. He didn't like living in town, too many people, too many prying eyes. Coming into the hospital was even harder, but for every visit his brother had been by his side and was happy to do all the talking. To have to walk inside, by himself, and speak to the nurses, the doctors, to wait in the waiting room while everyone stared at him, well, it was pretty much more than he could handle.

Another deep breath and he was ready. As ready as he'd ever be, anyway. Opening the door, he nearly fell as he was getting out, seven weeks in the cast and he was still awkward. As he walked into the hospital, he noticed a woman staring at him, and he felt a cold sweat break out along his spine. If she kept staring at him, he would have a full panic attack.

"Sheriff, are you okay? What did you do to yourself?" The woman hurried over to him, genuine concern on her face. Simon opened his mouth to answer, but he couldn't get the words out.

"Simon! Good to see you, come right through," the receptionist called to him. He exhaled, his relief flooding him as he nodded to the receptionist. The woman who had confronted him looked confused, but Simon just shrugged and walked through the fracture clinic door.

He knew that in the five years since he helped destroy the curse, he looked better, and living with his brother for nearly two months saw him eating regularly, showering every day, and even trimming his formerly wild beard. As the days passed, he looked better, healthier, and once again was looking like his brother's identical twin. He didn't get out much, though, and being mistaken for his brother was something he wasn't used to anymore. As a kid, and a young man, it was commonplace. Even their wives would have trouble telling them apart, but it hadn't happened for over a decade.

The fracture clinic was unfortunately a popular destination it seemed, there were no quiet seats on their own, the only room in the waiting area was right next to a rather loud family. Simon hesitated, if he remained standing then everyone would look at him, if he took the seat he would be subjected to elbows and children and be too close to too many people.

"*Simon Wallis, room seventeen,*" the crackly electronic voice announced, saving his dilemma.

The doctor was waiting for him at the door, a sympathetic smile on his face. "Good to see you, Simon."

"Thanks for calling me in so quickly." Simon took a seat as the doctor closed the door.

"Your brother had a word with us earlier. Pays to have the town Sheriff as your brother."

Simon nodded. "I guess it really is all about who you know. He told you I had social anxiety?"

The doctor sat and tapped at his keyboard. "No, we already knew that. He just asked that you not have to wait in the crowded waiting room. I saw him on his way to the E.R. I guess he was off to see the guy from the woods." The doctor stood and started to take off Simon's sling and have a look at the cast. "After last week's x-ray, I'm happy with your progress, we can take the cast off today."

Simon frowned. "Woods?"

"What? Oh, the guy? Yeah, the one that had a heart attack this morning. I think there was another guy that's missing. So, give me a moment, I'll get this cast removed for you quick smart."

"It can wait. I need to find my brother."

"Simon, it will only take a moment, quite literally. Then you can go find your brother, I'll even get a nurse to take you to him. Just give me half a minute, and I promise you, I'll get this off before you know it." Simon stood, but a nurse entered with the cast saw. He groaned but sat back down and suffered the ministrations of the nurse as she removed the cast, then cleaned his arm. The doctor sat there the whole time, smiling, but Simon realized he was just there to keep an eye on him and stop him from fleeing.

In what seemed like an agonizing amount of time, but was more likely only minutes, he was done. The nurse led him to the emergency department and left him outside a curtained bed, the blue drapes concealing what was behind it. Simon wasn't sure what he should do, if he should call out, or enter the drapes.

As he stood there, he could hear the sounds of the hospital, the beeping of instruments, the soft shuffle of nursing shoes, the muffled voices of people, both patients and medical staff. There were scents, too. Disinfectants tried to overpower the scent of shit and blood and fear, but those scents were there, underlying and unobtrusive, but always there.

As he stood, uncertain and unsure, the sounds of the hospital seemed to fade away, disappearing from an ever-present noise to a soft background sound, then to nothing.

In their place the faint, barely audible sound of almost heard music drifted in and around the busy room. Although the sound was very low, muted, a near-silent symphony of something that resembled music, it was just far enough away that he couldn't quite identify it, but it was all he could hear. The hospital had become as silent as a mausoleum as Simon turned his head, trying to pinpoint the origin of the strange sound.

A screech broke the silence as his brother pulled back the curtain surrounding his daughter's bed, the curtain rings sliding on their holders completely eliminating the sound of the music. He turned to face his brother, his face pale, a greasy sweat on his brow.

"Simon, how did you go? Good to see the cast is finally off!"

Simon looked at his brother, his mouth working to find the words his brain didn't want to concede.

"Simon? Are you okay?"

"It's back," Simon whispered. "Brother, it's come back."

Simon's eyes rolled back in his head and he collapsed.

CHAPTER NINE

"Two cars. Both locked, and in both cars the passenger seats have stuff on them, doesn't look like they had any company." Shirl peered into the back seats of the cars. "Timber guy wasn't much tidier than the council guy. What a pig sty! There are enough takeout wrappers to feed a small African nation for a month in there."

"Message from Michelle," Mike said, putting his cell back into his pocket. "She checked the plates we called in and she confirmed it was a timber company car, the driver is one Patrick Halls, and he was on his own, as far as they knew. They'll check that to be sure and conform asap. We gotta walk into the woods a bit, see if we can see anything."

Shirl sighed. "I know, and any other day before today I'd say go for it. But right now? Shit, Mike, you sure we gotta?"

"Just a little way. If we hear or see anything, we turn and run, no stopping to ask questions, no checking with each other, we just run, okay?

"Okay. You wanna hold hands?"

"Fuck off, douche bag," Mike laughed, but it was a forced, hollow sound. "Let's grab our parkas and some flashlights before we head in."

"I'm taking the shot gun. Mainly just to make myself feel better but I'm taking it."

Mike nodded and waited for Shirl to pop the trunk and retrieve the heavy weapon, before grabbing a parka each and the flashlights.

"I'll just check in with Michelle, let her know what we're doing," Mike said as he leaned into the police-issued radio on his shoulder. He spoke briefly, and registered the concern of their receptionist, before clearing his throat and pulling his parka around his shoulders. The deputies headed along the path, the sharp contrast between the bright, warm sunlight and the shaded, cold woods a shock to their senses. Shirl clicked on his flashlight; it wasn't dark enough to warrant the brilliant beam, but it made him feel better, and Mike didn't comment.

They walked a few hundred feet into the woods, Shirl shining his light around, but they couldn't see anything that might be of any assistance in finding the missing man. The path was hard packed dirt, here and there the rusty-colored pine needles showed a bit of a scuff like a foot had disturbed them, but there was no way to tell if this had been caused by the two men, or even when it had occurred.

"You know, I've always found it strange that there's never any trash in the woods."

Mike frowned and looked at Shirl. "People are tidy?"

"No, I don't think it's that. I mean, there's no cigarette butts, no candy wrappers, no soda cans, nothing. Not even a bit of paper that could blow in. It's always immaculate, you know, not a single piece of trash anywhere. Even when we have delinquents on community service and we make them clean the roadsides, there's always a tiny bit of something left behind, you know, little bits that are too small to pick up, or just things that you might have missed, or walked right past. Here, there's nothing, quite literally, not a single thing."

"You know I never thought about that before but you're right. I can't see a single thing to show a person has ever walked through here. But nothing about these woods surprises me. Scares the fuck outa me, yeah, but it never surprises me."

Relieved that there was no fog, nor the half-heard sound of music, the men turned and made their way back to the cars, both silent, the oppressive eeriness of the woods taking away their will to speak.

As they cleared the woods the radio in the squad car could be heard through the closed windows, and Mike jogged ahead to answer it. Shirl stopped to take off his heavy coat. Once outside the woods, the day was warm and pleasant; there was no need for the coats, no need for his flashlight.

"That was Alex on the radio," Mike said as he walked back to Shirl, who was standing at the cars that were parked beside the path that led into the woods. "He said something happened on the other side of the woods, near the school. Couple of girls hysterical, saying they were attacked by something when they cut through, taking a shortcut. Wants to know if we can check it out."

Shirl looked at his co-worker and best friend. His face was creased with worry, making him look far older than he was. "I don't care what the boss says, it's back. Clearly, it's back, and the whole madness has started again."

Mike sighed. "You wanna drive?"

"Nah, you take it. You know where to go. How old are the girls?"

Mike started the car as Shirl strapped his seatbelt, then carefully made a turn to get them back onto the main road. "Harry's age, I think. Alex said one of them is from her class, or something. I think you better call in the others, and check with Jake and Aaron about the timber guy. See if they know how many other guys there were supposed to be."

Shirl picked up the mic but looked over at his partner. "What was it all for, all the deaths, all the sacrifice, if we didn't kill it, Mike? Did Colin die for nothing?"

Mike was following the quiet road that wound around the outskirts of the woods. Not many people had a need to come this close to the forest, and the road didn't lead to anywhere other than the various hiking paths through the woods, with the occasional parking lot and amenities at the start of those paths.

When Mike didn't answer, Shirl put in a call back to Alex, asking about the timber guys.

"No, no one else. Timber company says they've had no contact with, um, where's my paper, oh, here, with Patrick Halls. He was meeting Fat Albert to check out the woods for some timber cutting contract."

"Other people can hear the police radio, Alex," Shirl rolled his eyes. "Let's keep it a bit more P.C., okay?"

"Sorry, yeah, okay. Anyway, they haven't heard from him, and his cell is ringing out, like, it rings until it goes to voicemail." Alex's voice cracked over the radio. *"I haven't heard back from dad yet. I mean, the Sheriff. I'll update as soon as I hear something."*

"I can see why that boy didn't go to college," Mike shook his head. "So, message the boss, let him know the updates, and he can make the call as to who we get in and how to start the search. Or searches, I guess. I see the ambulance. I'll pull in right beside it."

The deputies donned their hats as they alighted from their squad car, the red and blue lights of the ambulance reflecting on Shirl's sunglasses. Mike had a notebook in his hand and Shirl had a small camera, both men looking grim as they approached the small crowd that had gathered around.

"We need to get some crowd control here asap. Put a call in, also get Alex to organize some more guys to come over here." Mike walked ahead as Shirl spoke into the mic on his shoulder.

CHAPTER TEN

"Simon? Simon, can you hear me?"

He could hear the woman's voice, but he couldn't recognize it.

"Simon? Can you open your eyes for me?"

He groaned and tried to lift his head, but a cool hand on his forehead prevented that. With great effort he started to open one eye. It felt like someone had glued it shut and he strained to lift the lid, the lights assaulting his senses and making him shut the eye again.

"Good effort, Simon, very good. Now give it another try, okay? Let's get those eyes open."

Simon forced both eyes to open, just a little, and tried to focus on what he was seeing.

The ceiling was white, and there were things hanging from it, metal things, and a soft light glowed above him. A face slipped into his field of vision and he closed his eyes again, then opened them, trying to focus.

"Good to see those baby blues, Simon. My name is Dr. Singh, and I just want to check that you are okay. Now, see my finger, I want you to follow it, okay? Just with your eyes."

Simon squinted and realized that he was in hospital. The face was that of the doctor, the woman who had been asking him to open his eyes, and now she wanted to check he could track her finger as she moved it back and forth in front of his face.

She seemed satisfied with his reaction and wrote something down on a clipboard.

"What happened?" Simon didn't like the sound of his voice; it was dry and croaky. "Why am I in the hospital?"

"You passed out, you big idiot." Sam leaned over so Simon could see him. "You didn't want Harry to have all the attention."

Everything came flooding back to him, and Simon rubbed a hand over his eyes.

"All your vitals are fine, but I think perhaps you are a little dehydrated. When was the last time you had something to eat or drink?" Dr. Singh asked. "Perhaps that is why you passed out?"

"Yes, yes I'm sure that's it. I didn't eat any breakfast, and I think I missed dinner last night." He hoped his brother would keep his mouth shut and just let the doc finish.

"Okay, I'm going to get someone to bring you a sandwich and something to drink, you can sit up, but take it slow. If you are still feeling okay in an hour or two you can leave, okay?"

"Sure thing, doc, thanks."

She smiled at him, her large brown eyes crinkling with warmth. "I'll be back to check on you later, okay? I don't want you to get up until I come back."

"I'll keep an eye on him," Sam said as he stood and pulled back a curtain on one side of the bed. "He's right next to my daughter, Harry, so I can keep an eye on both of them."

The doctor smiled at them both and left, as Simon sat up, lifting the pillow behind himself. He looked across at Harry, the girl appeared to be sleeping.

"Is she okay? She looks very pale."

The Sheriff sighed and sat down in a large vinyl chair. "She's always pale, Simon. But yeah, she's okay, I think, for now. She woke up after they brought her here but was hysterical, the doctors had to sedate her. She kept screaming that her friends were in danger. They just couldn't calm her down. She hasn't woken up yet."

"Did she say what they were in danger from?"

Sam took off his cap and scratched his head, his face lined with worry. "Apparently not. She's been out the whole time I've been here. So, Simon, I'm guessing you didn't want the doc to ask you any more questions, because I know you ate more than both Alex and me combined last night."

"Yeah, I know, and you're right. Sam, I heard music. Well, not really music, but the sound it makes when it comes. It's back, and it's letting me know it's back."

Sam looked at his brother. "When did you hear the music?"

"Just before I passed out. All the sounds of the hospital disappeared, and I heard it."

"Did that happen before, you know, back then?"

Simon shook his head but didn't speak as an orderly came in with a small tray containing a sandwich and a glass of orange juice. He thanked the man, then looked at his brother. "I was sure we'd killed it. I mean, five years! Five years of nothing, then it starts again."

"What happened? Something must have triggered it, there has to be a reason it's back."

"I have no idea. I need to get out of here so I can start to figure out what's going on, I can do some research, or something. I don't know, I just don't know what could have happened."

"I do. I know." Harry spoke softly, but clearly.

Both men turned to look at the pale teenager as she struggled to sit up in her bed. Sam leapt to his feet to help her, lifting her into a sitting position and adjusting the pillows behind her.

"I'll get a doctor, just hang on a sec." Sam started to move away but Harry grabbed his arm.

"I don't need a doctor. I need to get out of here. Dad, it's back, and it's really angry. It's so much worse than last time. We need to stop it; we need to get out of here and do something."

"They'll want to keep you at least overnight, honey."

"Why? I just passed out. Tell them I have my period or something."

"I can't say that!" The Sheriff looked very uncomfortable. "I can talk them into letting you go, maybe, if you seem okay. That means not going anywhere till the doc looks you over. You were hysterical, Harry, you didn't know where you were or what was happening. You were completely out of it."

"Hysterical? Really? What was I saying?"

Sam shook his head. "I wasn't here. Something about your friends being in danger, you were screaming it out."

Harry looked worried. "Who did I say was in danger? Do you know?"

"Harry, if the thing is back, and that fact is still debatable, but if it is back, then anyone who goes into the woods would be in danger. Do any of your friends ever cut through there?"

Harry shook her head. "Never, not ever. They're terrified of the woods, and my friend Ronni, Veronika, her sister went to school with some of the boys that were killed five years ago, so she is super-duper scared."

"No one will be safe if it is back," Simon spoke quietly. "And most of all, *we* are not safe. None of our family, or anyone that saw it back then, is safe."

Harry chewed her lip, worry darkening her face. Sam looked weary, he had been through this before and he did not look forward to going through it again.

"I should go see what's happening with the guy that had a heart attack, see if he's awake, and if he's lucid. We need to know exactly what he saw." The Sheriff stood and took a few steps before turning back to face his daughter and his brother. "You two do and say everything you need to, let the doctors think you're both fine to come home. I'll be back as soon as I can."

Harry offered him a forced smile as he turned back and walked away. She looked over to her uncle, a man who looked so much like her dad that it made her head spin every time she looked at him.

"Why are you in here?"

"I had my appointment to get my cast off today," Simon replied, lifting his arm to show her. "But then I had a bit of a turn and fainted."

"A bit of a turn? Is that old speak for getting hysterical, like me?"

Simon shook his head, a bit of a smile catching his face, just for a moment. "No, I didn't get hysterical. I heard the music. All the other sounds in the hospital went quiet, then I heard the music. I passed out after that."

Harry tipped her head to one side, thoughtful. "That never happened before, did it? I mean hearing the music unless it was near?"

"No, it didn't. And it's not in any of the journal entries from anyone else, either."

"So, it's different this time. I mean, what happened to me wasn't really any different, that sort of thing happened before, like, maybe not the same but similar, but not anyone hearing the music." Harry ran a hand through her long hair. "That's new, and we need to figure out why it's doing things differently."

"You think it will help figure out why it's back, and maybe how to kill it?"

60

Harry nodded. "Not just kill it but stop it from ever coming back."

"I kept going through things in my mind for a long time. I often wondered if Shirl should have hit it with the log."

"What? What should he have hit it with?"

"No, not hit it, I think maybe the medallion needed to work a bit longer. Really burn it up, or just let it work a bit longer. It all ended too neatly, too quickly, and now I think I was right."

"Easy to say after the fact. Why didn't you say anything before?"

"Because I'm crazy, right? I just think crazy things all the time. I was hoping that this was just one of my crazy theories, and when nothing happened after a couple of years, I thought I was wrong."

"You're not crazy, Uncle Simon. And as it turns out, you were right. I wish you weren't, but you were. So now what? We burn it with the medallion again?"

Simon frowned. "There has to be something else, something that goes along with the medallion. You had some weird knowledge back then, kiddo. You could put your hand over the book and see what you were supposed to do. It was like you were psychic, for a little while."

"Yeah, I remember. But it wasn't like I knew what to do, or could see it, it was more like someone was telling me what to do, like a voice whispering in my head, almost. No, not almost, there *was* a voice. A girl's voice, I think. She would tell me things, but they were whispers, hard to hear. I wasn't sure if it was my own voice telling me what to do, or someone else's. Anyway, they stopped when we killed the monster. Or when we thought we did, anyway."

"You two are looking much better!" Doctor Singh smiled as she walked between the two beds. "Let's have a check of those vitals, shall we?"

CHAPTER ELEVEN

"Any word back from the Sheriff?" Shirl walked towards Mike, with one of the deputies by his side that had come in early, summoned by Alex's call.

"No, not yet, but Bob has called, he'll be here with his men and dogs any minute." Mike pulled out his cell phone. "You want I can call the hospital and get them to bring the boss to the phone?"

"Nah, I'll call. You get the deputies organized for the search. Not worth them going in without Bob. I'm pretty sure they won't find anything, but let's just make sure we've got every base covered. Oh, the school guy, um, the teacher, he said they'll call the parents and have them meet at the station."

"Okie dokie, but I'd be calling the boss right now, this is getting out of control awfully quick."

"On it." Shirl dialed the hospital as Mike took the deputies together for a huddle. He spoke on the phone briefly, then put it away. Mike noticed and called him over.

"So, what'd he say?"

"Hospital is going to get him to call, they weren't sure where he was. Harry's awake, though, and she seems fine."

The braying of dogs interrupted them as the search-dog handler and his friends joined the deputies. "Heya Shirl, Mike, gents," Bob greeted them then hawked a wad of phlegm off to his side. "What'll we be a-searchin' for?"

"We've got four missing girls, Bob. I haven't got anything with a scent yet, though."

"S'okay, Shirl. Me an' the guys can take a walk through with our dogs, and if we don't find nuthin' someone can get us some scents to follow then."

"You're a good man, Bob."

"Nah, just doin' me job, s'all." Bob tipped his cap and led his dogs into the woods, followed by his men, and then the deputies.

Shirl met Mike's eye and nodded, the two men grabbed their shotguns and followed the procession.

"Your nuts all the way up to your belly?" Mike asked, his voice low so only Shirl could hear him.

"Dude, my nuts are somewhere near my ears. I feel more scared now than back when we saw that thing head on."

"I hear yah. First sign of fog and I'm outta here."

The dogs let out little yaps and barks as they followed the path, excited for a hunt. The group walked for a few minutes, slowly, making sure that each side of the path was searched, carefully shining flashlights into the trees.

The dogs howled, excited, and someone shouted. Mike and Shirl moved ahead; passing the deputies on the narrow path wasn't easy, but they got to the front of the line where Bob was barely holding his dogs back.

"It's a girl, me dogs have foun' a girl!" Bob exclaimed as Shirl pushed passed him.

On the side of the path, against the base of a tree, Harper lay unconscious. Shirl bent to touch her neck and jumped as she moved and groaned.

"She's alive!" Shirl shouted. "Call an ambulance!"

Mike spoke into his radio as Shirl checked the girl as best as he could without moving her.

"Looks like her ankles are smashed, like she fell from up high. I think maybe some broken ribs, hard to tell, I don't want to hurt her by touching her too much." Shirl stood and looked at Mike. "She's covered in puke, too."

"We've never found one alive before," Mike spoke quietly. "This is new. This isn't how the thing works."

Shirl nodded, then stepped back from the girl. "Bob, take the dogs on, see if you can find the others. If you found one, the others could be alive, too."

Bob nodded and spat. "It's good for the dogs to fin' a live one, for a change. Me an' the boys'll fin' the other'n for yahs, too!"

"I'll leave a couple of guys with the girl to wait for the ambulance, we'd better keep up with the dogs. I'll tell you something, though, this day is getting stranger and stranger."

Shirl nodded to two of the deputies and then walked beside Mike as they followed the dog handlers, the dogs now more vocal after having a win.

"Maybe it doesn't kill any more? I mean, fat Albert got out alive, and while we haven't found the timber guy, doesn't mean we won't. What's the bet Bob's dogs will turn him up?" Mike shone the flashlight to his side of the woods, searching as he walked. "I can't tell you how much I hope we do."

"Me too, Mike, but I'm not going to hold my breath just yet. One girl is great, but we've got three more teenagers and the guy to find before I'll start feeling lucky."

They walked the path for a half hour, but the dogs didn't find anyone else. As they turned to walk back, Shirl's phone buzzed and he pulled it out.

"Finally, it's the boss!" he exclaimed as he answered it.

CHAPTER TWELVE

"I told you already," Kelli sobbed, snot streaming from her nose and mascara running down her cheeks. "He wasn't talking to me, Dyon, he was talking to Kyah!"

"I saw you, whore! I saw him and you, and you was laughing and stuff, and Kyah wasn't nowhere near you guys!" Dyon stood and began to pace. "I'm so sick of this. Every time I look away, there you are, hanging all over some guy, tits poking out, touching him, and making a whore outta yourself and a fool outta me! I'm done, it's over, and I don't want nothing to do with you anymore!"

Kelli started to cry harder. "It's not fair! He wasn't talking to me, I swear! I don't want no one except you, I'll die if you leave, I'll just die!"

Dyon stopped pacing and turned to her, his face twisted in a sneer. "Die then, I don't give a shit. I'm done. I am one hundred percent done. Over it. I couldn't be more over it if I tried." He picked up his keys from the hall table and walked out the door, slamming it behind him. Kelli threw herself onto the sofa and sobbed, her face buried into her arms. She *had* been flirting with Rowan, and it wasn't the first time, either, but it was the first time that Dyon had seen her.

She sat up and wiped her nose with the back of her hand. If Dyon was going to leave her, well, good! She knew Rowan would have her in a second, and not just Rowan, any one of the guys would be all over her in a flash once they knew she was single. She walked to the bathroom, mentally making a checklist of the guys who she could have now that she was single.

The bathroom mirror showed her what a mess she was. Her hair was tangled and messy, her eyes red from crying, along with her nose. She had mascara tear stains down her face and bags under her eyes. She looked more like thirty-five than twenty-five.

She peeled her clothes off and hopped into a hot shower, lathering her hair and thinking of what she could do with it. She was going out tonight, she was going to have a good time, and show everyone she was over Dyon already. In fact, maybe she would have a good time for a while, and not be in such a hurry to get another boyfriend. Maybe being single for a little while would be fun, she could be with any guy she wanted, and not have to answer to some crazy boyfriend getting jealous just because someone looked at her!

Her home was right on the edge of Macy street, bordering the woods. She used to like it when she was a teenager, she could slip out the window and take off for hours at a time, and her parents never knew. Now that she was a grown woman, she didn't have to tell anyone when she was coming or going, and to make life even easier her father had turned her bedroom into a self-contained apartment, with its own entrance, own bathroom, kitchen and living room.

It paid to be the only child, sometimes!

It was still early, but she wanted to get down to the diner. Her afternoon shift started at four, working through till nine. After she finished, she would hit the local bar in a big way, dancing until the sun came up, kissing anyone she wanted, and finding at least one guy to take her mind off Dyon for at least a couple of hours.

She tied her hair in a high ponytail, everyone liked it that way, the long, black, glossy hair always catching the eyes of men, and they always asked her to let it loose and see her shake it out.

Checking the mirror again she was happy with what she saw. Gone were any traces of her crying fit, her make-up was immaculate, her eyeliner straight, and her lips pout-perfect! That extra unit of filler had been worth every penny. She blew herself a kiss and smiled. Maybe she would get another unit next week.

She pulled the door closed behind her as she left, the keys for her Hyundai swinging in her hands when she stopped, a frown forming on her face. Why was it foggy?

She hated summers on Macy street, the fog often drifted along there, and her parents would never let her go outside on a summer's eve, but nothing had happened for the past five years. No fog, not even in winter, and her parents had stopped worrying about her going out at night. She looked past the fog and her frown deepened.

Dyon's car was still there. Had he changed his mind, and was waiting to say he was sorry, that he wanted her back, and would drive her to work? She sashayed up to the car, her eyes half closed and lips pursed, ready to make him beg to take her back

He was not in his car. The driver's door was wide open, and as Kelli drew closer, she saw that Dyon's keys were on the ground, along with his trucker's cap, but he was gone. She looked around, trying to see if he was near, but all she could see was the fog.

She didn't want to walk the path into the woods. While she had a bit of time before work, she didn't have a lot, and didn't want to waste it looking for her errant ex-boyfriend.

Reluctantly, she walked to the edge of the woods and looked in, but it was too dark and foggy for her to see anything. She heard something though. Music? Was there music, sort of far away, playing very softly?

"*Dyon!*" she called, her voice echoing back to her as it bounced from tree to tree. "Are you there? Dyon? What're you doing?"

No answer to her call, just the weird music, if it was music, almost half heard in the distance.

She decided to turn around, go to work, and not worry about Dyon. Maybe she'd give her Pa a call later and see if the car was still there, and he could take care of things.

A scream broke the eerie silence of the woods, a scream so wrought with pain and fear, so loud and anguished, that it made Kelli scream with fright.

The scream sounded again and she ran, panicking and terrified, and unlocked her door before falling inside in a heap. She groped for her purse which had been on her shoulder and had flung backwards when she ran. Her cell phone was in there and she called emergency services with shaky hands.

Another scream broke the quiet and Kelli slammed her door, locking it in a terrified act of self-protection.

The call wouldn't connect, so she ended it and tried again, but couldn't get a signal. She started to shiver, thinking it was just fear, but then noticed that the fog had started to seep under her door and it was freezing. It swirled around her feet, like a living thing, twisting and moving, flowing and ebbing, and she screamed again.

Her apartment still had a door to the main house and she ran there now, trying to outrun the strange fog that seemed to have a life of its own. She could hear the pained screams again from the woods and feared that it was Dyon, that something bad was happening to him.

She slammed the door as she ran through it; her parents were not home as both would be at work until at least five. They were old school and still had a landline telephone that hung on the wall in the kitchen. All she could think of was getting to the phone and calling for help.

She needed someone here, someone who could help her, help Dyon, find him and stop those horrendous screams.

She dialed the phone and heard the ring tone with a great sense of relief.

Michelle, the receptionist at the sheriff offices answered, just as the scream sounded again, but this time it was closer, louder. It sounded like it was in her apartment, just on the other side of the separating door.

Kelli screamed in response, she felt her bladder let go and her heart race.

"Hello? Please tell me your location, I can have a car there in no time. Hello?" Michelle's voice sounded tinny, and so very far away.

"M..M... Michelle, it's me, Kelli Allen, oh my god send somebody right now!"

The scream sounded again, and this time she thought it came from right against the door, that whoever was screaming was in her apartment.

"HURRY! Oh my God, hurry, something is happening, oh please, you've got to help me!" Kelli sobbed into the phone, but all she heard back was a buzzing sound. Michelle had gone. She didn't know if the receptionist had heard enough to send someone, or if the call had cut before her cry for help had been heard.

The fog had started to seep under the door that joined the house and the apartment, streaming like a gas, swift and silent. Kelli let the receiver drop from her hand and spun around, terrified, not knowing what she could do to protect herself.

In her hands she still held her car keys and she gasped. Her car! She should make a run for it out of the main house door. Her car was in the drive that was closer to this door, and whatever was screaming would have to get out of her apartment and around the building before it reached her. She could be in her car before then and be on her way to safety.

She looked back at the apartment door, wondering if the screamer was still there, not thinking that it could possibly be Dyon screaming in pain, not thinking what it could be, just panicked and unsure. The scream sounded again, louder, almost as if it were on this side of the door now, and that was all she needed to trigger her. She ripped the door open and ran, her keys held out before her, pressing the door release on the tab as she ran.

Her car beeped its response as she grabbed the door handle, relief flooding through her as she pulled the door open.

She felt something grab at her dress but she didn't stop, didn't turn around. She jumped in the car and pulled the door to slam it fast behind her.

The door hit something; it wouldn't close.

She turned to see what had blocked the door's path and her mouth fell open, her eyes wide in shock.

Something stood there, something so tall that she couldn't see its whole body, something that towered way over the roof of her car. The arm of the thing reached for her, a long, black clad, waving arm. The slithering, boneless looking thing grabbed at her, the fingers white, slim, and impossibly long.

Kelli screamed then, she screamed and screamed, her horror and fear all she had left as the thing closed its grasp around her neck.

CHAPTER THIRTEEN

"The number comes up as the Allen's, on Macy street. She sounded like someone was murdering her, Alex." Michelle was white, hearing the fear in the young lady's voice had shaken her to the core. "She was absolutely terrified. The call cut out before she could tell me what was happening."

Alex was standing at the reception desk with two other deputies; John, a swarthy middle-aged man who had been a deputy since he'd left high school in his late teens, and Vikki, a bright, robust girl he'd gone to high school with, before she'd headed off to two years of community college. She had dropped out in the second year and returned to Campbelltown and joined the sheriff's office later that year. He looked over at his sister's brother Ayden, who just came in to start his shift. "I think you need to take Vikki and check it out, John. But be careful, you know Macy street is right on the woods. Hurry, guys, lights and sirens, and check in as soon as you can, okay?"

John nodded and rushed with Vikki to the back office where the squad car keys were kept.

"It's just like before, isn't it? Like five years ago?" Michelle had started to cry; her fear was starting to eat at her resolve.

"We don't know that Michelle, but you know we'll take care of it, right? Just like we did then."

"Just how did you take care of it, Alex? How did you stop it? How can you know you can take care of it this time? It's getting out of hand; this is far worse than anything that happened before!"

"Hey, Michelle, it's okay, right?' Ayden spoke soothingly, smiling at the receptionist with the most reassuring smile he could muster. "Alex is right, we can take care of this. But right now, we need you to pull it together, we need you to be on reception so we can focus on what we're doing, we need to get a plan of action happening and coordinate with everyone to make it work. Can you do it, Michelle? Can you help us out here?"

The harried woman nodded and sighed. "Sure, Ayden, sure. I can do this. I just need a moment. Give me a minute to go to the bathroom, grab a coffee, and get my nerves under control, okay?"

"I'll cover the phones, you go, take all the time you need." Alex stepped behind the reception desk and waited until Michelle had gone through the door to the rest of the station. "Have you heard from my dad yet?"

Ayden shook his head. "No, not yet, but I rang the hospital and they said Harry is awake and seemed fine. I still can't get hold of my mom, though."

"She did say that reception could be iffy while she was at Metro General. You know what it's like, no cell phones allowed in the hospital."

"I've sent her a text, and I made sure I worded it so she wouldn't panic."

"So, she'll panic then, won't she?"

Ayden sighed. "Maybe that's not such a bad thing. You know what's funny?"

"Not much these days."

"Poor choice of words, I guess. What I meant was, I don't think the timber guy ever saw the thing before, and neither did the school kids. But I did, and you, and Harry, and mom and your dad. Even Shirl and Mike saw it. Yet it's not coming after us, it's coming after people that had nothing to do with it before."

"Yet." Alex looked up at Ayden. His blue eyes, normally twinkling with humor and fun, were dark and serious. "It hasn't come after us *yet*."

The desk phone rang and Alex answered it, his voice professional and even cheery. Ayden gave him a little nod and walked through the door to the back rooms and offices. He checked his cell, but there was still no answer from his mom. Sitting at his desk, he logged onto his computer and started to fill in requests for assistance from the next town. They would need more help in Campbelltown than their own deputies alone could provide.

Aaron and Jacob walked in from the loading dock at the back, and Aaron paused to hang up the keys to the squad car. Ayden looked up at them as they entered, each one turning and giving Michelle a nod as she walked back on her way to reception, a hot coffee in one hand and a handful of cookies in the other.

"Stress eating." She gave them an embarrassed smile and used her hip to push open the door adjoining the front office.

"Michelle under stress?" Jacob asked.

Ayden stood as Alex walked through the same door Michelle had just left by. "Yep, she's getting the calls. It's enough to stress everyone, I'm afraid."

Aaron looked at Jacob and his colleague nodded his head. "Guys, we need to know what's going on. I mean, not just the missing people and shit, but what is *really* going on. Everyone seems to have an idea of what's happening except Jake and me, and that's not fair."

Jacob took his cap off and scratched his close-cropped hair. "Remember we didn't grow up here, we have no idea on the weird history of this town."

"Alex, can you give the imports a rundown of the, um, thing? You know more than I do, having been here your whole life. Plus, it's your family that the thing was after. I'm only included by the poor decisions of my mother."

"Yeah, sure. But it will have to be the quickest version ever, we don't have time for the full feature-length episode. Sit down, guys, I'll tell you what I can."

Ayden went back to work on his computer, but he had one ear focused on what his friend was saying.

"You guys won't believe me, and that's okay, but here it is. The woods of the town have always been here, and local people don't go there in the summer. Like, never. And other times of the year you'd be stupid to even look at them, but people do cut through."

"Well, it's the quickest way to the other side of the lake. The road and path take forever to get around," Aaron agreed.

"Absolutely. Ayden and me used to cut through there all the time after school. There's a track that leads through the edge of the woods and it takes you into town, or other tracks can take you through to near the park, or the hills, and there's even a few hiking trails that people use. I think one of them is wide enough for mountain bikers, but we don't get many of those." Alex paused and looked over to Ayden for reassurance, and the deputy nodded at him to continue.

"Anyway, it's like a town legend, I guess, that there's something in the woods. A thing that will kill you if you ever see it."

"A thing? What kind of thing?" Jacob looked incredulous. "And if it kills you if you see it, how does anyone know about it?"

"Yeah, those scary stories always get me. 'Pass this note on or you'll die, the first person didn't do it and they keeled over dead' type thing, but if that happens, how do we know the first person didn't share it, coz they're dead, right? Or something like that."

"I'm getting to that, guys. I'm trying to cut out most of it or we'd be here all day. Anyway, before it comes there's this creepy fog, it's freezing, and kind of moves like it has a mind of its own. And you swear you can hear music, sort of, off in the distance, but you can't be real sure. If you see any of that you gotta run, and run as fast as you can, coz the next thing is the creature. There's stories 'bout people going missing in the woods since before the town was even here, right back to when the wagon trains came through here. The local Native American tribe had heaps of stories about it, too, when they used to live here, up where O'Grady's ranch is now. Well, they still live here, but they all live and work on the ranch."

Alex pushed to check the reactions of the two young men, their faces only showing him solemn expressions.

"Anyway, about five years ago it came for us, for me, and Harry, and Ayden, and our parents. Not just us, but a whole heap of people. A lot died. But my Uncle Simon and my dad found a way to stop it, and we thought we killed it. Simon and Mike were there, they helped, too. For five years nothing happened, and we really believed it was gone."

"Until today," Ayden added.

"Yeah, until today. We didn't even give much thought to Albert's report, not really, because people around here all grew up with stories about the monster, and if he was hallucinating, and he was around the woods, well, it made sense that he thought the thing was after him. It's only now when we have so many more reports that we're realizing maybe we didn't kill it, we maybe just hit pause on it for a while."

"How do you know it's the same thing, not, um, son of thing, or whatever?" Aaron asked.

Alex frowned, trying to figure out if the deputy was making fun of him or not.

"Well, we don't know, not really, but the truth is that something is out there in the woods, and that something is killing people. Again."

"Killing people? Who's been killed?" Jacob stood up. "I only heard some people were missing?"

"Some high school kids have gone missing," Ayden explained. "One girl has been found hurt, one got out okay but is beyond hysterical. Shirl and Mike are there, searching as we speak. Got the dogs and search teams in the woods right now."

"So, what do you guys think? You on board with the story, or what?" Alex asked them.

"Seriously, jury's out with me, but I can see you two believe what you're saying, and I can't deny some strange things are happening right now. And after talking to the super-fat dude's co-workers, I'm inclined to think there's definitely something going on here," Aaron said.

"Yep, they pretty much gave us the same story as you just did. So while I can't say I'm one hundred percent on board, I'm thinking that there is something happening, and we gotta just suit up and do our jobs," Jacob added. "Anyway, anyone heard back from the Sheriff yet?"

The intercom buzzed and Michelle's voice answered Jacob's question. "*Sheriff on line three, Alex. I already let him know about the Macy street incident.*"

"Thank you, Michelle. How're you holding up?"

"*Fine Alex, thanks. Line three.*"

CHAPTER FOURTEEN

"We've come almost right through to Macy street, Shirl." Mike turned to look at his fellow deputy. "Nothing. No bodies, no blood, not so much as a lost shoe. The search is a bust."

"We found one girl, Mike, and that's a success, I'd say. Anyway, the boss said to make sure we covered every inch, and that's what we're gonna do."

"This sucks. Anyway, that path takes us back around behind the madman's house. Let's take that, see what we can find."

"It's Simon, Mike, not the madman. The boss'll skin you alive if he hears you call his brother that."

"Yeah, sorry, old, bad habits. I'll go ahead and steer Bob onto the other path."

Shirl nodded and pulled out his cell to check it, then radioed in to let the station know which way they were heading. He didn't want to be caught in these creepy woods without anyone knowing where he'd led the team. He certainly didn't intend to be here when night fell. Even though the thing seemed to be quite happy to work its evil during the day, he had no desire to face it when these woods were even darker.

He motioned the guys behind him to follow as he took the fork to the second path, his stomach complaining that they'd missed lunch, as well as his usual afternoon snack. He couldn't see himself sitting down to a meal anytime soon, the best he could hope for was the boss calling in a food van to feed the volunteers. Bob, along with his dogs, was a paid helper, but the guys with him, and the few others that had come along to help, were doing it out of their own time, and the Sheriff always looked after the volunteers.

The dogs were very quiet, they had been excited after finding the girl, but the longer they searched the less noise they made. That wasn't normal behavior for the dogs, they would normally be yapping and barking, eager to follow a scent, all working each other up into a frenzy. Shirl had seen them like this before, five years ago, when they had searched the same woods. The dogs knew that there was something wrong, something strange, and they were solemnly silent.

Alex had sent a deputy with some clothing items from the missing girls to give the dogs the scents to follow, and something from the missing timber company man should arrive soon, though he was pretty sure they wouldn't find anyone, either living or dead.

He felt his cell vibrate and pulled it out again; it was a message from the Sheriff. Their conversation earlier had been terse, the fear that the creature was back confirmed when Harriet and Simon's collapse was relayed to him, along with the heart attack victim's terrified description. The Sheriff had been as confused as Harry and Mike with the creature's choice of victims. Like Alex, he'd thought those that had seen the monster five years ago would be the first in line for attack. The thought didn't help with his growing anxiety over being in the woods, a place he had not been near for the last five years. He knew Mike felt the same way, and also had been avoiding the woods, not even going to Simon's house with the boss when he needed to grab things for his brother.

Mike was standing by the side of the path waiting for Shirl to catch up. He gave him a reassuring smile but didn't feel the sentiment behind the gesture.

"Bob's okay?" Shirl asked him.

"Yeah, just quiet, same as his dogs, same as everyone, really. It's even creepier than I remember in here, Shirl. The dogs feel it, too."

"They're not the only ones. I was hoping we'd never have to come back here, Mike. The boss sent a message, I just got it on my cell."

"Yeah? What'd he have to say?"

"There's been another, um, incident. On Macy street. Girl and a guy missing. Girl was on the phone to Michelle when she was taken. Vikki and John are checking it out."

Mike shook his head as he walked beside Shirl but didn't say anything.

"This is crazy. Nothing for five years, not a single incident, now all of a sudden everything's gone ass up. Something must have happened to start all this. I don't believe the thing just waited till it felt like it, I really think something may have triggered it."

"You think maybe the timber company guy had something to do with it? The threat of the trees being cut down?"

"Yeah, maybe. I mean, I don't know what else happened recently. I'm not into the stars or horoscopes or that kinda shit, so I don't know if any planets aligned to make it easy for the thing to come back. You know, age of Aquarius type thing. I think it has to be something more than that, something big, and I think you're right, the trees coming down is a pretty big deal."

"Personally, I'd be pretty happy to see the last of these woods, Shirl. Cut the whole fucking lot down. Burn it, for all I care. Just get rid of them. But would cutting everything down get rid of the thing?"

"I'm thinking yes if it reacts like this. Don't think there's going to be much tree cutting if the thing is killing anyone who come near the woods, though."

The dogs started to bark, some howling, and a sense of excitement rippled down the line that perhaps they had picked up a scent. The pace picked up as the dogs became a little more animated, and the two deputies squeezed past the volunteers to reach the front and see what was happening.

"Aye, they've found something to sniff, boys!" Bob hailed them as they approached. "We can barely hold 'em back!"

The dogs were straining ahead, but not as much as they normally would when they had a scent. They were fairly subdued, instead of a frenetic hive of excitement, they just pulled a little on their restraints, with less than half of the dozen or so dogs making any noise at all. One of Bob's helpers had moved a little ahead, his dogs slightly more eager, and Shirl found himself hoping that they would find maybe one, though hopefully all, of the missing high school kids.

The dogs in the front became more vocal, barking around the base of a tree, their snouts pointed towards the canopy. The rest of the dogs joined them, howling and yapping, all facing upwards, all showing some excitement at finding their quarry.

As one, the dogs suddenly fell silent, dropping to the ground in crouched positions, tails tucked in and faces pushed against each other, fearful and shivering.

"I'm really not wanting to point my flashlight up there, Shirl," Mike whispered. He didn't need to shine his light, the volunteers and other deputies were already pointing their flashlights towards the tops of the trees, searching for whatever had frightened the dogs.

One of the dogs screamed in fear, and very quickly all the dogs were howling in terror, their eyes rolled back in their heads and their hackles raised.

"Oh my god, oh my fucking god!" someone behind Shirl yelled, and he realized that there were some flashlights pointed at the dogs. They were huddled together, a mass of fear and terror, and something was dripping on them. Every drip resulted in a scream of fear, a painful, horrifying cry that set the men's hair on end.

"What is that? Can you see what that shit is?" Mike sounded on the point of hysteria. The dog handlers were trying to pull their dogs away, pull them back, but the dogs were writhing and twisting on the ground, unable to walk.

"It looks like blood," Shirl said as he shone his flashlight over the dogs. All the deputies and volunteers crowded around to see what was going on.

Bob reached forward and touched one of the drips on the closest dog and shook his hand, then rubbed it on his pants before turning to Shirl. "It's freezing cold, so cold that it burned mah damn hand, Shirl. I gotta get my dogs outta here, get them back on the path and look for the scents. This'll turn 'em off ever searching again if I don't hurry."

"Sure, of course, head out, Bob. You two there," Shirl indicated two of the deputies huddled close by. "Grab the evidence bags and get some samples of the blood-stuff. Just make sure you don't touch it!"

The dog handlers dragged and cajoled their canines until they could get them moving reluctantly along the path.

"Don't look up, Mike." Shirl moved towards the tree as the dogs were slowly shifted away.

"Why?" Mike asked as he looked up, and immediately his face was hit with a drop of the cold blood. He squealed and jumped back, rubbing his face in pain.

"I told you not to look up!"

"Fuck's sake, Shirl, that's the first thing a person is going to do." Mike kept rubbing his face where the blood had landed. "It's like when you say *don't look now*, people are gonna look straight away. You shoulda said *look out for the blood.* That woulda saved my face. *Fuck* that hurt. No wonder the dogs were yowling!"

"Okay, everyone, look out for the blood. At least it didn't hit you in the eye. Now the blood is dripping from something, and my flashlight is pretty powerful, but I can't see shit except for branches. Anyone got anything stronger?"

A few *nope*s, and *no sir*s were his reply, so he shook his head and backed away from the tree. "We need to call this in, get some spotlights or something. Harley, you and Frieder stay here and wait for the shit to arrive, the rest of you, let's go." Shirl pointed after the dogs. "We need to finish this before nightfall. No way I wanna be here when it's dark."

The two deputies Shirl had mentioned moved away from the tree but stood their ground as Shirl called the station on his radio. Mike had a handkerchief from his pocket, trying to scrub the spot on his face as he followed the volunteers and deputies on the path behind the dogs.

"Leave it alone, Mike, or it'll leave a mark."

"Shut the fuck up, Shirl. I am seriously over this shit. One more thing and I am hightailing it like a jackrabbit."

"You'll have to catch me first. Here's hoping we find some warm ones before anything finds us, if you know what I mean."

Mike put his handkerchief back in his pocket and continued by Shirl's side, both men lost in silent reverie. After a while the dogs started to make a little noise again, their brush with the strange freezing blood forgotten as they gave an occasional yap or howl. From the back of the search party Shirl and Mike shone their flashlights to the sides of the path, up in the trees, and back again, making sure no evidence was missed.

The dogs started barking louder, a more excited sound, the howls echoing through and around the darkened woods. Shirl nodded at Mike to indicate he should join him as he made his way to the front of the line, his heart in his throat at the thought of what they may find.

As they made their way to the front the dogs got louder, their barking became fearful and frenzied, and Shirl was nearly knocked to the ground by a volunteer pushing past him, running back the way they had just come.

The dogs were escalating as Shirl broke through the line and he stopped, not sure what the dogs were barking about.

"Over there," Bob pointed. "The guy you was looking for, he's there."

"Patrick? The sawmill guy?" Shirl asked, not seeing anything other than trees and shadows.

"*What the fuck!*" One of the dog handlers started to back up. "I'm outta here. You guys should run. Fuck me, get outta my way!" He dropped his leashes and ran, and the other dog handlers did the same, all except Bob who was trying to gather up the loose dogs.

"Leave them, Bob," Mike spoke quietly. "Take the ones you have and go; they'll probably all just follow you."

Bob looked up at Mike, then turned back to try and grab all the leashes. The dogs had started to back up, their barks turning to howls, and some turned and ran after their handlers.

Shirl finally saw movement and shone his flashlight into the woods.

It was Patrick, as far as he could tell. He was still a little far, and the trees hid most of his body, but the man was walking towards them. He moved strangely, sort of jerking and bobbing like a marionette, the invisible strings operated by unseen hands.

Shirl's flashlight caught the man's form and he gasped, inadvertently taking a step backwards. The man had his head down, like he was watching the ground as he walked, and the light picked up splatters of red soaking his white shirt. Mike grabbed Shirl's arm; the grip tight, almost painful. Bob had managed to catch most of the flailing leads and was kneeling down, trying to snag the last few, the dogs howling and pulling him backwards as he struggled to keep his balance.

The man, Patrick, was closer now, and lit by several flashlights as everyone's attention was riveted to the sight, unable to move, frozen where they stood, mesmerized by the stumbling, jerking progress as he lurched towards the path. As the man drew closer, he lifted his head, and everyone gasped. The man had no eyes. There were dark gaping holes where his eyes had been, his cheeks were splattered with blood, and his chin and the front of his clothes looked soaked through. He opened his mouth as if to speak, and they could see that he had no teeth, his bloodied, ruined gums dripping blood and gore down his chin as his mouth moved silently.

"*RUN! EVERYBODY RUN!*" Mike screamed, pulling Shirl with him, then grabbing Bob's shirt collar with his other hand when the man had not moved. "*FUCKING RUN, NOW, GET THE FUCK OUT OF THE WOODS!*"

Bob dropped every leash and ran, Mike and Shirl only just ahead of him. The dogs flew passed them, silent now as they raced away, their leashes whipping the volunteers and deputies as they passed.

They all ran as fast as their legs would carry them, and when they came to the fork some turned towards the Macy street exit, while others continued the way they had come. Mike and Shirl turned, and did not stop running until they breached the edge of the woods, some men falling to the ground in relief, Shirl and Mike stumbling onto the sidewalk as Bob nearly bowled them over.

"Let's all move back from the trees, guys," Shirl called out as he moved away from the woods, turning to see a squad car and police tape around the first house.

"What's going on here?" Mike asked, walking to the car.

"Vikki and John were checking out the two missing people, remember?" Shirl told him, as he kept glancing over his shoulder, expecting to see the jerking movement of the hapless sawmill employee.

"They must be in the house." Mike walked up to the car, finding the doors were open and the engine was still running. He looked back at Shirl, confused. Beside the car was a shoe, a smaller one, though still police issue. "That looks like it would be Vikki's." Mike picked it up, then sat it in the car. "She wouldn't be walking around with only one shoe on, Shirl."

"She wouldn't have left the car running, either." Shirl took stock of how many deputies were with him. All the volunteers had run the other way and he had three deputies still with him, now standing, their attention pulled between the abandoned squad car and the entrance to the woods. Shirl ordered two of the guys to check out the house, and the third to radio into the station and let them know what happened.

"It's definitely escalating, it's so much worse than back then," Mike shook his head, as if to clear it. "We need to do something, we need to figure out if we can stop it again, and this time, stop it for good."

"I agree. We need to talk to the boss, and his brother. Mainly his brother. I think they're the only ones that can get us out of this mess."

CHAPTER FIFTEEN

"Doc says I can take you both home," Sheriff Wallis announced as he walked through the drawn curtains. Harry and Simon had kept the one dividing their two beds open but closed the ones that surrounded the other three sides, making them a semiprivate area in the emergency wing. "You need to get dressed, Harry."

"I can't dad, apparently I threw up all over my clothes."

"I had Ayden bring you some from the station, here." He tossed a bag on the bed and pulled the dividing curtain closed. "Simon, you okay to get your shoes on? Is the arm working okay?"

Simon shrugged as Sam bent down to retrieve his brother's shoes from beside the bed, then helped his brother put them on and do the laces up.

"I can't believe this." Harry sounded angry.

"What is it, possum?" Sam opened the curtain to see his daughter standing there, wearing a very large, bright floral sweatshirt, and old faded sweatpants. "I don't even think these are real clothes, they look like homeless cosplay 101."

"They'll do to get you home, it's not like we keep a set of designer clothes at the station. Alex just messaged me, things are escalating, more people are missing, including two of my deputies. There's a situation in the woods right now, the sawmill guy turned up with no eyes and teeth, just like Brent." Sam spoke quietly, he didn't want anyone overhearing what he was saying. "I think we need to sit down, all of us, and figure out what to do. We can't have this thing killing anyone else if we can help it."

"We should go back to my cabin, the journal is there, we need it to figure this out." Simon stood and tried to pull his jacket on, his arm still a little stiff. Sam reached over to help him, his face creased with a frown.

"No, I don't want us that close to the woods. I'll get Shirl and Mike to call past the cabin and grab it. Your spare key still over the front lintel?"

"I think the cabin would be the best place, Sam, I'm really more comfortable there."

"If we are going to have this many people, Simon, we aren't going to fit in that cabin. We'll go back to my house and I'll have Alex and Ayden meet us there."

Harry found her bag with her soiled clothes and wrinkled her nose as she peeked inside. "I can't wear my shoes, either. I'll go barefoot, it's okay." She tied the top of the plastic bag. "Where's mom? Have you heard from her?"

Sam pulled the curtains back to allow them to leave. "No, I haven't. I've messaged and so has Ayden."

"Did you ring her?" Harry asked.

"Yeah, I tried. Her cell's turned off. C'mon, let's get out of here."

Harry handed her bag to her father and followed him outside, Simon bringing up the rear, his gaze on the floor. He didn't like to make eye contact with anyone, so it was easier to just keep his eyes low.

Wallis left his car directly outside the front door, making it easier now for them to make a hasty exit. He leaned over to help his brother with the seatbelt, then smiled when Simon was able to do it up by himself.

"That must be a good feeling," Harry commented.

"I'd be dancing with joy if it were any other day, but it seems trivial now, with everything that's happening."

The Sheriff sighed and turned the car out onto the main road, switching on the police radio as he did. It crackled to life with news that the volunteers who'd ran from the ravaged visage of Patrick had not emerged from the forest, and everyone was refusing to enter to search for them.

"Have you told the boys to meet us at your house?" Simon asked his brother.

"I did, I rang them from the hospital. I've also told Shirl and Mike to grab the journal, they're just waiting for the word from you as to where it is. Also," he paused as he pulled into his drive, lining up Harry's door with the path to the front door of the house, saving her bare feet from the gravel drive. "Do you have it?"

"It?" Simon seemed confused. "No, the journal is at my cabin."

"Not the journal, Simon, the other thing, the power necklace. Do you have it at my house, or is it at the cabin?"

Simon reached into his pocket and withdrew a folded handkerchief. He opened it up, revealing the medallion they had used to end the creature five years ago. "I always carry it, always, everywhere I go."

Harry reached over, is if to touch it, but then withdrew her hand.

"Let's get inside, the others should be here soon. So where is the journal? I need to tell the guys, so they don't turn your place upside down looking for it."

"It's in a box beside my bed. They'll find it no problem, but they'll also need to bring the whole box, it's got all my research in it. Everything I know about the curse is in that box."

Harry got out of the car, waiting until her father and uncle alighted before turning to Simon.

"You're right, you know. It *is* a curse. A curse that should have stopped when the soldiers were killed."

"We know that already, Harry." The Sheriff pulled his cell from his pocket. "Simon told us that last time."

"But the curse was meant to stop when they were all dead, the girl was meant to end it. She tried, but, um…" Harry tipped her head to one side as if listening to a far-off voice. "He killed her."

"The monster killed her?" Simon asked.

"No, the soldier. He shot her. He shot her in the back."

"How do you know that?" Simon closed the car door and walked around to face Harry. "How could you possibly know that?"

"Let's get inside, Harry, here's the door keys. I'll just ring Shirl and let him know where to find the journal."

"Okay, yeah, good." Harry looked at her dad, her eyes sad, her gaze not quite focused.

"I'll have a quick shower; I still smell like puke."

The Sheriff waited for them to go inside before dialing Shirl, his face lined with worry. "You guys at the cabin yet?"

"*Nearly there, we're just at the bridge.*" Shirl's voice sounded hollow. "*This is escalating boss, the fog is now flowing out of the forest from all sides. We need to find a way to stop it.*"

"Yep, that's the plan boys. Just hurry and be careful. The thing knows where the cabin is, so put your running shoes on. Grab the box beside the bed, it has the journal and Simon's research, then hightail it outta there."

"*See you soon.*" Shirl hung up as another squad car pulled in behind the Wallis' car. Alex and Ayden climbed out, their faces as grim as the Sheriff's mood.

"Thanks for coming boys. I gotta tell you, I'm getting more and more confused and worried. Harry has started to talk weird again, like she did before."

"What did she say?" Alex asked.

Wallis filled them in, then turned towards the house.

"Hey, have you heard from my mom?" Ayden's voice was full of concern. "She would normally be in touch by now, wouldn't she?"

"Not yet, but don't worry about anything, she did say she was going to be hard to get hold of. No way for her to know we'd have an emergency here."

Ayden nodded and followed Alex and the Sheriff into the house. Simon was in the kitchen and had already started on making sandwiches. Alex put on the coffee and pulled out a chair at the kitchen table. "I think we need to set up at the dining table son, we'll have too many to fit around this one. Shirl and Mike will be here soon, they're just grabbing Simon's research. Can you fire up your computer?"

Wallis' cell vibrated on the table where he'd placed it and he picked it up. "It's a message from your mom, checking in, finally. I'll call her from the other room. It'll take me a minute to fill her in. Ayden, can you help Simon make some food, and then check on your sister if she doesn't come downstairs in a reasonable amount of time?"

Ayden shook his head. "A teenage girl having a shower in a reasonable amount of time? Who is he kidding?"

CHAPTER SIXTEEN

It had been a long day for Lisa. Her drive to Metro City was uneventful, but it took a good hour. She had travelled to the Metro University Hospital every week for the last two years. Her course placement at Campbelltown hospital required her to attend the small teaching hospital once a week, and the rest of the days involved the commute to the city. Her decision to pursue a career in nursing had surprised most people, but after everything that happened five years ago, she felt a need to help people, and with her children older and almost independent, a new career was something she looked forward to.

It was a tiring day. Even though she was older than all the other student nurses she was given the same duties, the same treatment, and she wouldn't have it any other way. Lisa really enjoyed the days spent on the hospital floor much more than the time in the classroom. Most days she didn't stop to eat as the hospital was a busy one, barely finding time to race to the bathroom when she needed to.

Working in the hospital meant she had to turn off her cell, and her family knew that, knowing that they had Sam to turn to if there were any problems. She didn't need to worry about anything with the Sheriff there to look after her kids, knowing that not only was Harriet a priority of his, but that her son, Ayden, was treated like Sam's own.

She had shifted in with Sam four years ago, letting their relationship mature for a year before making the move. She had been so happy living with the man who fathered her daughter. She had loved him for many years but had felt that he did not share the same feelings. Everything they had gone through five years ago had drawn them together, and Sam had let his guard down, finally, and embraced the woman and her family as a larger part of his life.

They got on so well that Lisa would be hard pressed to think of a single argument they had, they were happy to discuss their disagreements and work to a conclusion. They had rediscovered their love of a conversation with each other, and even after four years in the same house they would often talk into the wee hours of the morning.

Her children had thrived living with the Sheriff, his steady, even temperament and calm demeanor a positive influence, and he always had time for them. Ayden and Alex were as close as brothers, they had grown up together, and had always been treated as equals by the Sheriff. They still both lived at home, the family was a close one, and after all they had been through, neither young man was in any hurry to make a home of their own elsewhere. They were both good boys, never getting into trouble and doing well at school, and even though Lisa had been a little disappointed that they both chose to enter law enforcement instead of college, she understood that, like her, the effects of the traumatic experience with the creature five years ago had inspired them to help others, and, perhaps, feel like they had some control over their lives. The boys were much loved members of the force, the townsfolk treating them with respect and affection. They loved their job, they loved working with Sam, and Lisa could not ask for any more than the boys being happy.

Harry, thankfully, had no desire to become a deputy. She was more interested in going off to college in the city, though hadn't quite decided between a career in fashion, journalism, or maybe becoming a nurse like her mother. She had also toyed with the idea of becoming a writer, though other days she wanted to be a pop star. Sam had smiled at every future career choice Harry mentioned, and no matter what the girl chose to do Lisa knew her father would support and encourage her in her chosen path.

The last five years had been good to the blended family, her house had steady tenants, her investments from her husband's life insurance paying a small but adequate income. They had recently decided to take the whole family on a holiday to Europe come next summer, after Harry finished school for the year and Lisa graduated. It was something for everyone to look forward to, and Lisa had begun to believe her life was just about perfect.

She didn't worry when she turned her cell on and saw missed calls, or the several message alerts. She had been expecting the school to call at some stage as parent/teacher interviews were coming up, and it wasn't unusual for Sam to call her to try and catch a quick chat. There was a missed call from the hospital, but she thought it was just the nursing manager calling to check her hours.

It wasn't until she got in her car to drive home that she actually read her messages, then listened to her voicemail. She felt her stomach grow cold, the steady reassurance from the school and Sam to let her know not to worry about Harry's collapse, but asking her to call as soon as she could, did not inspire her to feel any calm at all.

She rang the hospital first and being told Harry had been discharged with her father and was fine made her feel a little better, so she tried Harry's cell. The call rang out, Harry's cheery voicemail also not alleviating her growing anxiety.

She checked her texts and felt her stomach twist with fear. Something was happening, and though Sam hadn't said what it was, she also had a couple of messages from her son asking her to ring as soon as she could.

She didn't want to ring Sam or Ayden, she didn't want to know what was happening, though she knew it was better to find out sooner rather than later. Taking a breath to steady herself she sent a message to Sam to call her straight away. She knew he would call as soon as she got the message and so she sat there with the phone in her hand. When it did ring, she jumped, but answered it quickly.

"What's going on?" she asked.

"*Are you sitting down?*" Sam replied, and Lisa felt the twist of fear grip tight.

CHAPTER SEVENTEEN

Shirl looked behind him, twisting in his seat, as the squad car bumped and rattled over the rustic bridge.

"How's the fog looking behind us," Mike's voice was tight, worried. "Is it any closer?"

"No, it's still heading towards the park, though. Sun's getting low, we need to motor on this, I do *not* want to be here when the sun goes down."

Mike turned to Simon's cabin and pulled in the open gate. "You know we won't be safe in town, either. If the thing wants us, don't matter where we are. It'll come for us no matter what."

"Yeah, I know that, but I still don't wanna be out here in the dark. Okay, you grab the key, and let's get this done."

As one the two deputies got out of the car and hurried up the front verandah, Mike retrieved the key from its hiding spot and unlocked the door. "We need to get the box from the bedroom," Shirl instructed. "It has everything in it."

Mike turned on the bedroom light. "Shit."

"What wrong?" Shirl stepped into the room beside Mike. "Oh, shit."

The bedroom had dozens of boxes, all stacked against the wall beside the bed.

"Did Simon give you any clue which box it could be?"

Shirl shook his head. "The boss said it was a box beside the bed. All these fucking boxes are beside the bed."

"Hopefully it will be obvious once we look in them as to which box we need. Okay, just start searching."

Mike grabbed one and opened it, then pushed it aside. Shirl did the same, working as quickly as they could to get through each box to find the one they needed. Mike lifted one heavy box onto the bed and opened it. "It's not in here, we're nearly through the lot and it's not in any of these boxes."

Shirl grabbed the last box and looked in it, kicking it across the floor when it held old clothes, not any paperwork, not any journal. "This is crazy, I don't want to go through them all again, there must be other things on top of the papers."

"Fuck me, Shirl, there's another box over there, on the other side of the bed," Mike pointed as Shirl ran around the double bed.

Ripping the top off he looked up, his face triumphant. "Yes! This is it, the journal's on top and it's got other papers and writing pads in there." He closed it and picked it up, squirrelling it under one arm. "Let's get the fuck outta here."

A knock on the door gave them both a start and Mike walked to the door to open it.

"Wait a sec, Mike. Why is someone knocking on the door? Everyone knows Simon's not here, and besides, no one comes to the door here, everyone thinks the house is haunted."

"Don't be stupid, someone has seen the cop car and that's why they're knocking."

He reached the door and opened it, stumbling backwards at what he saw.

Patrick stood there, the front of his clothes soaked in blood, his head hanging low, his arms by his side.

"*Shut the fucking door!*" screamed Shirl.

Mike kicked the door shut and bolted it, then jumped away from the door as if Patrick could reach through and grab him. "Holy fuck, Shirl, holy fuck. He's here. What the fuck are we gonna do? How are we getting outta here?"

Shirl hitched the box on his hip and shook his head. "I don't fucking know. Jesus, I don't fucking know! But if that corpsey thing is there, the monster can't be far behind. Fuck." He looked around the room, desperately searching for something that would help him. "I don't know!"

"Look!" Mike pointed at the door, where a stream of white fog was flowing from underneath, swirling around and approaching the deputies.

"Jesus fucking Christ, Mike, that means the monster is coming!"

Mike had a hand on his head, trying to think of something, trying to think of a solution.

"All we can do is shoot him. We need to get outta here, it's not safe. Shit. Fuck. Shit-fuck. Okay, okay. I'll open the door and you fire, hit that fucker in the head. I'll shoot too, and we make a break for the car. Okay. Okay, you ready?"

Shirl sat the box down on the table and pulled his police issue revolver out of the holster, flicking off the safety before picking up the box again. He nodded to Mike, and the deputy pulled open the door.

Patrick was gone.

"*RUN!*" Shirl screamed and they ran, Mike pulling the door shut behind him but not stopping to lock it. He had the squad car keys out; he had not locked the doors to the car but had taken the keys inside with them.

"There he is! Hurry, Shirl, get the fuck in the car!"

Shirl didn't stop to look where the walking corpse was, he just ripped the door open and flew inside, the box on his lap. Only then did he look up to see Mike taking aim at the ravaged face of the sawmill representative, pumping four quick shots into his head.

Patrick stumbled back at each shot but did not fall. Mike hesitated, waiting to see what the man would do, his gun still pointed, ready to fire. Patrick stood for a moment, the bullet holes clear in his head, his eyeless sockets no longer dripping blood. He stood motionless for a moment, then started to walk towards the car.

"*MIKE!*" Shirl reached over and opened his partner's door. "*MIKE!*"

He fired again, this time into the legs of the sawmill rep, smashing the knees and hitting the thighs of the man. This brought him down, he fell to his ravaged knees, but immediately struggled to get up. Mike got in the car then, starting it and gunning it into reverse, skidding around as he raced away from the cottage, from the walking corpse, from the flowing fog that was surely heralding the arrival of the creature.

CHAPTER EIGHTEEN

"So, let's work out what we know." The Sheriff had seated everyone around the large dining table, with Ayden taking notes. Shirl and Mike were still pale and shaken, both gripping the glasses of whiskey Sam had handed them as they told of their escape from the cabin.

"Do we know what time mom will be here?" Harry asked.

Sam looked at her, giving her what he hoped was a reassuring smile. "She's about a half hour away, possum, she's not stopping anywhere till she gets here."

Harry nodded as Alex bit down on the last sandwich. "Should we wait for her? I mean, she'll have some ideas, don't you think?"

"Well, honestly, no, I don't think so," Simon was sitting opposite his niece, a pile of paperwork in front of him. "I say this as none of us have any idea, really, of what to do. We never thought we'd be going through this again."

"Back to my point then," Sam tapped his forehead. "Then we hash it out. So, what do we know? I think the first people affected were the sawmill guy, and fat Albert. Is that right?"

Ayden nodded. "Yeah, then the high school kids were next. Then John and Vikki, then seven volunteers helping with the search. I think that's all."

"Me and Shirl," Mike added. "We had a brush with the crazy, as well."

"Yeah, sorry, Mike and Shirl." Ayden wrote that down.

"We have survivors, we've never had that before." Simon shuffled papers on his desk, pulling out a rumpled, stained piece that was covered top to bottom on both sides with his spidery scrawl. "Well, not in our lifetime. There were some notes in the journal about people that got away from the creature or one of the zombie people, but they were all taken before the night was over."

Shirl gulped down his whiskey in one swallow. Mike just looked at everyone, wide eyed, his Adam's apple bobbing.

"Five years ago, all the kids that were in the woods were taken in the first night, so we gotta figure that the two girls that got out of the woods are not going to make it through the night. And the one that was found unconscious, well, she and Albert are in the hospital, but I'd be shocked if they're still there in the morning."

"What high school kids?" Harry asked. "What girls? Are they the high school kids you're talking about?"

The Sheriff nodded. "A group of girls were walking through the woods this afternoon, after school, and they were taken. Two got out, one was found when Shirl and Mike were searching, but she was in a coma."

"Do I know them? I mean, do you guys know their names, so I can see if I know them?"

"You may know them, but seriously, I think it's better that you act like you don't." Alex ran a hand through his hair as he looked for the right words. "What I'm trying to say is that you may know them, I think they're your age, maybe. But if you get distracted now, you might miss something, something important. We need you to focus, sis, because you may be the only one that knows how to stop this."

Harry frowned. "Why do you say that? Not about the girls, I kinda understand, I guess, but about me being the only one that could stop it?"

"Because you are." Simon reached over and lightly touched her finger before withdrawing his hand. "You've got some kind of connection, some link, I feel, to the girl that the curse was made for. You know you do, don't you?"

Harry looked at the faces around the table, each one was looking at her, wide eyed and hopeful, waiting for her to say something that would lead them to the end of the creature.

"I don't know how to stop it. I don't know anything."

"It's okay, Harry, if you get an idea, or a feeling, anything, really, just speak up." Sam looked at everyone, wanting to take the attention off his daughter as she was clearly uncomfortable. "Right, so we have a list of those affected so far, good. But we don't know what started this thing back up, and with such a vengeance. I've never known it to go full metal jacket on day one. Simon, don't we normally get a bit of fog, and one or two people go missing, tops?"

His brother nodded. He reached over for the journal, once held so close and protected, now just another piece of research. While Sam was pleased that his brother no longer had the obsession, he did worry that it would come back with the return of the cursed creature.

"We need to find out what triggered it, what started not just the attack, but what brought it back. I think whatever, or whoever, that is, well, maybe that will tell us why it's super aggressive this time." Simon tapped the journal but didn't open it. "There's nothing in here about that, and my notes and research about the original curse didn't tell me anything, either."

"We can maybe Google something, maybe see if we can find out about the curse, or the medallion, or the people that made the curse?" Alex asked.

"You can maybe do that while we're talking?" Sam nodded at the laptop in front of his son. "I'm assuming you can do that and still talk as well."

Alex gave him a condescending smile and tapped on the keys of his laptop. Simon leaned over to look at the words he was using, then pulled a piece of paper out of his stack and handed it to Alex. "There are some things you can start with here; these are things I found out when I used to go to the library."

"Her name was Ix iLa'al," Harry spoke softly, her voice quiet in the room full of men. "She died on her stomach, her blood filled the earth and gave birth to the trees."

Everyone turned to look at the blonde-haired teenager, her brown eyes were soft, unfocused, and her skin very pale.

"What did you say?" Sam asked.

"She was the daughter of the king, from a long line of kings. Her brothers were Hagan and Tadeas, the twin born sons of the king. She lived and died in twelve years of the sun. Her blood gave birth to the trees." Harry's eyes rolled back in her head and she fell backward, her chair crashing to the floor before anyone could catch her.

Mike was the first to scoop the girl up, everyone was on their feet and crowding around her.

"Put her on the sofa!" Sam called, and Mike carried her into the lounge room. Harry's eyes flicked open as he gently lowered her onto the plush sofa and she looked confused.

"Why is everyone crowding around me?" She looked at the faces and blushed a little. "I passed out again, didn't I?"

"Hey, look at the bright side, sis," Alex reached and touched her forehead with his hand. "You didn't upchuck all over yourself this time."

She pushed away her brother's hand and pulled herself into an upright position. "I remember now. She talked to me. The girl, she was in my head, she was talking to me."

"How?" Simon kneeled on the floor in front of her. "How did she find you? Or, I don't know, why? I mean, there's been hundreds of years, why is she just contacting someone now?"

Harry leaned forward and placed a hand on her uncle's shoulder. "I did try to speak before now," Harry's voice was different, it had grown soft again, and seemed tinged with a gentle accent. "For many suns and moons I tried to speak to those who came before this one. For many suns and moons, no one could hear me. Some came close, and some would catch a word or a thought."

Harry's eyes had rolled back into her head again, but she did not pass out. Instead she straightened and turned her head as if she was looking at all those gathered around her, though her eyes were still showing only the whites.

"Are you Ikee lala?" Simon asked.

"I am Ix iLa'al, daughter of the king, princess to our lands. My blood birthed the trees of the forest, and I died by the hands of my kidnapper."

"I don't get it," Shirl knelt beside Simon. "How are you talking through Harriet?"

She tilted her head to one side, as if listening for a far-off sound. "She is the first daughter, the first female

105

child born in generations. This gives me a connection, a way to speak, instead of just watching, just listening, unable to help."

"Why now? Why didn't you talk to us before, when we were fighting this thing?" Sam asked.

"I tried, and I helped, but the girl was too immature to accept my attempt to reach her. Only now, when I have been trying for five years, has she allowed me in."

"She was the same age five years ago as you were, when you died, wouldn't that have been mature enough?"

Harriet let her hand drop from Simon's shoulder and a tear trickled down her face. "My life was very different to what you live now. I was loved. I was loved more than most, but then I was taken. What was done to me, what the soldiers did to me, it was not anything that a child should live through. When a soul is wounded like this, it cannot be easy to talk to another, it cannot be easy to accept such pain and fear and anger into your own soul. This girl was not ready."

"What girl? Who wasn't ready? Oh my god, what's wrong with your eyes Harry?" Lisa pushed through the men surrounding the sofa. Harry collapsed back as Lisa grabbed her daughter. "Will somebody tell me what's going on?"

CHAPTER NINETEEN

"The cops have been there all day, Mat. I think we should maybe skip tonight, dude, we'd be better off doing it tomorrow or something." Kye hooked a finger into his belt loop, thinking this made him look cool. "My old man will skin me alive if I get caught."

Mat was doing up the laces on his shoes, and he stopped and looked at his friend. "The cops being there is precisely the reason we should do this tonight, dickwad. They are all busy elsewhere, and we've got a clear run while their attention is on the woods. If we don't hit Hooley's now, we probably won't get another chance. Or are you a big, fat, pimple covered pussy?"

Kye sighed. "You know I'm not a pussy, I done proved that last week! It's not fair if you gonna keep bringing up that I'm a pussy when you know I'm not."

Mat laughed and continued doing up his shoelaces. "Anyway, we need to do this while my Pa is out of town. You know we ain't got a chance to do nothing when he's here. He'll have me doing chores and shit."

"Okay, okay, I get it. Where's the others?"

The door opened as he spoke, and a tumble of gangly teenagers joined the boys in the small double-wide Mat had been living in. While there was plenty of room in his father's large ranch house, he liked the sense of independence he felt living in the self-contained mobile home at the back of the hay sheds. During calving season, the double-wide would be used to house the travelling stock workers, but for now it was all Mat's and he was reveling in his independence from the watchful eye of his overbearing father.

He stood as his friends greeted him, handshakes and shoulder thumping, a hug or two, then he turned to the tarnished mirror on the side of the door. He ran a hand through his dark hair, his high cheekbones and copper-colored skin a throwback to his indigenous heritage. He bore none of the red-haired genes of his great-great-grandfather, except for the blue eyes, the rest of him taking after his great-great-grandmother's side.

He tucked the small gold pendant under his shirt, something he'd never questioned having or wearing, It had been passed to him from his grandmother and was passed down to her from a time gone by. His grandmother had told him it would protect him, and he was to wear it always, never take it off, even in the shower. He wasn't overly religious, nor superstitious, but he always wore the pendant, and, like instructed, it never left his neck.

"Where's Ryder?" Kye asked when he noticed a particular friend missing.

"He couldn't come, his sister Callie is in hospital," Brax, a lanky teenager with a mop of ink black hair replied.

"Fuck, what happened?" Mat asked. "My sister Zoey goes to school with her. *When* she goes to school, that is."

"Dunno exactly. Think some piss head fingered a bunch of girls in the woods, there's cops all over the place near Macy street and the school side."

"Yeah, Kye said there were cops everywhere. So, change of plans. We take the cars the long way, along Hiking Track road. No one'll be there, and they won't be looking for anyone playing up if they're busy looking for a kiddie fiddler off in the woods."

"Those girls are like sixteen and seventeen, dude, and there's some choice meat there. I'd be fiddling too if I had a chance."

This resulted in a raucous outcry of support and agreement from the six boys in the room and Mat shook his head, hooking his keys from the little yellow plastic hook by the door. "Okay, my comrades, let us ride into the night!"

The boys piled themselves into two cars, laughing and whooping as they roared off into the night. They were far enough away from the ranch house not to disturb the house staff, but the farm hands heard them, shaking their heads in disapproval as the boys drove off into the dusk. One touched his chest, his fingers seeking the pendant that was hidden beneath his clothes and whispered a silent prayer to a god long forgotten by many.

The road around the woods was a long one and not well travelled. In fact, at this late hour it was deserted, if not for the two hotted up cars travelling way too fast, racing each other dangerously along the two-lane black top.

They drove that way until they reached the center of town, then slowed and behaved a little more sedately, not wishing to draw any attention to themselves. They cruised around the town, driving past the main shopping mall and strip shops until they were satisfied that the town was quiet, and no passersby might see them and call the police.

Pulling up outside the rear delivery dock of Hooley's Wine and Spirits, the boys quietly climbed out of the cars, spray cans in hand.

"Keep the engines running and the doors open, in case we need to cut and run," Mat instructed. "And keep fucking quiet, okay? Hooley is still inside, and I don't want him to hear anything."

With nods and thumbs up all around, the teenagers got to work painting obscenities and crude images of genitalia. Kye was working on the back door when he stopped and signaled Mat to come over.

"Door's not locked," he hissed.

"No shit! Fuck me, we're drinking tonight!"

They opened the door slowly, hoping there was no alarm. The back room was dark and seemed deserted. Brax pulled his cell phone from his pocket and turned on the flashlight option, and a couple of others did the same.

"Bingo! Fucking jackpot!" Mat laughed but made sure his voice was no louder than a whisper. "Grab a few boxes but be quiet. We don't want to get caught!"

The boys grabbed what they could indiscriminately. No one checked labels, they just took what they could and sneaked outside, placing the boxes in the trunks of their cars as quietly as possible. Mat found a box of cigarettes and allowed himself a soft whistle of triumph. Kye grabbed any discarded spray cans that the others had left behind and threw them in with the alcohol, then the boys left, again driving quietly until they were out of town. Mat was in the lead and turned off Hiking Track road at one of the parking areas on the side of the woods. He pulled up at the far side of the lot where his car would be shrouded with the moonlight shade of the tall pines, and the other car pulled up beside him.

The boys jumped from their cars with cries of triumph and excitement, their good luck something to be celebrated. Boxes were pulled from trunks as the boys stepped over the chains that surrounded the lot and sat on a great big pine that had recently been cut.

"What have we got? C'mon, guys, who's opening the first box? We need to have a party!" Kye yelled.

Brax ripped open his box and pulled out a long bottle. "Sparkling wine. Is that good?"

"Who cares, just open the fucking thing. What've you got, shit head?"

The red-haired boy pulled open his box and looked at the label. "Sango something? I can't pronounce it. Anyway, it says sparkling red wine. I think my mom drinks it; it tastes like berry soda." He prized open the screw top and took a swig, his face screwing up as he swallowed. "Ah, yup, sour berry soda."

The boys all laughed and shared the bottles around, lighting up the stolen cigarettes and blowing the smoke into the growing dark. The parking lot had only one light, the amenities block another, but where the boys were sitting, they were almost completely enshrouded with darkness. It was a clear night, not a cloud in the sky, and though it was summer, it was briskly cold, the chill in the air easily disguised with cheap wine and cigarettes.

These were the good times, away from their parents, away from school, away from chores, from impending manhood and the threat of having to live on the straight and narrow. It wasn't too far until work and marriage and mortgages, and they boys knew that all too well.

Kye was lying on the ground, a half empty wine box as his backrest as he practiced blowing smoke rings into the night, the full moon an ethereal backdrop. His head was slowly spinning, the sweet, sparkling wine having gone straight to it, giving him a warm, fuzzy feeling.

"Hey guys," Brax paused to belch, eliciting laughter from a few of the boys. "Why is Campbelltown called Campbell*town*? I mean, it's not a little town, really, it's almost a big city. Not a really big city, like, but almost, um, like a small city. Am I right?"

"You fuck knuckle, Brax. I don't even understand what you're saying!" Kyle laughed and coughed at the same time, then laughed at his cough. "Who the fuck cares, anyway? It's an asshole of a town, with assholes living in it."

"We live in it," Mat laughed.

"Yeah, and you're an asshole!"

This made everyone laugh even more, and they shared more wine, more cigarettes, and more joviality. The night grew longer, the moon moved overhead, and the boys fell quiet as they drank.

From the woods, a soft, low-lying mist began to creep. The boys mostly had their back to the woods and could not see it, the tree they were sitting on laying parallel to the last row of tall pines.

Swirling and ebbing, the fog drew closer and closer, silently encroaching on the happy bunch, a soft, almost imperceptible glow emitting from the fog as it moved.

"It's getting cold, guys, don't you think?" Steven, Mat's friend since grade school, asked.

"Fucking freezing is what it is." Mat coughed into his elbow and threw his empty bottle behind him. "I'm gonna take a piss then we should head out. I need some fucking sleep coz I got like a whole week's worth of fucking chores to do before the olds get home."

"Yeah, I need a piss, too. I wonder if the bathroom is still open?" Kye pulled himself to his feet, swaying a little as he stood.

"Why you wanna know if the bathroom is open? You wanna squat like a pussy girl?" Mat laughed drunkenly at his joke. "You know we can just piss standing up wherever we are, don't you?"

He jumped atop the log and unzipped but stopped before removing his manhood. "Fuck me, anyone see that?"

Kyle staggered and turned to look up at his friend, nearly falling over as he did so. "What, you need a magnifying glass to see your micro dick?"

Everyone laughed at that, but Mat stepped down from the log and zipped up. "Shut the fuck up and look over there, you bunch of brainless jerks!"

"Maybe he does need a magnifying glass!" one of the teenagers laughed, as he turned to see what Mat was yelling about. He could see something beyond the log, something glowing and moving, like a cloud of milk, and he stepped backwards, fast, pointing to the woods.

"We need to get the fuck outta here! Shit, guys, will you fucking look? We need to move, now!" Suddenly sober, he scurried back to the cars, his alcohol forgotten. Mat was doing the same, though he picked up a carton of wine, running it to the car. The rest of the boys were confused, until Brax screamed.

They all turned to see what frightened him so, and saw the fog rise up, at least as high as them, then rush towards them all like a tidal wave. Everyone ran to the cars then, all thoughts of cigarettes forgotten, the leftover wine left sitting where they had placed it.

Kye shook his head to try and clear it, but that just made him dizzy and he fell. The fog rushed over him as he landed heavily on the ground, his feet tangled and his confusion intensifying. Mat turned to see his friend being engulfed by the white fog and ran back to help him. His friends started to scream, they yelled and called to him to stop, but he leapt over the chain link fence, the fog parting to let him through as he ran.

Hurry up, come back, and *shit, fuck, oh my god* assaulted his ears as his friends screamed and called to him, but he ran to where he saw Kye fall. The fog cleared in front of him, but the boy was gone.

"*KYE!!!*" Mat screamed, but he was answered with only his friends calling behind him.

The fog still swirled, it flowed and ebbed, dancing around the parking lot and climbing the light poles, but everywhere Mat turned, it parted to let him through. "Guys, Kye is gone! Come help me find him!"

No one came, no one answered him, total silence was all that he heard. The fog seemed to want to avoid him, it parted as he ran to the edge of the woods, trying to spot his friend. He was reluctant to enter the woods, there were too many stories that had been told through his childhood, too many rumors and legends shared for him to broach the woods on a summer's night.

He called a few more times, but only the echo of his voice returned to him.

From the cars he could hear his friends calling his name, so he reluctantly turned to them, scooping up the last carton of wine as he walked, hiking the cigarettes up with his other arm as he carefully stepped over the chain that surrounded the parking lot.

His friends were terrified, and while he felt the cold bite of fear deep in his soul, he had also started to feel confusion rise, a sense of foreboding lifting to be replaced with an awareness that the fog, while surrounding his friends and the cars, would not come near him.

His friends seemed not to notice, they just called to him to run, to come to the cars, to *get the fuck away from the woods.*

"Kye's gone, I can't find him," he said as he put the cartons in the open trunk.

"I don't give a shit, dude, just get your fucking ass in the car. We need to motor out of here, like now." Brax had already opened the door of the car and had one leg inside.

"We need to call the cops, someone, we need to get help!" Mat yelled at him.

"Are you fucking serious?" Brax screamed into his face. "The first thing the cops are gonna ask us is what the fuck we were doing out here! They'll see the booze and the smokes, for fuck's sake, we've even got spray cans in the trunk! There's no way we're getting away with anything, and you know Kye's gone. Jesus Christ, Mat, you grew up here just like the rest of us, you *know* he's gone. You *know* the stories, now get the fuck in the car, we are outta here!"

Mat turned one last time to look back at the woods and his breath caught in his throat. Brax was right, Kye was gone. The fog was now so high, it was nearly as high as the dark, distant treetops, and it was coming at them with a speed that defied belief. He ripped open the driver's door of his car and fell inside, the keys ready in the ignition where he had left them.

Both cars were full, the boys had climbed in and slammed doors, and were now screaming for Mat to drive, *fucking drive, dude*, and he gunned the car to life, skidding as he turned and raced away from the strange fog.

He glanced out of his rearview mirror and saw the fog spill out onto the road, before turning his attention back to the way home.

CHAPTER TWENTY

Lisa was nursing the whiskey that Mike had pushed into her hands, her face pale, her eyes wide. Harry had taken her place back at the table, assuring everyone that she was fine. Ayden was back at his notepad, while Alex was fixing another pot of coffee.

Sam sat beside her, his hand on her shoulder, trying to afford her some comfort. Mike, Shirl and Simon were huddled around the laptop, trying to decipher something that may help them.

"It's more than I can take in, really, I mean, I believe you, but seriously, my rational side just can't absorb that a ghost is trying to communicate through my baby girl." Lisa sipped the whiskey and turned to her daughter. "I just can't reconcile this, I can't."

Harry smiled at her mother, the color now returning to her face a little. "It's okay, Mom, I understand. You know it's not the first time, though, right?"

Lisa just stared at Harry. "First time? Like, it happened before?"

Harry nodded. "She tried to talk to me last time, five years ago. I kind of understood, I mean I tried to do what she said, I think, but I also didn't want to, I don't know, give in? That's what it seemed like, in a way, giving in, kind of."

"You weren't really giving in, not really." Simon turned to Harry. "You just didn't understand what she wanted."

Harry smiled at him. "Exactly. I mean I didn't even really understand that it was her, or her spirit, or whatever. I think that I believed it was me just having my own ideas and, um, insights? I think that's it. Anyway, it's sort of different, this time. I can really tell when she is talking to me, I can even sort of almost see her. Well, not really see her, but it's like an impression, I can tell she has really long, dark hair, so long that she can sit on it. And she is really tiny, like a small child, not like a midget or anything, just a short person. And she was sad, like, really sad. She knew she would die, I think, but that's not even what made her sad. I think it was losing all her people, her home, everything that mattered, everything that meant something to her."

Lisa nodded. "She must have had such horrible things happen to her. Is that why she's still here? A restless spirit, she can't rest until she finishes something?"

Harry shook her head. "No, it's not that, not as far as I can explain, but she does need to stop the K'aas."

"The K'aas?" Simon leaned forward. "Is that the name of the curse, a K'aas?"

'That's the name of the monster," Harry told him. 'It's the curse and the monster all wrapped up in one, they're the same thing."

"Searching that word," Alex said as he leaned over Shirl and Mike and started typing on the laptop.

"I think we need to talk to the girl, what's her name, Ix? Anyway, we need to talk to her again," Sam stood up and began to pace. "She's obviously the key, she can tell us why the thing is back, this K'aas, but more importantly, she'll tell us how to get rid of it."

Harry hung her head, then looked back at her father. "I don't know how to call her, or summon her, or whatever it's called. She just sort of comes without any warning."

"Maybe we could have a seance?" Simon suggested. "If she *is* a spirit, that's like a ghost, right?"

117

Sam looked at his brother, ready to shoot his idea down, but then shrugged. "Who knows? This is the kind of stuff you see in movies, all made up and written by kids who haven't finished college. We could be doing the right thing or making things so much worse. What do you think, pumpkin?"

Harry shrugged. "I'm not against it, but I don't think it's necessarily the right thing to do. Maybe we just wait and see if she comes back on her own."

"Or we could just try talking to her," Ayden suggested. "Ix iLa'al, are you there? Can we speak to you, please?"

Harry tipped her head to one side, and Ayden was ready for her to give him a sarcastic answer, but instead she just blinked her big brown eyes before they rolled backwards in their sockets and she smiled gently.

"I am here, boy who is brother."

Lisa gasped and stared at her daughter. "Harry? What's happening?"

The girl turned her head to face her mother. "Harry has let me speak, for now. She is here, but she is listening, she is not talking."

"We need to ask her things; we don't know how long she'll stay!" Simon exclaimed.

"Yes, absolutely, you're right. Um, Ixy, can I call you that, Ixy?" Sam asked.

Harry smiled but didn't answer.

"Okay, that's settled, I guess. Anyway, you said the thing was called, um, what was the name again, Alex?"

"The K'aas."

"Okay, yeah, The K'aas. We need to stop it and stop it for good this time. Can you tell us how to do that?"

Harry/Ix iLa'al tipped her head to the other side. "You have the means to destroy it. There are three things, the number of three. You need that which you used before. The talisman. You have that. You need the words that I can tell you. But what you do not have, you need to find. I cannot tell you where to find it."

"Okay, that's good." Simon had a pad and pen and was scrawling things down. "So, you can't tell us where to find the last thing we need, but can you tell us what it is, so we know what we're looking for?"

She nodded her head, just a short bob, and placed her hands flat on the table, palms down. "You need to break the images that were made to hold the curse and bind the K'aas. If you do not break them, all will be wasted. You must break these first."

"What do you mean?" Simon asked.

"You mean like the little stick figures Harry broke up last time, the ones in the rocks? There were no more, she broke them all up!" Sam lifted his cap with one hand and ran his hand through his hair with the other.

"Those were for the curse that followed me. They were broken, and the curse would have been broken, should you have said the right words. The K'aas would have been banished, unable to return. Because the words were not said, he was able to linger, to lie waiting, until he was summoned again. It is the one who summoned him that has made new figures to bind him. You need to find that one, you need to break the figures, and then you can end this curse."

"That's good, that's fantastic. We just need to find out who summoned the creature, is that right?" Sam nodded, a hopeful smile flitting across his face.

Harry's eyes were no longer rolled back, instead, she blinked a couple of times, then shook her head. "She's gone. I can't feel her anymore."

Lisa started to cry.

"Mom, are you alright?" Harry's lip quivered; she rarely saw her mother shed a tear.

Lisa got up, found a box of Kleenex and blew her nose. "I'm sorry, I'll be alright in a minute. Maybe some more whiskey?"

Mike jumped to his feet and retrieved the bottle, topping up her glass, then doing the same for himself and Shirl.

"We thought this was all over five years ago. So many people died then, so many people suffered, including us. And not only is it back, and killing again, but it's using my daughter as a mouthpiece!"

"Mom, no, it's not!" Harry stood and walked to her mother. "The girl isn't the monster. She's just a poor girl that had something really bad happen to her. Really bad. And she's trying to help us stop it." She placed her arms around her mother and hugged her. "She's not evil, Mom, she isn't"

"How do you know that, baby? You can't trust a ghost that takes over your body!"

"I can feel that she's good. I can't explain that, I know it's crazy, but you have to trust me. She's good, and her brothers were good. She showed me, I can't tell you how, but she showed me a glimpse of what her life was, when she was just little, and she was always happy. She had a good life and a family that loved her. I know it's hard, Mom, I do, but she's going to help us. I know it, I do, and I need you all to trust me."

"I do," Simon said.

"We all do," added Mike. "We really do, you were the cog in the wheel that kept the whole machine going last time, and it looks like you are going to be the pilot of this crazy ride this time."

"Enough of the wacko metaphors, Mike, let's all sit back down and go over things again." Sam pulled out chairs for Harry and Lisa. "Harry, anything else you can tell us about the girl would be great. Can you do that?"

Harry nodded. "I can. She showed me everything. It was like a movie in my head, and I know it was only a few seconds, or something, but it seemed like it went on for hours. Anyway, I'll tell you what I know."

CHAPTER TWENTY-ONE

She knew the soldier would never give her a chance of escape. Her feet were shackled, and more often than not her hands were also bound. When he rode, he tied her to himself, and when he slept, he chained her to him, her hands bound, her feet chained, but her will was never broken.

She was proud, she had been raised as the daughter of the king, a princess, and never would she let scum such as this one, this base creature not worthy of her thoughts much less her attention, never would she let him break her.

It wasn't easy, though, maintaining her reserve. She was young, very young, not yet of an age that should be with a man, not yet grown. Why this soldier found her interesting, why he longed to keep her as his concubine, was beyond the girl's comprehension. Why these people came from faraway lands to rob her people, to take their gods and their idols, strip them of all their riches, then rape, pillage and burn, was also beyond her understanding.

They appeared riding their horses several moons ago, their armor glinting in the morning sun, their heads helmeted and their ways strange. Her father, the king, had shown these strangers kindness and welcomed them, feeding them and entertaining them, showing the soldiers their ways, and their gods.

The girl kept away from these men, as was her place as a virgin, she was not permitted to speak with any man that was not her family. For her, being the princess, it was even more important that she was held chaste, for her future would hold marriage to the heir of a neighboring kingdom, to seal peace and prosperity for her people. The girl had prepared for this her whole life, she had been schooled in the ways of her people, their beliefs and ethics, their customs and traditions, and was happy to obey them with her customary grace and good nature.

Her brothers had first noticed the soldier watching her, placing himself in her path, tracing her every move so as to get a glimpse of her. They had warned her to keep a mind on him, to be careful, and to never stray too far from their protection.

Her brothers were revered in the kingdom, their identical features, their unusual, bright blue eyes, their strength and intelligence, all lent them to be loved and respected as young gods, ready to rule in their father's place once he passed.

When the brothers felt that the soldiers were planning something they tried to talk to their father, but he was too trusting, too enamored with these strange visitors, and he paid his sons no heed. The brothers tried to talk to their father's advisers, however they feared the wrath of the king and would not risk angering him by bringing the boys' concerns to him.

They saw the soldier becoming bolder around their sister, finding ways to approach her, to engage with her, and once they even saw him reach to touch her hair. They understood he did not know their customs, but they could not understand why a grown man would find a child attractive and try to gain her affection.

They followed their sister more closely, never letting her from their sight, and despaired of finding a way to make their father understand their concerns.

That was when they decided to make the curse, make something that would protect their sister, protect their village, and drive the soldiers away.

The first part was easy, they approached the shaman and explained what they needed, and he provided the words they would need to make their plan come to fruition. They fashioned the chain and the base of the medallion with their own hands, working at night, away from prying eyes. The stone was harder to locate; they had to leave their sister for a whole day as they travelled to the valley of the moon to find the right size and shape of stone that would carry the protective magic.

By the light of a full moon they spoke the words and performed the ritual, sacrificing seven sheep and seven lambs, taking their skins to make a parchment. On the parchment they wrote words and drew the sigils. The curse was nearly made. They spent the next day making little clay figures of the soldiers, letting them dry in the sun before painting them in the colors of the soldiers, their white skin, their drab clothes, and the armor they wore.

The following night they took a soldier, slitting his throat and draining his blood. They wrote on their parchment with this blood and coated the medallion with it before they burned his body on a pyre, the parchment arranged on his chest. The burning and the blood sealed the curse.

The next day they gave the medallion to their sister with the instructions that she was never to take it off, it would be the one thing that would protect her from soldiers should anything happen. The next step they would undertake that night, and it would protect the rest of the kingdom.

However, the brothers had miscalculated, and the soldiers made their move before they had a chance to finish the rest of the curse. Their sister was seized, and all they could do was watch helplessly as she was tied, her clothes rendered from her body, and she was thrown over the shoulder of the man who would ravage her.

They spoke their curses together as the soldiers had his men force them to their knees, a handful of hair grabbed to pull their heads back and expose their throats. They finished the words as the blade cut their necks and took their young lives, their last thoughts of their sister and the unfinished curse that would save their people.

They were thankful they had told their sister some of what was needed, but she had no chance to do anything before she was taken.

The soldiers made the king watch as they raped his daughter and burned his kingdom before slicing his stomach open and spilling his intestines over the blood-soaked ground. They left him crying for his sons as he gathered his insides, vainly trying to push them back into the wound before he expired. His crown was ripped from his head, the jewels around his neck rudely grabbed as he breathed his last, no mercy or pity given by these invaders.

The girl didn't sob or cry out as she was defiled but could not help but gasp in pain as the soldier entered her again and again.

He left her alone, just briefly, after tying her to a post, and she took the chance to say the words her brothers had taught her, the words that would summon the K'aas and bend it to servitude. The words would tie it to the soldiers and would make it hunt each one down until the girl ended the curse and the reign of death and destruction.

That night the creature had appeared.

The fog came first, a low-lying, soft white mist that rolled through the kingdom, around the huts and buildings, swirling its freezing white strangeness around the soldiers, putting out their fires and making them nervous.

The music was next.

The song of the K'aas was fearful, a frightening sound, long and loathsome, and loud enough to split the ears of those it was hunting. It filled every fiber of the soldiers, making them crazed, and they turned on the last of the native people, killing them where they stood, slicing the throats of any men that had survived the initial affront as they tried to fight it, tried to bring it down with their crude pistols, tried to hack it with their swords and knives.

Nothing worked against the tall creature, nothing could stop the many arms that sprang from its back to grab the men, lifting them high before tearing them apart and flinging their remains to the ground. The K'aas killed many that first night before they could run, the girl smiling as each soldier cried out, begging for their lives, screaming their horror and their fear.

When the dawn finally broke the K'aas withdrew, the song and the fog following the great evil creature. Those soldiers who survived that first onslaught rallied and made the decision to run. They gathered the horses and then, taking as many riches and girls as they could carry, they fled the kingdom.

The girl had hoped she would be left behind, but the soldier made sure she was the first to be tied to a horse, his horse, her tiny body draped over the saddle and tied so that she had no chance to escape. For hours she was held like that as the soldiers pushed their horses to their limits, travelling a great distance before the night fell.

That night the fog came again, preceding the song, and again the K'aas killed, reducing the soldiers by more than half. Night after night this happened, the soldiers soon learning that they needed to travel at night and rest by day, the creature always withdrawing by dawn's first light. The soldiers hung onto anything that was theirs, even when they seemed to have no use for it. They kept the empty horses with them, tethering them together and leading them from their own horses. The girl tried to plan her escape, she watched the soldiers' every move, her long hair often hiding her eyes, but not blocking her gaze. She watched everyone, always looking for a chance to flee. When she gave up hope of liberation for herself, she was quick to find ways for her fellow kidnapped girls to run.

Every night that the K'aas appeared to take revenge on the rapists and murderers, she was ready, she was prepared.

They rode like this for many weeks, the horses falling from exhaustion, only to be replaced with the spare horses that the soldiers had tethered to their own. Every now and then a kidnapped girl could escape when the soldier holding her was taken. If the girl was quick enough, she could leap upon his horse and flee.

At first the girls headed for home, but as they drew further and further away from their homelands the girls would follow at a distance, hoping to help rescue their companions.

One morning they found a clearing by a lake, a nice, meadowed land that was calm and peaceful. Overlooking the lake were a series of rolling hills, the grass moving in the breeze like waves of the ocean. The remaining soldiers pulled up here, hoping to sleep during the day, to rest for a little while before racing through the night again.

The girls that were left, only a half dozen or so, made a fire and prepared a simple meal, some trying to hunt for small birds or rabbits to add to their meagre supplies.

The king's daughter was never unshackled, the cruel chains cutting her delicate ankles as she shuffled about, but no matter what she did, the soldier who took her did not ever let her walk free.

She wandered a little way from the camp, the soldiers all exhausted, falling asleep fairly quickly in the warm summer sun. She found a strange array of rocks near the lake, arranged in piles as if someone had stacked them on purpose, some piles as big as herself, some only several rocks high, all placed around in an erratic display of nature.

She knew what to do when she saw one pile that had an opening just big enough for her to squeeze in. She found two hares inside, frightened at her intrusion, and quickly rung their necks. They would suffice for a meal and keep the soldier happy. She suffered greatly when he was unhappy, as he took his temper out on the poor child.

Inside the cairn-like pile of rocks she twisted twigs and bark with strings from her garment, and fluffs of fur from the hares. She made several simple figures to represent the soldiers and placed them about in a ritual pattern. Saying the words that her brothers taught her, she called upon the K'aas to take the men this evening and end the suffering of the girls. She would have to come back and break the twig figures to stop the creature, or it would take the girls as well. This was powerful magic, calling on all of their gods, good and bad, tying them to the tall, slim creature, and making it more powerful than before.

She gasped as a hand grabbed her ankle and tried to pull her from the rocks, so she twisted and wiggled and made her way out, the hares clasped in one hand, their ears providing the best hold.

The soldier smiled at her and nodded, pleased with her effort. He leaned forward and kissed her roughly, seeming to think that she was something to be loved as well as used.

She pushed him away and stood, brushing herself off as he lifted her over his shoulder and carried her back to the camp.

While she prepared a meal for the girls, she indicated for them to be ready, for them to flee when she gave the signal.

With bellies full and their other appetites sated, the men drifted off to sleep in the late afternoon, not intending to stay any longer than an hour or so. The girls stayed as quiet as possible, hoping the men would remain until nightfall, until the K'aas could come and free them from their torment.

As they had hoped, the sun set with the men still snoring away, none of them waking when the night darkened the sky and the stars shone their twinkling lights from horizon to horizon.

They only stirred when a soft wave of fog drifted over the meadow, swirling around the clearing and the piles of rocks, whisping here and there around the horses' feet, making them nicker and call out, the freezing fog causing them alarm.

The soldier jumped to his feet when the cold mist touched him, for the fingers of fog were icy, bitter cold, and the touch from this eerie apparition was enough to bring them to a fully aware state. He had hold of the princess, a grip so tight that she could not flee.

The song came next, the hypnotizing, strange sound that made some men crazy, made them slaves to the creature, unable to think or move for themselves. Those that were not under the spell of the monster ran to the horses, saddling them as swiftly as they could, but to no avail. The creature appeared, slim and tall, so impossibly tall, the long, waving arms coming from its back and waving in a bizarre and frightening way. The horses reared and panicked, breaking free and leaving the soldiers with no way to escape. The fog ebbed and flowed, then all at once it engulfed the men, and shrouded the encampment in a white haze so thick that none could see the monster, nor what it was doing.

One by one it took the soldiers; one by one they fell to the wrath of the deadly curse. The girls who were not tethered ran then, they ran to the hills, away from the fog, away from their tormentors, away from the horror that had defiled them over many weeks.

The girl knew that she had to get back to the little cave, she needed to now put an end to the curse so that the last soldier would be the last to die, and the land would not bear the curse of their actions, the curse of the K'aas.

She slipped from the soldier's grasp and shuffled as fast as her shackled feet would allow, trying to get to the little rock cave and break the curse. Behind her, the K'aas closed in on the last soldier, its long arms reaching to take him and tear him apart.

He drew his weapon and fired at the girl, hitting her in the back, the pellets littering her tiny body, tearing gaping holes in her flesh.

He had shot her out of a false sense of kindness, thinking he was saving her from the monster that was closing in on him. His last breath was taken as he placed the pistol to his chin and pulled the trigger.

The princess was dying, and dying quickly. She struggled to drag herself to the cave, so close yet so far, every ounce of her will getting her to within arm's reach. Unable to go any further she reached for the medallion that hung around her neck. Her hand was slick from the blood of her wounds, and it took a great effort to pull the medallion from around her neck. It was the one thing the soldier had let her keep, mistakenly thinking it was a sign of her noble birth. She flung it with her last ounce of strength and her aim was true, it landed far inside the little cave.

She died there, in the cold night, the swirl of fog receding from her tiny body, her blood seeping into the ground.

When morning came there was no sign of the soldiers, no bodies, no weapons, nothing at all. The body of the girl had disappeared as well, but where she had lain there grew no grass, the ground was barren, but a darker color than the rest of the earth, as if her blood had forever stained the dirt.

CHAPTER TWENTY-TWO

"What're we going to say happened to Kye?" Brax asked.

"We're not saying a fucking thing, you got it? Not a fucking word!"

The boys shuffled their feet, looking uncomfortable. "If we don't say anything, who'll know he's missing? No one will know where to look, Mat. They need to know where to look for him."

"Brax, think about it, you idiot! If we tell anyone where we were, they'll know it was us that hit Hooleys. We'll go to jail, we're all over eighteen. You wanna go to jail?"

Brax shook his head.

"It's not like they'll ever find him, anyway." Mark looked at the shocked faces. "You know I'm right, guys. No one that goes missing in the woods ever turns up alive!"

"He's right, Kye's a gonner. There's no hope for him. He was my best friend, don't think I'm just abandoning him, but he's gone, and we need to be smart." Mat scanned the faces of his friends to make sure they were all on the same page. "We need to keep our mouths shut. If anyone asks us, we need to all tell the same story, okay?"

Stephen put up his hand.

"Hey fuckwit, we're not in school," Mat snorted derisively.

"Yeah, um, shit," Stephen put his hand down. "I just wanted to ask what the story was, you know, the one we're all going to say."

"Yeah, we can't just say we were hanging up in your trailer, Mat. They'll ask us what we were doing." Mark nodded. "We need to say something that is not good, but not illegal, if you know what I mean."

"Well, why don't we say we were drinking and smoking? I know we're underage, but they'll believe us. And the Sheriff won't charge us for underage drinking," another boy suggested.

"Good thinking!" Another school friend leaned forward on the little built-in bench in the trailer kitchen. "We can all say we hiked a bottle from our parents, they'll believe that."

"Yeah, good plan," Mat agreed. "We don't need to get into any other details. We just were handing out, drinking and smoking. Yes, good idea."

"I think we need more than that," Mark said.

"I agree with Mark. We need to at least have a topic of conversation," Brax nodded at his wiseness.

"A topic of conversation? What are you, ninety? Just say we were talking about girls and tits and who fucked who. That's what they think we do anyway, so they'll believe that," Stephen said.

"Alright, that's the plan. We were drinking, smoking, and talking about fucking. And cars. Guys talk about cars. Done. Any questions?" Mat looked around at the faces of his friends, ignoring the sharp spike of fear in his stomach over Kye.

Everyone nodded, then jumped as someone knocked on the door.

"Who the fuck's that?" Mat got up and ran a hand down his shirt, straightening it. "My old's shouldn't be back yet."

"Maybe it's Kye?" Stephen suggested. Mat shot him a look of contempt then walked to the door, opening the latch without looking through the peephole.

"Fuck, Kye! It's Kye! What happened to you? You just disappeared! Fuck, Kye, come in!" Mat stepped back, but Kye didn't move.

He just stood there, his head hanging low, so that his face was hidden. He was shrouded in the dark of the night, the feeble light from the double-wide barely reaching him. He didn't move, and Mat frowned. "What the fuck is wrong with you, Kye?"

"Shut the door!" Stephen yelled.

"Kye? Dude? Are you okay?" Mat sounded unsure, now worried for his friend.

Kye lifted his head.

He had no eyes. His sockets were bloody, black holes, torn and ragged, they wept dark tears of blood down his cheeks. He opened his mouth, a bizarre grimace of a smile, showing his toothless, ravaged gums. The entire lower half of Kye's face was covered in blood, and it had dripped and splattered down the front of his clothes, soaking them through.

Mat stumbled backwards, shocked, and the boys at the table behind him started to scream, a high-pitched siren of terror.

Stephen jumped over the table and slammed the door, pushing the latch over and turning the bolt. He backed away from the door, pulling Mat with him.

"What happened? What the fuck happened to him? Did you see him?" Mat turned to Stephen. "Did you see his eyes? Did you see?"

Stephen shook Mat. "Snap out of it, dude!"

"There were no eyes, he had no eyes!" Brax's voice was high-pitched and filled with terror. "He had no fucking eyes!"

"I know, guys, I know! What the fuck are we going to do?" Mark had stood up and moved as far back from the door as he could. "That wasn't Kye, not really, was it?"

They screamed again when another knock at the door sounded, the banging loud, like he was hitting it with a closed fist.

Mat had his hands over his ears, as Mark's cousin Liam was on the floor, screaming "*Stop it! Stop it! Stop it!*" over and over. Stephen had a knife from the countertop in his hands, and the other boys just looked from one to the other in fear and panic. The banging continued and the boys, in complete terror and confusion, all backed away from the door.

The banging stopped.

Mat took his hands from his ears, and everyone looked at the door.

There was complete silence, except for Liam, who was still whispering his *stop it* mantra.

Another knock sounded and the boys screamed as one.

"*Open the door, Mateo, it's Peter,*" a voice called.

Mat looked at Stephen.

"Who's Peter?" asked Stephen in a hushed whisper.

"He's my uncle, my dad's brother. He works here at the ranch," Mat said, as he walked to the door and looked through the peephole. "It's him, and he's alone."

"*Open the door now, Mateo, hurry,*" the voice urged.

Mat opened the door and his uncle stepped inside, slamming the door behind him. They boys looked at the man, a copper-skinned, black-eyed man, his chiseled features and muscular physique reminiscent of the indigenous tribe that owned these lands long ago.

"What have you done, boy?" Peter asked Mat as he grabbed his arms. "Have you been near the woods on a summer night? What were you thinking?"

Mat shook his head, his terror reducing the brave teenager to a scared little boy.

"We just wanted to have fun, uncle. We didn't think…"

"No, you didn't think, did you? Do you realize what you have done?" Peter pushed Mat away from him and the boy stumbled before catching himself against the table. "You have brought the K'aas right to us! For generations we have kept it from our hearths, but you invited it right to us, all because you wanted to have fun?"

Mat started to cry. "I'm so sorry, I'm so sorry, uncle, I'm so sorry," he blubbered. "Can you stop it? Can you make it go away?"

Peter grimaced, then seemed to notice the other boys in the trailer. "How many of you went to the woods tonight?"

"Just us, and Kye. Uncle, Kye disappeared when we were at the woods, then he came back, but god, um, he wasn't the same, uncle, he was, he was…"

"Yes, I know what he was. I've seen it before. Too many times, my brother's son. Too many times. You have now cursed these friends of yours, they are cursed to die the same way Kye did."

"Nonononono," Liam started to cry again. "Nonono don't, don't say it, *nooooo*."

"But you can do something, can't you, Uncle? You can stop it? You've seen things before, and it didn't take you? Please, Uncle, please, I'm begging you!" Mat fell to his knees. "Please!"

Peter reached down and grabbed the pendant from under Mat's shirt and pulled out his own to match. "We are protected, boy, by our blood, by our birthright! These boys don't have that protection! You have condemned them, and most likely their families!"

"Can't you give us some of those necklaces too?" Brax jumped to his feet. "Just give us one each, so we can be safe, too!"

"Yes, please, oh my god my sister is only eight, please, can we have some too?" Stephen begged, the other boys all nodding and holding out their hands.

Peter sighed. "I don't have enough for all of you. Boys, I am sorry." The teens cried out in outrage, and he raised a hand to quiet them. "I can only offer you refuge, here, at the ranch. Call your families, call them and tell them to come here, tonight, as quickly as they can. I can't offer anything else. I can't say you can stay forever but I can make you safe while you're here. Come on, let's all get to the main house. Mat, you lead, and I'll bring up the rear. If we hurry, we should be safe."

"No! I'm not going out there, Kye is out there, and you don't know what else. I'm staying here, I'm not going out there!" Liam cried.

"Me neither, I'm stayin' here too," Mark stepped as far back from the door as he could. "You can't make us go out there!"

Peter looked to each boy and took a breath. "Sure, you can stay here. No problem. But the only reason your friend, or what used to be your friend, has not come in here is because Mat has a talisman around his neck that holds him at bay. Once he leaves with us you will be here, alone, with no one to protect you. You will be at the mercy of that thing, who will, I am sure, be ready to visit you as soon as we leave. Your choice, boys, but I feel you should rethink your decision."

All the boys leapt to their feet, their minds changed instantly.

"Good decision. All right, stay together, hold hands, I want you to huddle closely together in between Mateo and I, understand?"

He paused for a response, and the boys nodded and started to grab hands.

"You okay, Mat?" The boy looked terrified, but nodded, taking a deep breath to steel himself. "You will be okay, boy. Just keep your head up and walk fast."

"Imma run like Usain Bolt, Uncle."

"No, I think that could be troublesome, someone is bound to fall. Just grab one of your friends' hands and walk fast. Okay?" Mat nodded "Are we ready, boys?" There were nods all round.

Mat reached back and took Stephen's hand. "No homo, dude," he said, and Stephen barked a nervous laugh.

"Okay, move!" Peter ordered, and Mat opened the door and stepped out, straight into a cloud of frigid mist that parted as soon as he put his foot down. He took a sharp breath in alarm, but pulled Stephen behind him, who had hold of another boy's hand. The boys had hold of hands or hooked elbows, a huddled mass of teenage fear. They could see the fog as it lapped and slipped towards them, Liam sobbing and praying, the other boys either searching their surroundings for any signs of their fallen friend, or heads bowed looking at the ground only, trying to avoid any signs of anything other than their own feet.

"There he is!" shouted one teenager, and Brax and Mark started to scream.

"Just keep walking!" Peter yelled, but Brax broke free and ran, with two other boys following.

"You're going the wrong way!" Mat yelled, stopping, trying to call to his friends. "Turn around, you're going the wrong way!"

"Just keep walking, Mateo!" Peter ordered, and Mat started to jog, a faster pace than walking, dragging Stephen's arm as he guided them towards the house.

The three boys that had run towards the light source could no longer be seen, and Mat rounded the corner of a large, dark shed, his feet finding the path to the house as he hurried, the mist still banking each side of the group as they moved.

The house could finally be seen, a safe haven standing brightly lit like a sentinel against the night. There was a low fence that surrounded the house, and Mat opened the latched gate, allowing them entry and they all ran, breaking from their huddled formation towards the perceived safety of the long verandah and bright lights. As they tumbled up the steps, gasping and crying, Mat threw open the large glass door, the panes decorated in intricate patterns and colors, something unnoticed by the panicked teenagers as they stumbled over the threshold.

"What about the others? They went the wrong way!" Mat stood at the door, looking out, his face pale and frightened. "They ran towards the cattle sheds, Uncle. There's nothing there to keep them safe!"

Peter ran a hand down his face and turned to look out into the dark. The fog had filled the entire yard, swirling, flowing and ebbing like water, an incandescent glow of pure fear as it rolled up to the veranda to spill away again, repelled by something unseen within the structure.

"I can go after them. I'll try to find them. The rest of you stay here, you'll be safe. Boy, you there, hand me that flashlight." He pointed to a small table near the door where several flashlights stood, along with a hurricane lamp and candles. Mark handed him the light and stepped back, wanting to avoid the open door at all costs. "Close the door behind me. The sigils on the door will protect everyone. The house is built with the runes all over to protect it, so you are safe, but only while you are inside. Do not open the door. Do not come outside. Do you understand?"

Wide eyed, frightened boys all looked at him, their mouths open, as they nodded, heads bobbing like little birds. He gave them what he thought was a reassuring nod and stepped outside, not turning as Mat closed the door behind him. He strode across the verandah and looked down at the thick fog. It couldn't be more than ten or twelve inches deep, but it looked fathomless, and he was almost reluctant to put his foot down into the swirling mist. He glanced over his shoulder at the white, fearful faces staring at him through the glass panes, then turned back, and stepped off the verandah. The mist parted as his foot touched the first step, and he left the wooden decking at the rear of the house, eight steps all clear as he walked down each one, the mist parting in front of him as he moved towards the gate.

Peter had seen the kids run towards the cattle shed, the lights there making them think they were running to safety. The spotlights were solar powered, they would last an hour more, two, at the most, before their light faded, so he didn't need the flashlight just yet, but he didn't want to tuck it into his jeans pocket in case it fell out unnoticed.

He placed a hand on the gate and vaulted over it, jogging briskly towards the cattle sheds, hoping that he would find the kids alive. Or at all.

A scream split the night, and while it made him jump, he didn't react in any other way. He knew the scream didn't come from the boys, it was coming from further down, away from the hills. The sounds from the woods would often echo up the hills, sounding like they were very close by, when they were usually a couple of miles away. It had always been like that, the sounds of car horns, chainsaws, and the strange and eerie screaming

140

that occurred in summer when the creature was lurking around.

Peter had not heard the screams for five years now, but never thought that they were gone. He didn't know how he knew that; it was just a feeling in his gut. His ties to this land, to the creature, went back for many generations. He always felt connected to the creature somehow, always knew when it was about, when it was hunting, when it was disturbed. For five years he had not felt anything other than its slumber, but two nights ago he felt it rise, felt its anger, and its hunger. He didn't know why it was back or what had started the killing season. He had some ideas, but for now, he couldn't think about it, he couldn't concentrate on that, it was something he would ponder when he had more time. Right now, he had to focus on finding the boys and bringing them to safety.

He rounded the corner of a dark shed and headed towards the light, the mist getting thicker and higher as he jogged, nearing the height of the spotlights. It still parted as he moved, closing in behind him like swirling smoke, hindering his vision and making it hard to see anything other than the white fog.

He caught a movement from his peripheral vision and turned, hoping it was a boy, not an errant bull, when the mist lowered a little and swirled back, revealing the figure of a tallish youth standing there.

A twist in his stomach told him straight away this was not one of the boys he was looking for, it wasn't one of the teens that had taken off running looking for safety. He could only surmise that this was the boy Kye that his nephew had told him about, the one taken by the K'aas. He pulled his jacket tighter and kept walking, but the boy stepped into his path, blocking him, his head hanging low, his feet bare.

Peter stopped, looking at the boy, at the damp hair, the blood-soaked clothes.

The boy lifted his head, showing his bloodied, empty eye sockets, and his grinning, toothless mouth.

Peter tried to walk around the boy, but it stepped in his way again. He tried to step the other way, and again the boy blocked him.

"Seriously? That's what you're gonna do, dance with me?" Peter yelled at the ragged corpse. "We both know you can't touch me, so what do you think you're gonna do? Just keep stepping in front of me?"

The corpse boy tilted its head, as if it was trying to understand Peter's words, or maybe it was listening to something far off. Peter didn't care, he tried walking forward again, and when the thing stepped back in front of him, he lifted his leg high and kicked it, hard, square in the chest, pushing it off its feet and out of his way. The thing rolled back like a rag doll, limbs flopping without control, and Peter continued on as the fog swallowed the dead boy from his sight.

The cattle sheds were right in front of him, the heavy sliding door pulled closed, and that gave him hope. Peter had left the door open when he'd finished up earlier that evening, and there wasn't anyone else on this side of the ranch at this time of the night. The boys had to be in there, they had to have closed the door. He hoped that it had, for at least a short time, kept them safe.

He moved to a smaller door on the side of the building, and he wasn't sure if the boys knew of it or had closed it.

The door had one small light above it, and it shone like a beacon above the swirling mist. He moved to the door, the mist opening as he walked, and tried the handle. The boys must have locked the door. He banged on it, heard muffled screams from inside, and felt an immediate relief. At least two of the boys were in there, based on the screams, so he knocked again.

"Boys, it's Mateo's uncle, it's Peter, open the door!"

He could hear them talking to each other, their worried voices in hushed, panicked conversation. "Open up, I've come to take you to the house!" His call was met with silence, so he banged on the door again. "Seriously, boys, the thing doesn't talk. It can't talk. It's just me, Peter, and if you don't come with me, now, I'll leave you to the corpse that used to be your friend!"

The latch clicked and the door flew open. Three very frightened boys stood before him, their faces stained with tears.

"Come on, hang onto me, let's get to the house." He turned without checking they were all with him, but felt hands clutch at the back of his shirt and the belt on his jeans. He moved quickly, trusting the boys to hang on, their terrified clutches letting him know they were not letting go any time soon.

He rounded the corner of the cattle shed as the lights went out, plunging them into complete darkness. The boys scrambled but Peter kept walking, turning on his flashlight as he moved. He noticed the fog had a glow to it, a soft, strange light that formed right at the bottom of the mist and reflected through the swirling mass. The boys stopped screaming as Peter moved. He made sure he was moving fast, giving the boys no time to dwell, trying to just keep them moving, keep them headed towards the safety of the ranch house.

His flashlight caught something up ahead and he cursed and spat, sure it was the dead boy, but as he drew closer he saw it was the rear end of a large bull, the creature looking at them with startled eyes as it ran off into the mist.

He moved again, closer to the house. He drew around the large, darkened shed nearer the house and gasped as Kye stood there. No longer with his head lowered, he seemed to be looking at them with his eyeless sockets, his mouth moving like he was trying to speak.

He reached one arm towards them, the boys again screaming as Peter continued ahead, Kye stepping out of their way as they passed. They made it to the house gate, Peter leaning over to unlatch it, when the boys screamed again. He felt a tug on the back of his shirt that nearly pulled him from his feet, and he turned just in time to see one of the boys being pulled back into the fog, unseen hands whisking him away as he screamed.

"Run to the house!" Peter yelled at the other two, shoving them through the gate as he ran after the screaming boy.

He ran fast, following the sound, the heart-wrenching cry, the mist parting before him and closing behind him, the glow showing the faintest dark outline of the boy, his scream seemingly endless.

Peter pushed harder, he felt he was gaining, getting closer, he was sure of it, he was so close…

He reached out and grabbed a handful of the kid's sweater. Lunging forward he grabbed the kid's arm and dug his heels in, pulling them both to a stumbling, falling stop. The kid and he were face to face, their noses almost touching. The kid started to smile, opening his mouth to speak, when he was jerked away again. Peter jumped to his feet, but this time he had no clue as to which way to run. The mist was close around him, still, softly swirling, it gave no clue to which way the boy had been taken.

He knew he could do nothing, he had to get back to the house to protect the kids there. He turned and there was Kye, right in front of him, face split in a bloody grin.

Peter hit him, a punch filled with rage and loathing and hopelessness. The Kye thing flew backwards, the mist swallowing him up, and Peter marched back to the house, his anger and fear mounting and flushing him with a strange, prickling heat.

He slammed the garden gate behind him, the boys screaming at him to *hurry, run!* as he marched towards the doors. He did not increase his speed, he just walked to the door, the boys opening it and pulling him inside, and he turned as they slammed it.

A wall of fog banked up at the steps of the verandah and then fell back, the wave rolling and crashing as if the verandah had an invisible wall around it.

Further back, barely seen in the fog, stood a dark shape. It was tall, very tall, and seemed to be waving long, thin arms. The fog rose and crashed again, and the shape was gone.

CHAPTER TWENTY-THREE

The girls were frightened, they were cold, and they were hurt. Some were more hurt than others, but all had been raped, all had been beaten, all had been taken from their homes. The youngest was only seven years old, the oldest was thirty-three. The rest were all ages in between, though mostly younger, as was the soldiers' preference.

The princess had helped free most of them, others had run when they had the opportunity, taking a horse or two if they could. The girls headed towards their home, at first, but then pulled up, fearing for their fellow kidnapped friends. They followed the soldiers from a distance, grabbing horses as their owners were taken, making sure every girl had a mount to carry her. Occasionally the horse would have supplies tied to its saddle, even weapons. It wasn't much, but it was enough to keep the girls alive, enough to make them feel safe. They followed the soldiers for many, many days, tired, weak, but full of resolve. Every time a girl ran free, they collected her, put her on a horse, and followed.

Sometimes they grew braver, and skulked into the camp of the soldiers, taking a horse, cutting the ties of a girl or two, grabbing some supplies. They could never get close to the daughter of their king, however. The poor girl was in chains, her feet shackled, often her hands tied, and the soldier that took her, someone high up in a rank that meant nothing to the survivors, never let her far from his side or out of his sight. Not even once.

They watched from afar that night when the creature came to take the last of the soldiers. The princess had told them she would break the curse, she would end it, when the last soldier was killed. No one had thought that the last soldier would kill the princess before she could stop the curse, and none of the girls really knew how to stop it, not completely. They knew bits and pieces, like most from their homeland they knew how to summon it, but they did not know how to end it.

They were alone then, the last of the girls mounted on horses, the last of the supplies, what there was of them, stowed in the saddle bags, but they were lost, cold and hungry, and very far from home. They had seen their home burning as they were taken and they were sure there was nothing to go back to. Their families were dead, their homes burned to the ground, their animals killed, and their treasures stolen.

There was nothing for them there.

They waited until dawn, when the sun rose in blazes of gold and red, bright beams of glorious diamond rays touching the long meadow grass, glinting off the backs of the dew-covered bison in the distance, and warming their cold, barely clad bodies.

They sat on the grass of the meadow, far from the soldiers' campsite, and watched the morning rays touch the tops of the strange trees that had birthed from the blood of their dead princess. The trees now covered the valley, from one side of the lake almost around to the other, and stretched as far as their eyes could see.

They needed a plan, needed to decide what to do next. Now that they were free, now that the soldiers were dead, and now that the morning opened with them orphaned and homeless. They looked to the oldest girl, a dark-eyed beauty, formerly a concubine to the king. She was taken, despite her age, because of her grace, her lithe body, her exotic features catching the eye of many a soldier.

She sat, now, watching the sunrise, watching the birds and deer as they moved about the meadow, eating the grass and catching insects. She watched rabbits scurrying around and playing with each other in the warmth of the early morning sun. She gasped when she spied the silhouette of a man on a horse, and for a split second her fear thought the man was an escaped soldier, but he was joined by another, and another, until the crest of the hill was filled with many men on horses.

The girls grabbed up their horses, ready to mount and flee, but the older girl raised a hand, stilling their action. She nodded to them to let them mount the horses, but they stayed still, waiting for the men to come to them.

The men rode down, slowly, no weapons in hand, no bows drawn, stopping before they reached the girls. They sent just two men forward, two who rode up to the girls slowly, their faces open, their eyes kind, their manner respectful.

They looked at the girls, at the bruises, the torn garments, the rope burns, and their faces darkened. They shared no language but could clearly see the girls rode horses that did not belong to them, carried weapons made for the large hands of men, and were frightened and alone.

They took the women back to their village, to their people, who welcomed them as their own, who fed them, cared for them, and birthed the children that some of the girls bore from the soldiers.

One did not bear a child from the soldiers; she had already been pregnant when she was taken. She bore twins, two perfect boys, identical in looks, both with striking blue eyes and fair skin, both the sons of the dead king from her home.

Twins were rare and blue eyes even more so, and the people of the village treated these boys as special, teaching them the ways of their tribe, raising them as their sons, and marrying them to their daughters. The blood of the stolen girls blended with the tribe of people from this land, their myths and legends passing down to their children and their children's children.

They watched over the forest and kept the monster there at bay, the girls forging talismans from the gold the soldiers had taken and protecting the people of the village, their offspring, and their lands.

They held their myths and traditions close; they did not share their lore with the white man when he came to these lands, his wagon trains and people many, their ways and customs strange. The tribe was respectful and kept to themselves. As time passed, they drifted from their village, they assimilated with the white people, and they married within them, leaving their lands and their ways.

One family stayed in the hills, one family kept the lands that had belonged to the peaceful nation of indigenous peoples, and though they occasionally married a white person, they did not leave their lands. An enterprising young man appeared one day, having come all the way from Ireland, and he fell in love with a blue-eyed, copper-skinned beauty that lived in a small shack on the hill. He was a clever man, this Irishman, and he knew cattle and sheep. He knew them so well that he built an empire, along with a massive house, many outbuildings, and a fortune in the bank.

He sired twin sons, who sired twin sons, and in turn they sired twins. Each one identical, each one with his mother's dark features and his father's Irish name.

They all continued the running of cattle and sheep, their fortunes grew, but they never forgot where they had come from, and never forgot their myths and legends, passing the important stories from parent to child, from generation to generation.

They watched over the woods but never broached the borders. They respected what went on there, they respected the curse, and kept themselves safe with the small gold medallions that were passed to them from their families. Anyone who came to work on the ranch was a descendant of the local indigenous people, and each wore a medallion, each knew the legends, and each made sure to stay far away from the woods when the seasons turned, and summer began.

The owners of the ranch and the people that worked there heard the chainsaw that morning the K'aas was awoken, they heard the crash as the mighty pine was felled, they felt the fear in their stomachs, and they felt the ripple through the earth as the first of the mighty trees died.

The woods were part of their history, part of their culture, part of their very blood. They were direct descendants of the last king, they were the guardians of the lands and of the woods, and they were shocked and saddened at the threat of razing those trees to the ground.

They could not let the trees be cut; they could not let the woods be lost. The owner of the ranch and his wife left that same day to speak to the owners of the Crosspine Timber and Sawmill, leaving their lawyers to file injunctions with the local government that meant to clear and sell the land. They would fight the white men with the white man's laws, they would protect the woods, and they would make sure not one more tree fell.

CHAPTER TWENTY-FOUR

"So, this K'aas, the monster, it wasn't meant to stay, it wasn't meant to hang around and kill people for hundreds of years, right?" Shirl swirled his glass of liquor around. "They just wanted it to kill the bad guys, but now the thing kills everyone and everything that goes near the woods."

Harry nodded. "She tried to stop it once its job was done, but she couldn't. She died before she could say the words and rip up the little stick men. I can feel her pain and her frustration, I can feel it like it happened to me, like a memory of the pain, you know?"

"Yeah, I get it," Sam said. "So now we need to figure out who cursed the woods all over again, who woke the damn thing up."

"The way I see it," Lisa began, shifting in her chair. Her acceptance of the spirit talking through her daughter was not quite complete, but she was choosing to move on and try to find an end to this twisted story. "Is that it all started when the sawmill guy went into the woods. So it's the creature defending its home, maybe?"

"They were the first victims, the sawmill people, sure. But Jake called the company, Crosspine Timber and Sawmill, this morning," Alex lifted his notebook from his top pocket. "Seems this has been in the works for a while, and early Monday morning, two days ago, a large pine was felled as a test, to take samples and test for quality. I'd say that's the first trigger."

"Absolutely! Do you think the K'aas, that's what you called it, yeah?" Lisa paused for Harry to nod her affirmation. "That the K'aas was trapped in the trees, or

151

lives in the trees, and when one was cut down it was let out?"

"Could be, the woods have always been where the thing lived, so it kind of makes sense," Mike nodded.

"No, no, I don't think so," Harry looked at the faces around the table. "It doesn't feel right, somehow."

"The girl, Ix iLa'al, she said that the curse has been done again, so I don't think that the creature came out of trees, at least not by itself," Simon had his hand on the tattered journal. "The thing was summoned by someone, and I'd say it's a pretty even bet that it's someone who's either connected to the woods or protected by them."

"Do you have any ideas, brother?" Sam asked.

Simon looked at Harry. "What do you think?"

Harry shrugged. "I'm not sure, I mean, I don't really have any idea. I know there are protesters everywhere whenever a forest is threatened, but I don't think I've seen any around the woods. Have you guys seen anything?" She looked at the deputies, and they all shook their heads.

"Even if there were protesters, they'd have to know how to say the curse. Ix has been dead for centuries, so unless she, or her brothers, are haunting someone else's family I can't think that protesters are the ones that called the creature up this time," Sam sighed. "Any other ideas?"

"The girl, Ix iLa'al, she wasn't the only girl the soldiers took from her village, or town, or whatever it was called. There were others, weren't there?" Harry nodded at her uncle. "Well, what if one of those, or all of those, ended up here in the original settlement? Maybe they've passed down the traditions to their offspring?"

"No, not the town," Ayden pulled his chair back a little. "There used to be a tribe of Native Americans that lived here, in the hills, didn't there?"

"Yes! That's where Josiah was when he was found, wasn't he? Dad used to tell us those stories all the time, remember, Simon?" Sam asked his brother, and Simon started to flick through the journal. "The girls would have run off to the tribe that lived in the hills, and they could have passed down everything they knew!"

Simon found what he was looking for and looked up at his brother. "Josiah was with the native people for about a year, and they did mention that they had lived there since before time was counted. So, it would make sense. If they were the only people here back then, there wouldn't have been anywhere else for girls to go."

"The girls were given refuge, they were given love, they were given a life here," Harry spoke quietly, and Lisa gasped when she looked at her daughter to see her eyes rolled back in her head. "They were welcomed to the people here and became the people of this land. They birthed children, they kept our customs, and their children kept the customs. But there is more that you should know. There is more." Harry/Ix iLa'al stared straight ahead, her whitened eyes not focused on anyone. "My father had a companion, a wise and gentle woman. She birthed the offspring of the king, of my father, right here in this land, right here, overlooking the woods of the K'aas. The line of my father continued and does continue still. You need to find the descendants of the king, for only the royal blood could call the K'aas, only the royal bloodline would have the power and the words to make it kill."

"Do you know who that is? Can you tell us who might be your relatives, do you have a link to them because of your bloodlines?" Simon asked the girl.

"What? How would I know that?" Harry's brown eyes were back, and she seemed unaware of what had happened. "Oh, right, I'm getting it now, like a memory, sort of, when she talked to you."

"I wish we could find a way to talk to her a bit longer, or when we need her," Sam sighed.

"I'm not sure I want Harry to go through that, it's quite unsettling!" Lisa stood and grabbed the whiskey bottle. "I don't think I can ever get used to that."

"Wait, um, I think I can see something, sort of," Harry closed her eyes. "She had twins. The woman had twins, the one that used to be the friend of the king. Not a friend, a, um, a *concubine*? Isn't that the right word?"

"Yes, pumpkin, that's the right word," Sam shrugged. "I can't see how that helps. There were no birth records back then, no written records at all. No way we can find out who had twins centuries ago."

"My friend Ronni's sister went to high school with twins. The O'Gradys. They're identical twins, like you guys." Harry looked from her uncle to her brother. "It's weird, too, because their father is an identical twin as well."

"Why is that weird?" Mike asked. "Twins can run in families."

"Not identical twins," Lisa told him. "That's just luck, not hereditary. It would be rare for identical twins to have identical twins."

"There was a teacher at school, Mr. O'Grady. Homer O'Grady, he taught grades a few years ahead of us, remember, Simon? He was a twin, his brother, what was his name? Ben? Allen?"

"Ben. Ben O'Grady," Simon told him.

"Yeah, that's right. They were identical twins, too. They liked us because we were twins as well, they were always really nice to us. They went to school with our mom and were friends of the family. Homer was a teacher; his brother ran the ranch. He would be Ben and

Peter's father. Ben runs the ranch now, I think his brother lives up there, too. Ben has twin boys." Sam looked at Lisa. "What are the chances of at least three generations of twins?"

"Four," Simon corrected him. "I remember Mr. O'Grady telling me their father was also an identical twin."

"That's just way too many generations to be a coincidence. Ayden look up city records. How far does the twins line go?" Sam instructed.

"There's something else, Sam," Simon flicked some pages of the journal, and looked up at his brother. "Little Josiah? He actually married an indigenous woman, from the local tribe. She had twin brothers; they became employees of the sheriff's office. They had blue eyes, and their father was one of twins, too. Josiah didn't write much else, though he did have twins, one child died soon after birth. Sam, there are heaps of twins in our line, too. Even our dad was a twin, his brother died when he was tiny, I can't remember why."

"Measles. He died from measles when they were three. And their father was also a twin, but his brother died in the war. You're right, I've never thought about it much before, I just thought twins were hereditary. What's the bet they were all identical?"

"Wait a second here, back up, dad. Are you saying we're related to the Ix girl? That we're descendants of the king?" Alex stood up, then sat down. "I'm not a twin, so that doesn't really fit."

"Tell him, Sam," Lisa said, her voice soft. "He has a right to know."

"Know what, Lisa? Dad, what do I have a right to know?"

Sam looked grim. "You were a twin. So was Brent. Your brother, your identical brother, died three days after he was born. He caught a virus from a visitor to the hospital, and he was too little to survive. Somehow, you managed to beat it, but you were pretty sick for a few weeks."

Alex looked shocked. He turned to his uncle, his eyes filled with tears. "What happened to Brent's brother?"

Simon shook his head, then looked down at the table. "His mom nearly miscarried when she was about six months pregnant. Brent's brother died then, three months before Brent was born. We didn't even know he had a twin until the birth, the other baby was small, it didn't show on any scans. I never gave it any thought, really, we were expecting only one child, we had only one child."

"That's why we could stop the thing the first time around, isn't it?" Harry asked. "It wasn't just that we were twins and one girl, like the first people, but that we were actually related to them! Wow, this is super cool!"

"I'm glad *you* think so," Lisa poured another whiskey, but pushed it across to Simon. "Why didn't you figure this out before?"

Simon looked at the glass, then up at Lisa. "We knew we had Native American blood, but it was from so long ago, and so diluted, that we never thought much about it. I mean, I didn't really see any connection. Why would I?" He picked up the whiskey glass and downed the contents in one swallow. "I was too focused on the stone and the legend, I never thought we *were* the legend. It was only right at the end we knew that the twins thing had some sort of connection, but we thought it was just luck, you know? And Harry, being the only girl born for so long, for so many generations, well, that's all I saw."

"So, we're related to the O'Gradys?" Alex asked.

"From a long way back, but yeah, we are, it seems." Sam looked thoughtful. "Thing is, we may have other relatives, other sets of twins, and any one of them could be the person that started the curse this time."

"All the way back to the start of records," Ayden said.

"What?" Sam looked over at him, confused.

"The run of twins in the O'Gradys line. It goes back as far as records go. Though the twins got a little whack there, one set of twins were girls, not boys, one of them married an immigrant, that's where the surname comes from. They were the only girls born like that, any other girls were single births, and all born after twin boys. Though there weren't many girls. Anyway, that's their line. I can search for any others, or their relatives, you know, the other twins' families?"

"This could take all night. We should start with what we have and go from there. We have the O'Gradys, so let's see if they have anything to do with this curse. We may just get lucky first-time round." Sam stood up from the table. "We should go pay them a visit."

"It's after midnight, Sam. People will be in bed. You can't go up there now, in the dark. It's too dangerous with the monster lurking about, anyway." Lisa stood up as well. "I think you all should try and get some sleep, at least a couple of hours, if you can. You'll think better if you're rested, and right now that's what we need. Every brain working at full capacity."

Shirl stood as well. "I'll give Mike a lift home, then."

"No, I think it'd be best if you stayed here, if we're all under the one roof." Lisa looked at Mike and Shirl. "We've got a pull-out sofa in the living room, and there's a spare bed in the study. Or there are bunks in the spare room. I want you both here tonight, there's no way either of you should be out there, with that thing waiting to grab you." Lisa turned to her daughter. "I've got spare toothbrushes for everyone, Harry, can you grab them from the closet?"

"I'm on the sofa bed," Shirl nodded at Mike. "You can take the spare room. Are we safe in here, though? I mean, if the thing comes for us, are we safe? It's not like we have a weapon against it or anything."

Sam looked around at his companions, at his children, at his lover. "I hope we'll be okay, Shirl, I really do. What we have got, most importantly, is Simon's medallion. It held off the thing before, I can't see why it won't work this time."

"It will work, you know. It's the original curse, and the girl said we still need it. I believe her. Don't you?" Harry asked, and yawned. "I'm off to bed. Good night all."

"Good night, Pumpkin," Sam said, and as he bent to kiss her on the head the first scream split the quiet of the night.

CHAPTER TWENTY-FIVE

Alison had worked at the hospital for nearly fifteen years. She started at reception during her college years, then her nursing career kept her at Campbelltown General, a position she not only enjoyed, but reveled in. She considered it her life's calling. Not only was the hospital her second home, it was also where she met her husband, Donald, when the tall, handsome doctor transferred from Metro City.

While they tried to roster themselves on at the same time, this wasn't always possible, and more often than not at least one of them had to pull a second shift. Tonight, it was Alison's turn, and she had been on her feet since eight-thirty that morning. It was now well after midnight, and her feet hurt almost as much as her lower back. She was hungry and tired, but still in good spirits. Alison was pretty much always in good spirits.

She was doing her rounds now, checking vitals, administering medication where needed, answering the patient's alerts, and trying to maintain her colleagues' sanity. All going well, she should be able to leave in an hour or two, and she was looking forward to snuggling in bed beside her husband for a couple of hours, at least.

Her cell phone buzzed in her pocket, and she smiled. Donald had programmed her vibration alert with different patterns for different callers, and she knew the one set for her husband off by heart.

"Hello honey," she smiled as she answered.

"I've made dinner, would you like me to run it up to you, babe?"

"Goodness, no, honey, you worked until an hour ago, you must be as tired as I am. Just pop it on the bench and I'll nuke it when I get home." Alison walked to her next room, grabbing the chart from the door as she went.

"You doing your rounds?" Donald asked.

"Yup. Ange and Julia should be in soon, so I'm doing last rounds. I'm in the cardiac ward right now, everyone's asleep, so it's nice and quiet. I'll call you when I'm about to leave, okay?"

"Sure, babe, I'll wait up. See you soon, I hope."

Alison smiled again and popped her phone back in the hip pocket of her smock. She looked at the chart in her hand, flicking through the pages to check the patient history. She could hear music, or maybe a television, somewhere further down the corridor. It was quiet, barely heard, and didn't worry her. It could be that a television was left on in the day room, or maybe a patient was having trouble sleeping and decided to watch a bit of the latest movie or show.

She glanced down the corridor and frowned. There was something strange, something that made her place the patient chart back in the holder and walk down the corridor, her frown firmly in place.

There was something wrong, something strange…

Was that fog?

She had a small flashlight in one of her pockets; it helped with patients at night, better than turning on the overhead lights and disturbing them. The hospital had an evening policy with the lights in corridors, it was at quarter strength in the evening, and tonight was no exception.

She shone her little light towards the white mist that was flowing down the long corridor, the strange, soft fog rolled and swirled, twisting like it had a mind with rational thought.

She couldn't see where it originated, but she could see the fog flowing into the critical care ward and became increasingly worried.

She could only think of liquid nitrogen causing a fog like this, like a special effects smoke machine. Being one of the senior nurses, Alison often worked alone, but there were other nurses and staff in other areas. She moved closer to the empty nurses' station, leaned over the high desk and pressed the intercom.

"*Presley here,*" a hollow voice echoed in response.

"Pres, it's Alison. I think I have a problem in critical care."

"*You need help, love?*" Presley's deep voice, along with his lilting southern accent, was always soothing, and Alison smiled despite her worry.

"I've got something weird, looks like fog, along the floor. Could be a leak of some gas or something? Better send someone up here ASAP."

"*Right on it, Ali. Hang in there.*"

"Okie dokie. I'll just have a look, make sure the patients are safe." Alison released the button and turned back to the corridor. Her alarm grew, her heart starting to beat a little faster. The fog had risen, it was now knee height, and she wasn't sure if she should enter the fog with no way to know whether it was toxic or not.

"Hey! What's going on?" a voice behind Alison called, and she turned, breathing a sigh of relief. It was Marlo, the security guard, closely followed by Presley, a fellow nurse.

"It's this fog, or gas, I'm not sure where it's coming from. The only gas we have here is oxygen, and it shouldn't be doing this, so I'm confused."

Presley walked up to the fog.

"Don't touch it, dude!" Marlo called. "Move back, let me have a look at it."

Presley didn't move back, but he waited for the overweight security guard to join him. "There's no scent, no odor, from it. It looks like fog," Presley reached down and plunged his hand into the white mist. Marlo grabbed him and pulled him backwards.

"Dude! You don't know what that is!" Marlo gasped.

"It's freezing, super cold," Presley turned back to Alison. "That's like normal cold, but with a cape on."

Alison laughed, despite the bizarre situation. "You're an idiot, Pres. So what is it? It can't be fog, not inside like that. There has to be some explanation."

"Can you guys hear music?" Marlo asked.

"Probably just a TV on in a patient's room," Alison remarked.

"Yeah, maybe, but hun, this is critical care," Presley turned back to look down the corridor. "There ain't no TVs in this wing."

Marlo started to back up. "Guys, we need to get outta here," he said as he turned to look at Alison. "You know what this is, right? You guys know!"

Presley didn't back up from the fog, but he turned, his nose screwed up in confusion. "No, my boy, I do not know what this is. Other than weird fog, and music. Also, have you noticed this weird fog shit is glowing?"

"I'm outta here. You guys need to get outta here, too. Now, right now!" Marlo turned and ran towards the elevators.

"What the hell? I thought he was security!" Presley scoffed. "Why he so scared of a little fog?"

Alison stepped back, suddenly unsure. "I think he's right; I think we need to get out of here, Pres." She stepped back a little more, her eyes riveted on the fog.

"Girl, what's your problem? Why you freaking out? If it's dangerous, we need to be getting the patients outta here!"

"If they're asleep, they'll be okay. Pres, honey, trust me. We need to be out of here, like yesterday. We need to run and run now!"

Presley frowned at her, not moving, so Alison reached forward and grabbed his arm, pulling him along with her. The fog started to rise higher, and the music grew a little louder. In the shadow near the end of the corridor, Alison thought she saw something move.

"Fuck it, Presley, *RUN!*" Alison screamed, and headed the same way Marlo had fled. Her panic was infectious and Presley ran as well, not looking back, not wanting to see what had caused his friend such panic.

They almost flew around the corner, Presley stumbling, one knee touching the linoleum before Alison yanked him up and almost dragged him to the elevators. Marlo was just entering; he saw the two and held the door for them as they neared.

Presley slammed into the back of the elevator and Alison turned to stab the door close button repeatedly, trying to close it before whatever she saw in the corridor caught up to them.

The fog had followed them and was starting to flow into the elevator, the doors taking what seemed like forever to close.

"Come on, come on!" Marlo stabbed at the button on his side of the door and finally they started to close, moving silently across, just as the fog banked higher. They all stood, staring at the door, waiting for the elevator to move.

Nothing.

"What's going on? Why are we stuck here?" Alison looked at Marlo, her face pale and drawn with panic.

"I don't know!" Marlo started at the panel. "Oh, fuck me, we didn't press a floor!"

He reached forward to stab a floor number, but his hand brushed the wrong button and the doors started to slide back open.

"Shut the door!" shrieked Presley.

"Shut the door, oh my god, shut the door!" Alison again stabbed the close button. "Come on!"

The fog gushed in, filling the elevator car with a frigid white cloud, freezing cold and opaque, and Presley started to scream.

"There's something there!" His voice was panicked and high-pitched. "Look, there's something there!"

Through the fog, barely seen, but impossible to not see, a tall shape was advancing on the elevator. Alison saw it and started to scream as well, and Marlo grabbed his chest, stumbling backwards, his mouth working in a silent cry for help. As the thing drew near, the doors finally decided they would close, and moved together, cutting off the flow of the fog, and inhibiting the view of the tall figure.

Just as the doors were nearly shut, a slim hand broke through the gap, a white, bony, long-fingered hand grasped the door, followed by another hand, and another, and another.

Marlo fell backwards, his face growing dark, turning purple, and his mouth gaped wide open, a strangled noise issuing as he slumped to the floor.

"Ach ack ack," he uttered as even more hands joined the others, forcing the doors open. Alison tried to step back and she tripped on Marlo's splayed legs, falling against his ample belly. She screamed, Presley screamed, and Marlo exhaled, though no inhale followed that spent breath.

On the ground floor Julia and Ange, the late shift nurses, stood, takeaway coffees in hand, as they waited for the elevator to arrive.

"It's going to be a long night," Julia sighed as she sipped her coffee. "I barely got any sleep; the dogs would not stop barking!"

"Yeah, I heard you getting up a couple of times to try and settle them. I thought whippets were supposed to be non-barking dogs." Ange stifled a yawn.

"They would be, if the damn squirrels didn't keep teasing them through the patio doors. Oh, here's the elevator, finally. I was about to report it as out of order!"

The doors slid open, spewing out a waterfall of white fog. The girls jumped backwards, the shock of seeing the white gaseous substance giving them a fright. The fog dissipated instantly, vanishing to nothing, revealing a single figure, alone, in the back of the elevator car. Marlo was lumped on the floor, his head lolling to one side.

Coffees dropped, spilling across the shiny linoleum as the two nurses rushed in to help Marlo, his face turning black, his tongue, swollen and huge, protruding through his cracked lips.

"He's cold," Ange said as she felt for a pulse. "He stinks, like he's been dead for days!"

Julia drew back, confusion darkening her face. "I saw him alive as I was at the coffee machine not ten minutes ago, Ange. What happened? What was in that gas?"

CHAPTER TWENTY-SIX

The screams continued, the sounds of fear and horror splitting the night. There was no way to tell which direction they came from, they just reverberated across the town in an intermittent cry from the depths of hell. Calls came into the station from all over town, people were being woken by the screams and were understandably worried. Jacob and Aaron had been running the show with the senior staff away and were running out of steam. Their exhaustion was taking over when a call came in from the hospital, reporting missing people and the appearance of a strange fog.

Wallis had to leave the boys, Alex and Ayden, behind to continue the research with Harry and her mother, his brother somehow managing to sleep through the shrieks. Shirl and Mike drove their squad car behind him, lights flashing but no sirens. They had decided on the lights to add some feeling of comfort for those that were up and wondering what to do about the shrieks, hoping that everyone would stay indoors and away from anywhere, or anything, that could put them in danger.

Aaron was waiting for him out the front of the station as Wallis pulled up, and the Sheriff could see from the young man's expression that the night had not been a quiet one.

"What's the latest?" Wallis asked him as he got out of the squad car, Shirl and Mike pulling up on the other side.

"You better come inside, sir, there's a bit happening. Well, more than a bit."

"Well, boys, let's go. No use hanging around here." Sam followed them into the station, with his two Senior detectives bringing up the rear. At this time of night, the station would normally be a graveyard, Michelle would have left for the day and the reception desk would be unmanned, with Joan, the night receptionist, doing paperwork or helping with reports. Only a skeleton staff would man the station, though there were always men on call, and at least one car patrolling the streets of the normally quiet town.

Tonight, there were several people waiting at the reception desk, and Joan was standing, trying to answer the phone as well as deal with the people waiting to speak to her.

Wallis nodded his head at Mike to go help her and led Shirl into the back office. There were more men on tonight, the young deputies had done a fantastic job at keeping the station under control, but they were more than happy to let the boss take over.

"Sitrep. Who's first?" Wallis moved to his desk and sat down.

Jacob came over carrying a stack of reports, his face as tired and worried as his partner's. "Sir, it's going crazy here. I have to say, at first when the guys told us about what happened five years ago, we thought they were having us on, seriously. But as the night wore on, I have to tell you sir, I think maybe they were holding back on some of the details."

"Maybe more than some," Aaron joined them, his voice low so as to not be heard by his fellow deputies working at other desks and interviewing some members of the general public.

"I'd bet they held back a lot, boys, but I have to say, this day past has to be some shit storm the likes of which we've not seen before," Wallis sighed. "It's far worse than ever before, well, that *we've* ever lived through, anyway. How many missing that you know of?"

167

Jacob handed the Sheriff a list. "We have the sawmill guy, Patrick, the four schoolgirls, Vikki and John, and the girl and guy they were investigating, and the six volunteers. From the hospital, two nurses, the guy, Albert, the heart attack man from this morning. The girl in a coma, the one that they found in the woods, she's still there in the hospital, but hasn't woken up yet."

"The heart attack guy, fat Albert, he's gone?" Shirl asked.

"Yes sir, he's gone. We've got a massive amount of people that have disappeared, and that's not all that's happening." Jacob pulled his notepad from his top pocket. "Hooley's Drug and Alcohol was vandalized and robbed earlier tonight, and soon after we had reports of two cars speeding and racing along Hiking Track road. I haven't sent anyone out to look into that, I figured they'd be long gone by the time we got there, and I didn't want to have any men away when we could need them elsewhere."

"And have you?" the Sheriff asked. "Needed them elsewhere, I mean?"

"The screams have kept the phones busy, and there are people coming in to see what we're doing about it. It's been nonstop here, sir. We're also getting reports of people going missing, right from their own homes. Most of the time they see fog, or hear music, then someone goes missing"

"Jesus Christ, this is a mess. Not you guys, you've been doing a fantastic job holding the down the fort. Trust me when I say we've been working on this, ah, situation, and looking into our research from five years ago. We haven't got any strong leads, not yet, but we have a few theories that could bear fruit very soon."

Mike came through the swinging door, his face as grim as those around the Sheriff's desk.

"What've you got there, Mike?"

"Boss, I got some parents out front that say their kids are up at O'Grady's ranch, and they've had calls from their kids in a panic, telling them to get to the ranch so they can, in their words, 'be safe'. A couple of the kids said something is after them, and they can't leave the ranch house, or *it* will get them."

"What makes them think they're safe there?" Wallis took his cap off and rubbed his hand through his hair. "This thing just attacked the hospital, it's taking people from their homes, a ranch house isn't any safer."

"The parents said that one of the kids lives there, and his uncle has told them to get all of their families up there so they can be safe. Some have gone there; others are freaking out and want us to go and get the kids and bring them home."

Wallis looked at Shirl, then back at Mike. "Who's the kid that lives there, and who is the uncle? Is it Peter?"

Mike nodded. "Sure is, boss. Ben and his wife are in Crosspine, according to Joan. They took one of their sons, and their daughter, and left the other one here coz he works at the ranch."

"I wonder why they think they're safe," mused the Sheriff. He looked at the reports on his desk, flicking through them until he came to the one that he wanted. "The girl in the hospital, Harper Blackbird, I want a check on her background. Is she related to the O'Gradys?"

Aaron moved over to his desk and sat down, tapping at the keyboard.

"What're you thinking, boss?" Shirl asked.

"We've never had anyone survive before, not twice, anyway. The thing left her in the woods, and then didn't take her from the hospital. What's the bet she's related to the ranch folks? And if she's not, we need to find out why she's been spared."

"Got it, sir," called Aaron. "Sending it to your desk now."

Wallis shook the mouse, waking up his desktop computer, then keyed in his password. He frowned when he saw what Aaron had sent. "She's a cousin, all right, her great-grandfather was a twin, and was an O'Grady. His daughter is the grandmother, so she's linked, but not directly."

"Direct enough for the thing to drop her. Does that mean you're safe? You and your family?" Shirl was leaning back on the desk opposite the Sheriff's.

"I wish that were true, but no. My family has lost people in every single generation. Don't forget about Brent."

"No, no, I get that, and I didn't forget him," Shirl stood up. "I mean now, this time. If the girl, what's her name, Harper? If Harper is okay, and she's a distant relative, then maybe you guys will be okay, too."

"This could be a good theory. If it can't hurt any of you, then maybe we should have Alex and Ayden here, they'll be a lot safer than other deputies, maybe," Mike nodded.

"Ayden isn't related by blood, Mike. And we don't know that. There's probably over half the town that shares the same distant relatives, if you think about it. Our connection is so far back that it probably won't count."

"It counted five years ago," Shirl commented.

"Yes and no. It was the Wallis blood that helped us, and cursed us, back then. I don't know if that's got anything to do with it this time, though." Wallis looked back at his computer. "We're going to have to go to the ranch and have a chat with the O'Gradys. Everything keeps pointing back to them, everything we find seems to have its connection with the people at that ranch."

"You don't think you're jumping at straws here, boss, and not looking for other clues?" Shirl asked.

"It's clasping at straws, Shirl, and no, not really. I have a gut feeling on this one, with what the Ixy girl was saying."

"Ixy girl?" Aaron asked, coming back from his desk.

"Long story, remind me to tell you all about it after this is over. If we survive, god willing," Mike gave a nervous laugh. "Anyway, what are we going to do about all the parents out there? They're all a bit freaked out and too scared to go racing up the hill to get their kids."

"Bring them in, pop them in the conference room. I'll be in shortly to talk to them," Wallis stood up from his desk. "Shirl, you see if Joan needs anything, she's not used to this kind of bedlam."

"And I am?" Shirl shook his head. "Hell, I'm probably more used to it than she is, anyway. What do I tell people about the screams?"

"I've been telling people it's some kind of prank," Jacob offered. "Someone hacked the public address system and are doing it for fun. We're trying to track it down, but they keep changing their server."

"We have a public address system?" Mike looked shocked.

Jacob shrugged. "I don't know. It's just what I've been telling them."

"Remind me to promote you once we get through all this," Wallis smiled at the young man. "Okay, grab me a coffee and your notebook and meet me in the conference room."

"Come on Mike, let's go face the mob," Shirl turned to go through the sliding doors as they burst open, a woman dragging her teenage daughter by the wrist, the father dragging her by the other arm. Another couple followed them, their teenage daughter between them, the child sobbing uncontrollably. Three or four other teens followed, their faces a mix of embarrassment and fear.

"Help us! For god's sake, Sheriff, you have to help us!" the first woman screamed.

"Oh, for fuck's sake," muttered Wallis.

"My Veronika saw the thing, and her friend, Callie, did too!"

"They're marked, please, you've got to help us!" the second woman shrieked.

"Get them in my office, now, and wait with them. I'll take care of the conference room first and be in as soon as I can," the Sheriff told Aaron. "You two get out the front and sort things out. Mike, I want those parents in the conference room right now."

"What a shit show," Shirl followed Mike out the front.

"You can't hide us away, man, you know the stories as much as I do!" Veronika's father grabbed Wallis by the arm. "We won't be safe in the office alone!"

"You won't be alone, you'll have one of my finest deputies with you, and the station is full of people. My office is glass, see? Everyone can see everything if you keep the blinds open. You'll be safe, probably safer in there than out the front. Please just go in with Aaron, and I will be in as soon as I have a chat with the other parents."

"A chat? For god's sake, man, I think our situation is a little more urgent!" the father looked apoplectic, and the other man had now taken his place at his side.

"I'm aware of your distress, sir, but please keep your voice down. I have parents coming through who have children in very similar circumstances, so please, go into my office, and I will be with you as soon as I find out what is going on with their kids, okay?"

The men looked at each other, then nodded, turning to follow Aaron as he led them in.

Mike walked through with several people, and the Sheriff followed them in, taking the coffee from Jacob as he took a seat at the head of the table.

Mike gave him a grim smile as he closed the door, glad that he didn't have to deal with the parents any longer.

CHAPTER TWENTY-SEVEN

"This is wack. We didn't do nothin' wrong, so why is it after us, man?" Mark was crying, he hadn't stopped sobbing since he got back to the house. "Kye is gone, Brax is gone, oh fuck, somebody tell me why it's after us?"

"I think you should watch your language, for a start," Stephen's mother held her hands over her daughter's ears. "We came here because you said we were in danger, Mr. O'Grady, and all I see are eight terrified boys and a lot of fog around the ranch house."

Peter took a deep breath and turned to the woman, exhaling slowly. "Clearly you believed me, or you wouldn't be here."

"We're not stupid, Mr. O'Grady," her husband leaned forward, a cup of coffee cradled in his hands. "We grew up in this town, we know the stories. We have been hearing things happening today, all around town, strange things, well, things that haven't happened for a few years now. Then you get our son to call us, crying and panicking, and tell us to come here because we were all in danger. We got dressed and came here as soon as we could. But since we got here, all we've done is sit and drink coffee, and you haven't told us anything."

"We just want to know what's going on," his wife finished.

"I was hoping the other families would arrive, but it seems you are the only ones that listened to your son. I was waiting to explain what was happening until everyone was here together."

"Hey, hey my mom and dad are here," Liam held his phone up for all to see the message. "They should be pulling up now."

"Tell them to park as close to the house as possible, boy," Peter stood and walked to the glass doors.

The fog had settled down to a soft flowing ground cover, no more than a few inches high, and the strange figure had not returned. Liam and a couple of other boys joined Peter at the door, waiting for the car to arrive.

A black SUV turned around the corner and pulled up beside Stephen's parents' car, and the headlights turned off. Peter opened the door as Liam stood beside him, waving for his parents to hurry. As they opened the car doors the fog started to rise.

"Tell them to hurry," Peter spoke quietly, but his voice was tight with concern.

"Mom, Dad, hurry, can you hurry? Run to the house!"

The fog was building at an exponential rate, it was already at waist height and growing. Liam's mother seemed concerned, his father less so, and he waved at his son as he turned to lock the car.

Behind them, only a few feet back, the fog grew, the softly glowing, white mist was maybe twenty feet high, and banking, folding, ready to spill over the hapless couple who had only just made it to the gate.

"MOM!" Liam screamed. "MOM, DAD, *RUN!*"

The fog started to race towards Liam's parents, and Peter stepped forward. "YOU HAVE TO *RUN!*"

The other boys got up and crowded the door. They all started to scream and yell, urging the adults to *run, run now, hurry!*

Liam's mom seemed confused, the cold fog chilling her, making her disconcerted, and his father was turning to see what was making the people on the verandah yell.

Stephen's father had joined the kids on the verandah, and he was yelling as well, begging the couple to run, not to turn around, just run.

Liam's dad could see the wall of fog that was racing towards him and he turned, grabbing his wife's arm, then ran, dragging the woman with him as the kids screamed. The fog was gaining on them, the white wall collapsing as it raced forward, a large wave that threatened to engulf the running pair.

They made the verandah and fell up the steps, unable to see the fog that surrounded the house. As they fell onto their backs the wave crashed against the verandah as if hitting an invisible barrier, like a glass wall that stopped the fog from entering the house or its immediate surroundings.

"W..what was that?" Liam's mom gasped.

"Did you see that? That fog, that fog, it tried to eat us!" Liam's father scuttled back on his butt. "Did you see?"

Peter offered the man a hand and pulled him to his feet as Liam helped his mother up. "We need to get inside, everybody. Come on, please, it's safer inside."

"What was that?" Liam's mom was pale and could only walk with the support of her son. "Liam, honey, what *was* that?"

"Mom, it's the thing from the woods, you know, the one everyone tells their kids about to stop them playing up," Liam took his mother's hand. "Let's go inside, Mat's uncle will tell us what's going on, okay?"

"Yes, please, everybody, please all come inside, I don't want to provoke the creature any further than we already have."

Liam's father still had his mouth hanging open and kept glancing over his shoulder as he followed the others into the house. Peter closed the glass door, then ushered the group through to the casual living room off to one side of the kitchen.

The open fireplace was going, despite being a summer evening, and Peter walked over to it, throwing in a couple of logs and stirring the coals around. He waited until everyone found a seat on the overstuffed sofas and chairs, some of the boys sitting on ottomans or on the generous, plush rugs on the floor.

"Are you going to tell us what's going on, Mr. O'Grady?" Stephen's father prompted.

"Please, call me Peter. I feel like people are talking to my father when they call me Mr. O'Grady." He pulled a small stool from beside the fireplace and sat down, running a hand through his long black hair. "I can't tell you everything, hell, I don't need to, really, but I can tell you the obvious; the thing you grew up hearing scary stories about is real. What you saw out there was that monster."

"I didn't see anything except fog," Mark moaned. "And Kye, fuck him. Where's my mom and dad? Why didn't they come?"

"I can't answer that, boy, but feel free to try ringing them again. I made the offer, if they decided that we were being capricious, then you are the only one that could convince them otherwise. Same for the rest of you boys, though it'd be a safe bet that your parents have joined the other boys' parents at the Sheriff's station."

A few of the boys ducked their heads, embarrassed by their parents' refusal to drive to the ranch. "Not my fault my parents are untrusting assholes," one of them muttered

"Yeah, not just yours, dickwad," another teen looked around at the rest of the boys. "My parents hate the O'Gradys coz they got more money than the whole town combined."

"Not really the point, boys," Liam's father admonished them. "So, Mr., um, sorry, Peter, we are here, I see the Jones' are here, and I'm guessing that we are all that's coming by what the boys are saying. Please continue."

"Well, the fog, any music you might hear, and the shape of the creature in the fog, they are all signs you've been marked. It's true, once you've seen any of those, except maybe the fog, you're marked. You won't survive the next forty-eight hours."

He expected an outcry or protestations, but all he could hear was Mark's quiet sobbing. Liam had been reduced to rocking back and forth, but at least he was lucid. Peter took a steadying breath before continuing.

"My family, apart from my great, great, grandfather, have lived in these hills for longer than time has been counted in this region. You all probably know that. I know I went to school with your older brother, Sherry," he nodded to Liam's mom. "He and his friends would take pride in their racist bullying. Didn't matter then that my family was the wealthiest in the area, all that mattered was that I was native American. Even now, in this day and age, it's harder being a 'red man' than it is being white. What none of you may know is that the creature in the woods has been here as long as my people have, maybe even longer."

"I don't think we need a history lesson, Peter," Stephen's father barked. "You being bullied as a boy is tragic and all that, but shit, man, just get to the point. I mean, jeez, we are all scared out of our fucking minds." His wife grabbed her daughter, her hands clamped over her ears again. "Sorry, honey, but it's true. You know it's true. Anyway, Peter, if you can stop this thing coming after us, well, we'd be forever grateful. Seriously, we'd be forever in your debt."

178

"I'm not looking for debt or favors here, okay?"

"So why are you doing it, Peter?" Sherry spoke softly.

Peter got up and poked at the fire a bit, then sat down again. "I'm sick of all the killing. I'm sick of it. When things happened five years ago," he turned and looked at everyone in the room. "You probably didn't really know what happened, but your very brave Sheriff and his deputies damn near put an end to that monster. Damn near. I started to feel hopeful that it was gone. I mean, I knew, down in the pit of my stomach, that it was still there, but it was dormant, you know? And if no one called on it, it probably would have stayed that way for damn near forever."

"So what changed?" Mat asked. "What brought it back?"

"About three months ago the local planning department was approached by a big developer. They wanted to buy up land and put in a new housing estate and all the shebang that goes with it. You know, shopping mall, swimming pool, maybe, and if it passed town planning, a casino. Huge money earner for the town, a shit load of jobs for the locals, all round it was a gold mine waiting to be cracked. Monday morning, someone cut down a tree. Just one tree, mind you. But it was enough to get the Crosspine Sawmill people out here to make a decision to clear the trees, ready for the developers to step in. Someone had their thinking cap on. The money made in selling off the woods would provide more than a hefty pay day for the town, then add the development on top of that, well, you can imagine the dollar signs in front of everyone's eyes."

"How do you know all this, Mat's uncle?" Mark asked.

"Because, boy, they came to us first. They tried to buy the ranch land to put their development on."

"You guys said no?" Stephen asked.

"We told them to go fuck themselves. And lady, if you keep covering up your daughter's ears every time someone is going to swear tonight, you may as well sew your fucking hands on there for good."

CHAPTER TWENTY-EIGHT

"Did the kids say why they thought the, ah, thing, was after them?" Wallis asked.

The parents all shook their head, apart from one mother.

"Mrs. McKay? You know something?"

She looked at the other parents, and her husband, before looking at the Sheriff. "I promised my boy I wouldn't say anything. He made me swear. My son's trust is everything, Sheriff Wallis."

"Perhaps so, ma'am, but his life is worth even more than that, isn't it?"

She sighed and nodded. "He said the boys were drinking near the woods, off Hiking Track road. At one of those hiking picnic stop places, you know? Anyway, he said the fog came in," a few of the parents gasped, one woman's hands flew to her mouth in horror. "He said the fog came in, and that Mat and Kye were on the other side of some big log, or something, I can't remember, but he said Kye disappeared."

"What?" a woman jumped to her feet, her husband joining her. "Are you saying my boy disappeared? Oh my god, no wonder I haven't heard from him! Why didn't you say anything?"

"I just did. I don't know, anyway, he said Kye came back when they were at the ranch, at Mat's trailer. He didn't say anything else, really, just that we need to come there, we're in great danger, and we need to get to the ranch as soon as we can."

Kye's mother looked around the group frantically, but her husband pulled her back into her seat. "He said Kye came back, honey. It's okay, Kye's okay."

"Is he okay, Mrs. McKay?" Wallis looked at her, his brows raised.

"I don't know. He didn't say anything else. He just cried and begged me to come. Begged me to leave his father at home and come to the ranch."

"She was about to go, too, but I had the keys. She couldn't get to the car." He swung the keys around his finger for emphasis. "Was going to leave me there and save herself and her precious little boy."

Mrs. McKay stifled a sob. Wallis glanced at Jacob, and the deputy gave him a barely perceptible nod. This was something they would follow up after the night was over. Clearly there were issues at the McKay household, but that had to wait until the more pressing issues were dealt with.

"How did you know to come here if you haven't heard from your son, Mrs., ah," he glanced down at the papers in front of him.

"Stevenson. It's Helen Stevenson. And my husband Neil." The man gave a nod of acknowledgement. "We got a text from Kye's friend Mat telling us it was urgent, and we should come to the ranch. He wouldn't answer his phone when we rang back, so I rang Nina," she nodded to Mrs. McKay, "and she told me that her son rang, and told her to go to the ranch, too. We decided to come here. I don't want to go up there, I can't stand that family. All of them think they're better than us, they always have. Just because they have money, it doesn't make them any better than me or Neil, or anyone else in the town.

Wallis raised a hand. "I'm not sure that's really relevant at this time, Mrs. Stevenson. Okay, you haven't heard from Kye. Is there anyone else here who hasn't heard from their son or daughter?"

Everyone looked around at each other, and all shook their heads. "Well that's a good sign, I suppose. Do you know what your boys were doing near the woods?"

Again, all heads shook no.

"Well, that's something we will take up with the boys at a later time. Are all the boys that went up to the ranch accounted for? What I mean is, do you know how many boys were there? Was it just your boys and the O'Grady boy?"

A few shrugs, and *not sure*, *I don't know*'s.

"Well, normally I would advise you to go home and wait for news, and I'd send a car up there. I'm sure you'll agree that we're probably better advised to keep you here for now. Or rather, ask you to stay here. There's a coffee and soda machine in the hall outside the door to the left, bathrooms beside it. There's an outside line on the phone over there, just dial one to get out. I'll keep you updated. If I hear anything, if anything happens, I'll make sure you are all in the loop. Thoughts?"

"You're not going up there? To the ranch, I mean?" Mrs. Stevenson asked.

"Not until daybreak. I'll call them after I speak to some other people of interest I have in my office."

"The phone lines are out, I've already tried," Mr. McKay said. "I reported the fault, too. I thought it was the right thing to do."

Wallis gave him a tight smile. "So, we all good here?" He rose to his feet. "Good. If you need anything, press the red button on the phone. It'll buzz the reception desk; Joan will help you." He gave them a nod and left with Jacob following him.

"That went better than I thought it would," Jacob sighed as they closed the door. "I thought for sure they'd be screaming and demanding you do something."

"Me too, boy. Five years ago, we had a situation with several teens, and their parents were not as nearly so polite. I think maybe everybody remembers what happened then, and really don't want it to happen to them, or their kids."

"The other parents, the ones from five years ago, did their kids all make it?"

Wallis shook his head. "Even the parents of the kids didn't make it. They were all killed. The only kids that survived were Alex, Ayden and Harriet. It wasn't a good time, Jacob. I lost one of my deputies, a good man, and an even better friend. We need to stop this thing and stop it soon."

Jacob put a hand on Wallis' arm, stopping him from moving forward. "Those other kids, the ones in your office. They would be the next to go, wouldn't they? I mean, if I understood what Shirl and Mike explained, they are the most likely to be, oh, picked off?"

Wallis nodded. "Though this thing doesn't really have any rational order in the way it does things. All we know is that if you've seen it, or your family members have seen it, your chances aren't real good you'll see the end of the week. You have to know that the parents in my office, and the ones in the conference room, are most likely aware of that, and are shit scared. They will say things they wouldn't normally, so just keep cool. The calmer we are, the easier things'll go. At least, I hope so."

Jacob let go of his arm and they turned the corner to the main office. Wallis' office was a large glass room set at the back of the main office. He rarely used the office, it was more for sensitive issues, staff discipline, or private phone calls. All the deputies used the office and it was only a formality that Wallis' name was on the door.

There were blinds on each window, though rarely closed they did afford privacy should it be needed, and now, with the parents and kids in the office, all the blinds were open. One of the fathers was pacing the small space, the others looked to be in a heated argument, Aaron seemed to be trying to talk to them. The teenagers were all huddled in one corner, their eyes wide, faces pale, clearly terrified.

"Just great," muttered the Sheriff as he opened the door, allowing Jacob to enter as well before closing the door behind him. "Thank you for your patience, I was as quick as I could be."

"The deputy here says you won't put us up in the hotel for our safety!" Veronica's father was livid. "You can't expect us to go home, we wouldn't be safe at home!"

"You wouldn't be any safer in a hotel, Roger. I think the safest place is here. There are a lot of people, it's bright, well lit, and you have the full force of the Sheriff's department to protect you."

"Come on, man! You know Ronni is your daughter's best friend, just imagine how you'd feel if Harry saw that damn thing?"

"She did see that damn thing, Rog. She saw it five years ago, so don't ask me how I'd feel. You know exactly how I felt. Same as I know exactly how you feel." Wallis pulled out a chair and beckoned the other father to sit. "Look, I know that it's not the most comfortable room or anything, but the sofa is soft, the armchairs are well padded. All I can say is stay here till it's safe. You can go home in the morning if you want, though I wouldn't recommend it."

"Safe? Sam, how are you going to make it safe?" Ronni's mom cried.

"We're working on a plan. We've faced this thing before, and we won. We can do it again, Agnes, but I need to have the time to work on that. I can't do that if I'm running after everybody, I need time to work things out and put them into action. So, if I know you guys are safe here in the station, I can set about fixing things, this time for good. Does that sound like a workable plan?" He looked at the four adults, purposely avoiding the bruised looking eyes of the girls, and the fearful gaze of their siblings.

They all nodded, and Roger moved forward on his seat. "Are you leaving the deputy in here with us?"

Aaron gave the Sheriff a look of sheer terror, and Sam had to suppress a smile. "The walls are glass. You can pull the blinds all the way up. Nothing gets in here without everyone seeing. I need the deputy out there, helping us, not babysitting you guys."

With that he got up and nodded at Jacob to open the door, leaving the office without turning.

CHAPTER TWENTY-NINE

"So the thing knew that the trees were going to be cut down and it's fighting back?" Stephen's father asked. "Is that what's happening?"

"We heard a tree being cut down the other morning. The sound made its way up the hill, the chainsaw, the tree crashing down. I believe it was only one, but one is all it takes. Everything starts with one."

"We saw that tree, uncle," Mat looked around at his friends. "We were sitting on it, I didn't think nuthin' of it, but you know, I've never seen any of the trees in the woods fallen down. Like, never."

"You're right, Mateo. The trees in the woods never fall, they never drop branches, and they never, not ever, should be cut down. That forest is a sacred place to my people." Peter leaned forward, his elbows on his knees and his head in his hands. "I guess the tree being cut down triggered this attack. I'm not up on the lore like my parents, or my grandparents. My brother and I, well, we respect what happened before, we keep to some traditions, but not all of them, in fact, not that many at all."

"Grandma knows everything. She's always talking about things like they happened yesterday and stuff," Mat commented. "I don't listen, really. I wish I had. If we get through this, man, I'm gonna be cramming on ancient history like you never seen."

"I know the runes to write on the doors and windows, the sigils to place at the four corners of the house to guard it against evil. I know that, up until today, that thing has never come onto this land, onto the ranch. Not even when it was a settlement. This land was always safe."

"What happened tonight?" Sherry asked. "Was it just the fog?"

"It was more than the fog and it was more than the music. I don't know why that is. But from what the boys have told me, when they were near the woods the thing must have marked them, or chosen them, or whatever it does. It followed them here. This house is the only safe place that I know of in the entire district, so I made them call you, to try and keep you all safe."

"But for how long?" Stephen asked. "Like, do we just live here now? House arrest and shit?"

Peter stood and poked the fire again before turning back. "Honestly, I have no idea. I don't know what happens now, I don't know how to stop it. I don't even know how to protect you if you step off the verandah."

"Well that's just fucking great." Liam's dad leapt to his feet, stomping over to stand face to face with the tall man at the fire. "What the fuck are we meant to do? Just stay here forever? Fuck me, you Indians made this monster, you should all know how to stop the fucking thing!"

"Sir, I advise you to sit down, now. Right now." Peter spoke quietly, but his voice was dark, threatening, and Liam's dad took a step backwards.

"I, um, man, you know we're all just scared, right?" Liam stood and walked over to his father, placing a placating hand on his shoulder. "Let's just sit down and try and work things out, okay Dad? Okay?"

His father blinked and shook his head, as if to clear it. "Yeah, um, okay. Sure. Yeah, let's work things out."

"How?" Mat asked.

"How what?" Peter frowned at his nephew. "How do we work things out?"

"Yeah. I mean, I know you said you're not up on the lore and all that shit, but you gotta know some stuff, right? You gotta have some idea what we can do?"

Peter shrugged. "Honestly? I have no idea. I wouldn't know where to start."

"Can't you sacrifice a cow or something?" Mark added hopefully.

Peter snorted, throwing his hands up in the air. "A pagan ritual? Is that what you want? No, seriously, when I said that I would have no idea where to start, I meant that. My mother will know, and with her help my brother and I can put an end to this thing, once and for all."

"Great! Fantastic!" Liam's dad slapped his knee. "Go and wake her up, then. I know it's late, but this is an emergency!"

"If she were here, she would have already been awake. No, I'm afraid that she is not here. She went to visit her sister in Metro City, she's been away for two days. She was due to come home at the end of the week, but trust me, as soon as the phone lines come back, I will be ringing her, and my brother, and filling them in on what is unfolding here. In the meantime, I invite you all to stay. There are enough rooms here for everyone, and you are safe in this house. Mat will show you to the rooms, I advise you to get some sleep, and in the morning, we can work on what we can do."

"Sure, like anyone's going to be able to sleep," Stephen shook his head. "I am seriously never going to sleep again."

"I want to go to sleep," another boy said, his red rimmed eyes blinking rapidly. "I just want to go to sleep, and when I wake up, this is all gone, and I remember that it's all a bad dream."

"I can't give you that peace, boy, but I can tell you that while you are under this roof, nothing can harm you.

Nothing can enter here; nothing can step foot beyond the verandah." Peter gave him a reassuring smile. "Not even the fog can come onto the verandah. You are safe tonight, boy. And you need not leave until we've taken care of things, and make sure you are safe forever, okay?"

Liam shrugged. "I guess," he whispered.

"Okay, guys, follow me," Mat stood and beckoned everyone to follow him. "I got a spare bed in my room, too, if anyone wants to share."

"No way!" squeaked Mark. "I'm not going back out there to your trailer!"

"No, shit head, my old room here in the house. No fuckwit is going outside, or did you just blank out everything my uncle said to you?"

Mark gave a short nervous bark of a laugh and followed his friend. Peter watched them all leave, then stood with his back to the fire. The heavy drapes were not closed, he could see out of the glass door, as well as the long windows on the other side of the door. The fog had not dissipated, it still swirled and flowed, softly glowing in the dark of night. He didn't know why it was still there, what it was waiting for.

Further back, where the fog was much higher, he thought he could see a shape moving, a tall, very tall, and slim figure. Although it was not clear, he thought he could see it moving back and forth around the house yard, as if waiting for someone to step outside.

"Not tonight, you motherfucker, you're not getting anyone else. Not from my house." Peter strode over and closed the drapes, pulling them tightly, so nobody could see out, but, more importantly, nor could anything see in.

CHAPTER THIRTY

"I know you guys are going to hate me, but I need to leave you here to hold down the fort while I figure out what to do next." Wallis took a mouthful of his coffee, then grimaced. "This is the worst coffee I've ever had." He gulped down the rest and put the mug down.

"Sir, are you leaving Shirl and Mike here to help us?" Jacob asked, his fatigue making him look far older than his years.

"Yes, I will, for now. I need you to work out shifts to get some rest. Keep alert and stay frosty. I need everyone to watch for anything, any aberrant behavior, any weird things that happen. And," Wallis looked at the men surrounding his desk, taking in the faces, the trust they had in him, and the fear emanating from them. Jacob and Aaron were joined by three other deputies, Mike and Shirl stood to the side. "Watch out for each other. Make sure you have each other's backs. Don't leave the station, not for anything, unless you have no other choice. Shirl is in charge, Mike second. Order food and some decent java, and oh, I'm going to lock the doors. Make everyone buzz to get in. And if they look hinkey, in any way, then don't open the door."

"Hinkey?" Aaron asked. "Like, how hinkey? How will we know if someone shouldn't be let in?"

"Run it passed me or Mike," Shirl answered. "No one in, or out, without our say so. Got it?"

"I won't be leaving until it's light, so until then it's business as usual."

Jacob nodded, then stifled a yawn. Mike turned to Shirl. "I'll take first watch; you and Jacob get some shut eye in the staff room."

"Aaron, grab the takeout menus and see what everyone wants. I'll go lock the front door, Mike, you check the back, please."

"I feel like we're under siege," Orville, one of the deputies, commented.

"You're not far off the point, really," Wallis griped as he pushed the swinging door into the reception area. Joan looked up as he walked through, a bright smile on her face. "Phones any quieter?" Wallis asked her.

"Oh yes, once the screaming stopped, things quietened right down. Normal night now, I hope!"

"What time did the screaming stop?"

"About an hour ago. It's dead quiet out there now."

Wallis walked to the front doors. The Sheriff's station had long glass doors to the foyer, which was also glass, but was barred as well as fronted with concrete filled bollards. Wallis swiped his ID card to activate the electric locks, the *Press Buzzer for Entry* sign flicking automatically as soon as the locks were engaged. Walking back into the reception area, he turned off the automatic sliders and also locked the sliding glass doors.

"Oh, look, there's someone out there. I'll buzz them in," Joan leaned over to hit the button to allow entry.

"No, wait a sec, Joan. Don't let anyone in without either myself, Shirl or Mike looking at them first. Understand?" He turned to make sure Joan was listening to him. "Not anyone else, and no one in. Got it?"

Joan nodded, her face worried as she pointed to the figure out the front. "It looks like one of the volunteers, what's his name? You know the one, bit of a nosey one, the busy body."

"The red-haired guy that works at Shifton's Plumbing? Arlo, or Marlo, or something like that?"

"Yes, that's him! Should I buzz him in?"

"No, Joan, don't. Please call Mike to come out the front."

Joan hit the intercom, her brow furrowed. The man out the front started to bang on the glass wall, not seeming to know that he was about four feet away from the door.

Mike and Aaron came through the swinging doors, the banging continuing, and Aaron walked up to the sliding doors to get a closer look.

"It's Akron, the plumber guy. He's one of the volunteers that we marked missing today," Mike looked at Wallis. "What's he doing here?"

"For fuck's sake, did you see him!" Aaron stepped back from the door.

"Jesus lord and savior, that man has no eyes!" Joan had stepped from behind her reception desk but was now backing away from the doors. "Why does he not have eyes?"

"Aaron, step back from the doors," Wallis spoke calmly, as Joan kept backing up.

"Sir, he's bleeding, there's blood coming from his mouth, and he's covered in it, all down his shirt." Aaron turned to Mike and the Sheriff. "Should we let him in so we can help him?"

"Call an ambulance!" Joan cried, her voice shrill with panic.

"No, no ambulance. Aaron, move back, go turn off the foyer lights, please."

Aaron stepped back, confusion on his face. "What happened to him? What's wrong with him?"

"That's the hinkey that the boss mentioned earlier," Mike explained. "He probably won't be the first, either."

Wallis held open the swinging door. "Let's all go out the back. Aaron, flick off the reception lights as well as the foyer. I want the front dark. Maybe he'll go away."

"Hey, boss, there's someone banging on the loading dock door," Orville poked his head through the swinging door. "You wanna come see?"

"What's the bet it's another of the volunteers?" Mike asked as they all walked into the main office.

"You'd lose that bet, Mike," Orville led the way to the rear door. "Looks like a girl, but she's all dirty, and won't lift her head. I didn't want to open the door till you guys had a look."

The rear door was a solid metal safety door, but there was a close circuit monitor that showed the entire rear of the building, including the loading dock, and there was a metal peephole beside the door. Orville slid the peephole open and Wallis peered through.

There was a young girl standing there, her head hanging low, her hair, unkempt and tangled, fell over her face. She had only one canvas sneaker on one, the other foot was bare, and very dirty. She wore ankle length jeans, and these were torn, and covered with something dark. Her short t-shirt was filthy, and under the yellow light it looked like she had brown mud down the front of her, covering her shirt and jeans, and splashing on the ground as she knocked on the door.

She lifted her head slowly, very slowly, and looked straight at the peephole, as if she could see that Wallis was looking at her.

Only she couldn't see that, not because of the one-way mirror set into the peephole, but because she had no eyes. Her black, ragged sockets dripped dark liquid down her cheeks, splattering onto her chest. Wallis gasped as the girl smiled, her toothless, torn gums an assault on the Sheriff's senses, and he slammed the peephole cover shut.

"Don't open it. Turn off the outside light and come away from the door," Wallis ordered.

The deputies were staring at the girl through the small monitor beside the door, their mouths agape in horror. The girl lifted an arm and waved at the camera, slowly, her movements jerky and unnatural. Mike moved to the light switches and flicked them off, causing the cameras to change to a greenish, eerie night mode.

This made the girl look even worse, like a walking corpse, green-skinned and bloodied, and the men drew back as one from the monitor. "This is totally fucked up," Orville whistled through his teeth. "Pardon my French and all, but that is, well, fucked up."

"Let's get back into the main office, guys. I think we need to leave the freaks to their own devices and try to ride this night out." Wallis led the deputies, his stomach twisting with fear. He didn't want to spread panic, but all he could think of was calling his house and warning everyone there.

He had given strict instructions for everyone to go to bed and get some rest, but if he knew Lisa at all, she would be up, writing lists of things that may help, pounding the keys of the laptop looking for clues, and worrying about everyone, including himself.

"What do we do about ordering food, boss?" Mike asked. "I don't want the delivery guy to run into horror movie monster guy out there."

"Agreed. I think we'll just order in breakfast when the diner opens and have them deliver when it's light. The people we have in the conference room and my office will want to eat then, too, so let's just wait for a couple of hours."

Aaron nodded and walked off to refill the coffee maker, Joan helping him, not wanting to return to the reception desk. Wallis pulled his cell phone from his jacket pocket and tapped out a message to Lisa, just asking if she was awake. She answered instantly, so Wallis sent a message letting her know about the walking corpses and warning her.

He didn't want to alarm her any more than she was, however the need for caution was more important, and he needed his family to be safe. Lisa didn't answer for a couple of minutes, and Wallis chewed at his bottom lip, hoping that his house wasn't being paid the same sort of visit that the Sheriff's office was.

His cell chimed to let him know he had an answer, and he breathed a sigh of relief when Lisa assured him all was quiet there, and she had dispatched everyone off to bed. At least he knew his family should be fine until morning.

"All good at home, boss?" Mike pulled up a chair. "I didn't see your message, but I can tell by your face that you look worried."

"All good there. Though I didn't know if anyone would go knocking there, they haven't seen any fog, or creatures, or anything this time. Maybe it's not about us anymore," he leaned back in his chair and shook his head. "I know that's probably unrealistic, I know that, but a man can hope."

"You know as soon as we start poking around, you're going to paint a bullseye fair and square on you and your brother's chest, right?"

"With Harry and her, um, ghostly visitor, I think that bullseye is already there, and not just on Simon and me. Our family is going to be in the middle of this, whether I like it or not. All I can do is find a way to finally end this. And not just for them, Mike. For everyone. For this town, for all the parents that lose kids, for the safety of everyone. For too long we've just put up with this thing in the woods, because it only took one person, or two, and we seemed to think that was an acceptable loss." Wallis took off his cap and scratched his head. "We can't accept this any longer. First light, I'm going to pick up Alex and Ayden and head up to the O'Grady's and see what we can do."

"What if you don't find anything, boss? What if the O'Grady's have nothing to do with it?"

"Well, I have parents sitting in my conference room that make me think otherwise. If the O'Gradys didn't have anything to do with it, then why are they offering sanctuary to people in their house? You know the O'Grady's as well as anyone. They are closed people, Mike, they don't let anyone on their land without a good reason and a double-booked appointment. For them to invite a dozen or more people up there to spend the night, I'm thinking that even if they don't know why this thing is back this time, they must know how to keep it at bay, and they may have some clue on how to fight it. Maybe they'll even help us get rid of it."

"Well, that would be the ideal plan. Are you going to take Harry?"

"I think I would have to; she may be the key to this whole thing, yet again. Poor kid, it took her so long to get over what happened last time, I just don't know how she'll cope going through it again. Thank goodness she's older, and she's got a damn good head on those shoulders. Way too old for her own good, really."

Mike tried to stifle a yawn but gave up and shook his head as he yawned. "Been a long day."

"Go get some rest and take Aaron with you."

"But boss …"

"I'll call you if anything happens. I've got Orville and Harmen, and Joan for back up."

Mike laughed. "I wouldn't ever want to get on her bad side!"

"Off with you then, try and get a couple of hours." Wallis looked a little melancholy. "I'll wake up Shirl in an hour and get him to take over while I grab some shut eye."

"Phone, boss," Harmen called.

"Take a message," Wallis answered.

"It's Mayor Butler, he says he has to talk to you, now. He says his kid didn't come home tonight and he's not answering his cell."

"God save us all from the self-important members of local government," Wallis groaned. "Send it here, Harmen, I'll take it at my desk."

CHAPTER THIRTY-ONE

Peter knew he could go to sleep without fear of anyone, or anything, getting in the house, but he wasn't sure about the people inside. He didn't know if any of them would get up to leave, or even if the thing out there could control people inside with its strange, not quite heard music. He knew it could make people do what it wanted when they were in its woods, but wasn't sure if that translated to the ranch, or anyone in the house.

He had pulled the most comfortable sofa chair in front of the fireplace in the main room, his feet on an ottoman, a glass of very good wine in his hand. He wasn't tired, his mind was too full to allow any hope of sleep. He also felt it was his duty to keep those he had invited into the house safe, and if he wasn't sure if the thing could control them, he was even more unsure of what the thing could make them do, should it find a way to compel them.

All it would take was the scratching off of one of the sigils, or maybe setting the house on fire, forcing them all outside, and they would be in dire peril.

He checked his cell again, still no signal. It wasn't overly unusual here on the ranch to have no cell coverage, but it was annoying. He wanted to get hold of his brother, needed to get hold of him, and with no phone coverage he didn't have much of a chance.

He frowned, a thought coming to him. He sat his wine down and grabbed the laptop from the little side table near his chair and turned it on. Sometimes he could get an email through, even if the Wi-Fi signal was low. He checked the strength of the signal and the corner of his mouth hinted at a smile. He didn't know if his brother would check his emails at night, however he was absolutely sure he would check them before he even got out of bed in the morning.

He sat there, tapping away at the keys, letting his brother know exactly what was going on and telling him of the people sleeping at the house, when he felt the hair on the back of his neck stand up. He felt gooseflesh break out on his arms, and his breath plumed before him, even though he was sitting close to the roaring fire.

He felt the air turn frigid around him and his first thought was that somehow, the creature had come in, somehow, it had gained access. He looked around, setting the laptop aside, but could see no fog. There was no music, only the crackle and roar of the fire. He checked the windows and the doors. They were still bolted, curtains still drawn. He could no longer see the fog, so flicked on the flood lights that surrounded the verandah.

The fog had disappeared, the yard was clear.

Peter opened the doors and stepped out, looking beyond the house yard, but could not see any trace of the soft, eerie glow of the heavy white mist. He stood, waiting to hear the music, waiting for the fog to reappear, but there was nothing. No sound other than the usual song of crickets and night insects, and the occasional hoot of an owl. No creature, no fog.

He returned indoors, again locking the doors and drawing the curtains, shivering as he did so. The temperature inside had dropped, it was now far colder inside than it was outside. His breath formed a white cloud in front of him, and he felt the cold bite at his cheeks.

Confused, he stoked the fire and threw more logs on, but unless he was bent right over the fire, he could feel no heat. The house was as cold as a grave.

The lamps flickered and went out, the overhead pendant light went dark, and the only illumination was now the soft, red glow from the fire. Peter picked up the long iron poker and held it before him like a weapon as he scanned the room, not sure what he was looking for, not sure how he would fight anything he would find.

He didn't feel fear, he knew the small medallion around his neck would keep him safe, as long as he wore it the creature could not touch him, the walking corpse-zombies were unable to harm him, and he couldn't be hypnotized by the music. Of all the other people in the main part of the house, only his nephew wore the same medallion, only his nephew was safe. He knew that all of the staff, even those that held rooms in the other wings of the house, had medallions as well, so he was unconcerned about them.

"You need to sit down and listen," the voice made him start, and he turned to see Mateo standing in the hallway, wearing only his boxers and a t-shirt.

"Go back to bed, boy, it's not safe here." Peter turned back, scanning the room for anything that might be a threat.

"I have slept for many seasons."

Peter turned slowly, lowering the poker. "What did you say?"

"I have slumbered for many an age, for too many seasons. It is time for me to awaken, time for me to sleep no more."

"Mateo, are you okay? Are you sleepwalking?" Peter took a step towards his nephew, but something about the boy made him hesitate. "Mateo?"

"Your son sleeps. He is not aware of me."

Peter felt an icy cold hand grip his insides. "Who are you? Are you the creature? Have you taken my nephew to try and kill us all? He wears the medallion; this shouldn't be possible!"

The boy shook his head. "My name is Hagen. I lived a long time before now. I lived very far away from here. I died when I was no older than this boy. This boy is not your son?"

"Not my son. My brother's son. He is Mateo. He is from the land here, from the people here. Why are you doing this? How did you get past the medallion? What is going to happen to him?"

"This son of your brother will be okay. The medallion is old magic, it is from my time, from my people. It protects against the K'aas, but not against my people. I will speak only when I need to, and I will leave this boy unharmed. Please sit, and I will speak of my story, I will speak of the time we called the K'aas, and I will speak of my sister. I will speak, and you will listen, and we may end the curse of the K'aas."

"You made the creature?"

Mateo shook his head, and Peter realized that the boy did indeed look to be asleep. His eyes were half open, the lids heavy, and his head hung a little. His expression was relaxed and calm, unlike the words that were issuing from his mouth.

"We called the K'aas, my brother and myself, to protect our sister, Ix iLa'al. To protect our father, and our people. It was not meant to be alive now. It was not meant to kill anyone else. Only the people we cursed."

Peter backed up to his chair and sat down, so cold that he shivered violently now. He noticed Mateo did not appear to be cold despite being so scantily clad.

"How come you're here? You said you died far away?"

"Our blood, the blood of our sacrifice, was carried here. Our heads, our hair…" Mateo's hand reached up and made a sweeping motion across his scalp. "They took this here. Our spirit is tied to this land. To this curse. To the K'aas."

"If that's true, if you are tied to it, why haven't you shown yourselves before now? I mean, it's been centuries, many ah, what did you call it? Oh, many seasons, yeah. So many seasons, so many ages, you let so many people die. Why didn't you show yourselves before?"

The boy tilted his head to one side, as if he was listening to something far away. "We could not. We did want to come. We did want to speak. We did want to stop the K'aas. We could only watch, only wait."

"But now you can? What changed?" Peter found it very disturbing that the voice emitting from his nephew's mouth sounded just like his nephew. He expected an ethereal, deep, ghostly specter sound, but all he heard was his teenage nephew's voice. It was flat, and spoke weirdly, but it was all Mateo's sound.

"The curse was not just ours, no longer was just from us. There was another whose blood mingled with ours, whose blood touched the talisman, whose blood joined the curse."

"This happened now? Whose blood is it? Did they start the curse up again? Is that what happened?"

"Many seasons ago the blood was joined. The boy touched the talisman with his blood, and he was bound to the curse. His family was bound to the curse. Was bound to us. Was bound to the K'aas."

"Who? What family? Oh, hang on, I think I know. It was the Wallis family, I'm sure of that. They've been here since the town started, and they've lost more family members to that thing than anyone else. I think they've lost more people than all of the other deaths combined. Am I right?"

"The family is cursed, yes. They are all cursed, now."

"So, what woke you up?"

"We wake, always wake, when the days grow longer, and the sun is higher, and the warm season is here, we always wake. We were not able to speak, but we were here, watching, and waiting."

"Okay, so, again, how come you're here now? What gave you the, I don't know, the strength, the opportunity, the spell, whatever, to possess my nephew, after so many seasons?"

The boy tipped his head to the other side and attempted a smile, though only one side of his face seemed to move. "The one was born. The one that would allow my sister to speak."

"The one? You mean Mateo, my nephew, the boy you are speaking through now?"

"This boy is not the one. This boy is a brother, we did need a brother to speak, we did need a brother born at the same time as another to speak. But he is not the one."

"Wait a minute, you needed a twin, is that right? You needed a twin to speak through?"

Mateo nodded.

"But I'm a twin, and so was my father, and my grandfather. Hell, I think every generation in our family has a set of twins. So why didn't you talk through one of us?"

"The one needed to be born. We could not speak until the one was born."

"A single birth? Hell, we have many of those. I have an aunt who was a single birth, and there have been many born in my family tree that weren't twins. Even my brother has a single child as well, Mateo has a sister. Why couldn't you speak through one of those?"

"This child was to be born from a different mother, from different blood. Our sister was from different blood, not from our mother, but still a child of the king."

"Who writes these rules?" Peter snorted. "This is madness!"

Mat frowned and leaned forward a little. "There are no written words of these rituals and traditions. Our ways are ancient, and mainly forgotten. We did not make the decisions. We have tried, for many seasons, to make contact. We have tried to talk through many, many brothers. For some, this did not work. For some, this made them go mad. They gave themselves to the K'aas, thinking that was what they should do. We tried to talk through the cursed family, but to no avail. The ability of our sister to speak through the one has shown us to try a different family, and tonight, we came to the son of your brother. He did not hear us, did not listen, so I had to wait until he was asleep. My brother, Tadeas, will speak through this boy's brother."

"That's not possible," Peter ran a hand through his hair as he gathered his thoughts. "Mateo and his brother were born too early, and there were problems. Mateo is fine, he survived okay, but his brother didn't. He has cerebral palsy, he's in a wheelchair, and he can't speak. My brother thinks he's okay, brain wise, but I'm not convinced. So, your brother lucked out. He won't get a voice with Luca."

Mat smiled, this time his whole face managed the expression. "We are strong. I do not worry about my brother. He will find a way."

Peter shrugged. "My brother has spent a fortune to find a way. Nothing has worked. The kid is a vegetable, believe me. I think we'll be dealing with just you, honestly. What now? What's the next step? I've got a house full of people here, and there are people getting slaughtered by the minute in the woods. What do we do?"

"We can stop the K'aas, we can stop it forever. Would you help us stop it?"

"Of course! For fuck's sake, boy, what the hell have we been talking about, if not stopping the thing? Just tell me what we have to do, and we'll do it. Anything!"

"You need to find who called the K'aas back from its slumber. There is one that knows the old ways and has summoned the K'aas."

"You don't know who it is?"

Mat shook his head. "We do not. We know that the power used was not wielded properly. The K'aas has been unleashed with no controls, with no boundaries. It will kill anyone and everyone, and will not stop, will not rest. We need to stop it, or I fear no one in this land will survive."

CHAPTER THIRTY-TWO

"Mayor Butler's son is missing as well, and we have reports of many people missing from their homes. This night is getting worse and worse, Lisa. I think we need to talk to this Ix girl again, as soon as possible." Wallis shifted the phone to his other hand. "You may need to wake Harry up and see if she can get the girl to talk."

"Harry was exhausted, Sam. I think she should sleep until you can get back here, and you can listen to her as well."

"We got about an hour till sunup, I'll leave here as soon as it's light. It's been quiet for about forty minutes here; I'm hoping that's all we see of the things tonight."

"Don't hold your breath," Lisa sounded tired. *"We've not seen anything here, so far, but I'm not holding my breath, either."*

"Boss, you gotta see this," Orville called out. "You better come right now."

"Looks like I spoke too soon, Lisa. I gotta go. I'll call you before I leave here."

"Love you," Lisa hung up and Sam placed the phone back in its receiver, his trepidation growing over what the deputy wanted him to see.

He walked to the swinging door and Orville was standing beside them, looking at the closed-circuit television monitor on the wall.

"What's going on?"

"Boss, that kid is back, but she's got a couple of friends with her."

Wallis looked at the monitor and whistled through his teeth in surprise. The girl was indeed back, and at her side were two boys, both staring into the station with eyeless sockets, both covered in blood, just like the girl.

"That there is Kye Sanders, the boy that hangs around with Mat O'Grady. I busted 'em a few weeks ago for tagging the deli on High Street."

"Can you tell who the other one is, Orville?"

"That's Butler's older boy, that one," Joan spoke softly behind them. "Those boys are all the spitting image of their mom. I'd recognize one anywhere."

"Well, I guess that's going to be difficult to explain to the mayor. Sorry, sir, your beloved boy is now a zombie," Orville was joking, but his voice was grim, matching his expression.

The back-door access buzzer went off, and Wallis groaned. "Let me guess, we got another walking corpse out the back?"

Orville touched the buttons beside the CCTV monitor, and it showed the back door. Patrick, the sawmill man, stood there, his appearance the same as the three hapless youths out the front of the building.

"This night is not getting any better." Orville turned the alert for the back door off and changed the view on the CCTV monitor to show both the front and back entrances. "You ever seen it this bad before?"

"You know we haven't. Jeez, we've never even really believed in this thing before, right?" Harmen walked up to the others. "I just checked on the parents in the conference room, they're all asleep still."

"Well, that's a small blessing." Wallis looked back at the CCTV, the three figures at the front just standing there, not knocking, not moving, the man at the back doing the same. "I need to leave here when it's light, we have a few leads I need to chase up. I hope these jerks are gone by then."

"Well, we could always try grabbing them and throwing them in lock up?" Harmen suggested.

Wallis looked at him. "I'm not sure that's a good idea. You don't know what bringing one of those in here will do."

"Yes, I know, but the cell block is completely isolated from the main building when we close the doors. We got triple doors there, if anything can get through those then we ain't safe in here anyway."

"You've got a point. We could try it, I guess." Wallis turned back to the monitor and tapped the side showing the back view. "He's on his own, and he's a bit of a weedy little guy. If we try it, we go for him."

"I'll get the taser. Dunno if it'll help, but it can't hurt." Harmen hurried to the weapons room.

"I'll grab the coyote net. I think if we throw that on him and drag him into the cells, might be better than touching him." Orville hurried after Harmen.

Wallis watched the man, then nodded at Joan, who had heard everything but not spoken. "What do you think? Are we crazy?"

Joan bit her bottom lip, then gave Wallis a strained smile. "I think it's a good idea, but I don't think you should do it."

"What do you mean? If it's a good idea, why shouldn't we do it?"

"No, you misunderstand me. I mean yes, it's a good idea and it should be done, I just don't think that *you* should be involved. You're our best hope for defeating this monster. If we lose you, I don't think we have a hope."

"Joan…"

"Look, Sam, I know you didn't talk about what happened five years ago when Colin was killed, but I also know the thing hasn't been back for five years.

Maybe, whatever you did back then, maybe you could make it permanent this time."

"Yeah, we agree," Orville turned the corner with Harmen, the coyote net in his arms. "We were just saying the exact same thing."

"Yup. We'll go out. We'll grab the thing, and you can man the doors," Harmen grinned. "We'll be maneuvering that net, boss, we can't do the doors too. And Joan's right, we need you safe. Okie dokie?"

Wallis sighed. "Okie dokie, I guess. Okay, let's get the cell block doors open, so all you have to do is throw him in, it'll be easier, I hope, and maybe safer."

The Sheriff led the trio to the cell block, two of the large doors open already, the third closed, but not locked. There was no one inside the cells, it was dark and cold, the heavy concrete walls keeping out any of the day's warming rays, and the night's cold didn't help the temperature.

Making sure there was an open cell and the route was clear, they gathered at the back door, deciding on the small access door beside the main loading bay.

"You stand back, boss," Harmen instructed. "Hit the emergency close door as soon as we get that bastard through. Ready, Orvie ol' boy?"

"Nope. Feel like I'm about to shit my pants, but let's do this. Open the door."

Wallis hit the green button on the wall and the door opened. One the deputies threw the large net, capturing the eyeless man where he stood.

Orville pulled the bottom of the net, scooping the man off his feet as he raised his arms in a small effort to escape. Both deputies pulled the net hard, sweeping it inside. Wallis hit the red button, the door slamming shut as the deputies ran, pulling the net with them, through the hall to the open truck bay, then into the cell block.

Wallis had run ahead and opened the door as the men threw the bundle of net and man into the first cell, Wallis again hitting the right button to lock the door. They stood for a moment and looked at the man who was lying there, wrapped in the net, unmoving.

"Let's get out of here. C'mon, we can watch it on the CCTV," Wallis urged, and the deputies followed him out. They locked the door to the cells, then the heavy, reinforced blast doors, finally the bay door closed, rolling down quickly, Wallis enabling the security locks before the men hurried to Wallis' desk.

The Sheriff touched the mouse to wake the computer, then keyed in the password to open the CCTV stream from the cells.

Joan was on the other side of the office, the bank of monitors showing every feed from the security cameras and closed-circuit television. "He's out of the net," she told them.

"Did you see how he got out of it?" Orville asked her.

"He just stood up, it was weird, like someone pulled him from the top, you know, like he had a string on his head. He dropped to the ground when you closed all the doors, though."

"He's still in a heap on the floor," Wallis confirmed.

"It's like whatever is controlling him had the signal turned off when you closed the blast doors, Sam," Joan explained. "As soon as you closed that door he just dropped."

"Interesting," Wallis frowned. "What does it mean, though? Have we found a way to block the creature, or did it just stop controlling him once he was locked up?"

"I wouldn't want to speculate, really, but my guess is he isn't of any use if he's locked up," Joan commented.

"Are we going to try and grab the kids out front?" Harmen asked.

"They're gone!" Joan pointed to the monitor that showed the front of the building. "The kids are gone!"

"She's right," Wallis changed the view from just the cell blocks, to one showing all outside cameras. "I wish we saw if they walked off or just disappeared. We don't actually know how they move around yet."

"The sun's starting to come up. Maybe that scared them away?" Orville offered.

"I'm thinking there aren't any brains that work inside these victims. I don't think they can feel anything, let alone be scared." Wallis stood and stretched. "Time to wake up Shirl and Jacob, let Mike and Aaron sleep a little longer, if you can. I'll be leaving once it's actually light out there."

"Sure thing, boss," Harmen nodded towards the coffee machine. "I'll fire that beauty up first; I think it's been cold for a couple of hours now."

"I don't want to speak too soon, but it looks like we made it through the night," Orville smiled.

"If anything happens now, I'm socking you in the jaw for jinxing us!" Harmen shook his head as he walked to the coffee machine.

"We'll just have to wait and see what reports come in. Remember, daylight doesn't seem to stop anything happening in the woods, so we could be in for a bad day." Wallis sat back down and pulled out his cell phone, checking for messages. "I'm hoping we can have this thing terminated before the day is finished."

"Amen to that!" Joan agreed.

CHAPTER THIRTY-THREE

"What am I doing here?" Robert snorted. "I don't know why we have to be here at the crack of dawn, for gawd's sake, it's not like the trees care what time we gonna chop them down."

"I like getting up early," Fred replied. "Means we get to knock off early, dude."

"Yeah, okay for you, you're not married. I got a wife at home that's not just fat, she ugly."

"You married her, Bobby, you chose her!"

Robert laughed. "She used to be pretty, and thin. Was mighty fine, lemme tell you. She could *sliiiide*, boy, so smooth you would cry like a baby. My friends were so cut when I hooked up with her!"

"So, what happened?"

"Babies happened. And twinkies. And tacos. Man, that girl, she love to eat. You have no idea!"

Fred reached over and slapped Robert's ample stomach. "She not the only one. And I am gonna bet she dint marry no bald guy!"

Robert laughed as he pulled the car into the parking lot off Hiking Track road.

"This the right one?"

Fred looked at the work order. "Yeah, we need to be at the second lot, not the same one as the other guys cut from. They want a sample from three different sites, then we can go."

"Fine. Wake up Dwayne, coz we stopping here first."

Fred leaned over the back seat and hit the snoring man on the knee, waking him up and grinning at the blinking, tired face. "Wakey wakey, hands off snakey!"

"Shut the fuck up, doofus. I weren't touching no snakey." Dwayne yawned and straightened up in his seat. "Why you wakin' me? I said to lemme sleep till we get there."

"Well, dude, we here!" Fred grabbed his cap and put it on as Robert parked the truck. "Time to be cutting down some mutha fucken huge trees!"

"Seriously, these trees are humongous!" Robert climbed out of the truck and walked to the back to retrieve the chainsaws, the other two guys following him. "I ain't never seen so many big trees. I reckon the locals'll end up protesting and shit, sayin' these are treasures or some such shit."

"Ain't no problem to me," Dwayne lit a cigarette as he accepted a chainsaw from his boss. "I just cut 'em down, don't give a shit if they treasures or important. Long as I get to cut me some trees and get me a paycheck, is all I care 'bout."

The trio stepped over the chain that was slung between knee-high bollards that surrounded the gravel parking lot. This was a more basic lot, no bathroom block, no picnic chairs, just a water faucet attached to a sign board that gave local sightseeing details and showed a map of the hiking trails.

They walked over to a tree that was far enough from the lot to avoid any damage should it fall the wrong way and sprayed a marking on the trees surrounding it. Robert took some pictures with his cell phone as Dwayne threw his cigarette butt on the ground, grinding it in with his heel.

"This looks good," Robert nodded at the tree.

"Shit man, they all look good. You ever seen so many trees that all look exactly the same?" Fred walked into the woods a little, just a few feet. "They all the exact fucking same. I ain't never seen shit like this before."

"Who cares? Let's just get this cut, I'm starving, I wanna get this done and see what the local diners got that's hot an' covered wit' cheese. I would eat a fucking horse if it had cheese on it." Robert laughed at his own joke and took the cover off the chainsaw blade, tossing it to one side.

"You seein' this?" Dwayne pointed at the ground just inside the woods. "This white fog shit, you seein' it?"

"I'm not blind, fuckwit, course I see it." Robert looked at the white mist that now flowed from the woods like a flood of water, swirling around their feet and racing towards the truck.

"Jeez, it's freezing! My feet are frozen, man!" Dwayne complained.

"You right, I feel it through mah boots, an' these boots got steel toes an' shit." Robert looked around, his expression confused. "Where the fuck is Fred?"

Dwayne frowned. "Dude just stepped into the woods a bit, where he go?"

"I ain't got time for no exploring shit. Go get him. Fucken idiot, I'll knock him a new one if he makes me late for my food!"

Dwayne looked at the fog that was now knee-high and shivered. He looked at Robert, unsure and a little scared. "I dunno, man, this fog is freakin' me out, like. It don' look natural and shit."

"What, you think some big fairy in the woods makin' fog on a fairy fog makin' machine?" Robert laughed. "Go get that dipshit so we can get this tree cut an' get outta here."

Dwayne sniffed nervously but entered the woods, immediately struck by how much colder it was than the parking lot, just feet away. It was darker, too, the further he walked, the less sun entered.

The fog was thicker, as well, and Dwayne swore that it was glowing. He didn't want to say anything to Robert, though, so he just cleared his throat and slapped his arms around himself, trying to warm up a little. "Freddy, dude, where you at?" he called, stomping his feet to try to get some feeling back. "Yo, dude, where you at? Freddy? Yell if you hear me, 'kay?"

No one answered. Dwayne walked a little further but made sure to keep the edge of the woods within sight. The fog was swirling around him now, as high as his chest, and he was losing feeling in his hands.

"*FREDDY!*" Dwayne's voice echoed back to him, then faded, leaving a deafening silence. He realized then that there were no other sounds, no birds singing, no bugs calling, not even the sound of the breeze in the treetops. He had been in many, many forests before, but not one of them was ever silent. Even in the dead of winter, there was always some sound, either from an animal, or from the melting snow, or wind, or creaking of the trees themselves.

Here there was nothing, just total silence.

"*FREDDY!*" he called again. "I swear to god, man, if you don' answer me imma knock yo ass into next week!"

He listened to the echoes die down, then another sound came to him. Somewhere, very far off if he had to guess, was the soft, almost unheard sound of music. Gently, and strange, like the sounds from an old-time carnival, almost, but the more he listened he wasn't even sure if it *was* music. There was a definite sound, though, and he wasn't sure if he should follow it.

"Goddamn, my nuts be 'bout inside my body now, so damn col' here. Freddy, imma leave yo ass here to freeze, I swear." He turned to head out of the woods. He needed to ask Robert what they should do now, as he was too cold to keep searching, and a little freaked out, if he was honest with himself. The music-like sound drifted to him again, but he ignored it, standing there, a little confused.

He hadn't walked more than a few feet into the woods, but he couldn't see the edge. He was surrounded by trees and darkness, and the endless, freezing mist. He frowned. Dwayne was sure he had not wandered too far into the woods, he had kept one eye on the edge, looking back every few seconds to make sure he didn't stray too far. He turned a complete circle, now disoriented, unable to tell which way he had come, and which way led to the edge of the woods.

"ROBERT!" Dwayne yelled. All he wanted was an answer so he would know which way to walk. "YO! BOSS! YOU HEAR ME?"

He waited for an answer, but he heard nothing. Nothing except that creepy music sound. He felt his testicles draw themselves further up as fear now gnawed at his belly, the music, the mist, and the darkness all fueling his imagination, and heightening his fears.

"HELLO? ANYONE?" No one answered.

He couldn't see the ground to find any tracks, he couldn't see any sunlight peering through the trees to guide him. He was as lost as Fred. "Now I knows how you got yo self all turned about, Freddy," he muttered, stamping his numb feet again. "I guess I just gonna walk an' see if I find a way, coz I ain't staying here no longer."

He started to walk, trying to find any recognition of his path, but with each tree identical to the next, he was floundering. He hoped he could at least come across one of the hiking paths, at least that would lead him to an exit, any exit, he didn't care. So far, he was sure he was still in the woods, not near a path, as the trees were too close together to have any sort of path between them.

"Naw, shit, you got no brains, Dwayney ole boy," he muttered to himself, and pulled out his cell phone. "Why you no think of this before?" He scrolled through to ring Robert's number, and hit the call icon. The phone didn't ring, and he drew it closer to his face. "No bars. Fucking fantastic. No fucking service."

He thought about playing his music real loud, maybe that would attract anyone in the woods, and decided that must have been what he heard before. Fred must have had the same idea and was playing his music for Dwayne to find him!

He stopped then and closed his eyes, trying to figure out the direction of the soft music. He knew it wouldn't give him a way out of there, but at least he wouldn't be alone. These woods were super freaky, there was no way he wanted to stay here by himself.

"Gotcha, superfreak," he started in the direction he thought the music was coming from. It seemed to be getting louder, so he felt relief, and hastened his step.

He would be much happier when he found his co-worker, even if he did owe him a punch in the arm for getting him into this mess. He couldn't see the ground through the fog, he couldn't see more than a few feet in front of him with the mix of darkness and fog. He pulled out his cell again, deciding that the flashlight function would be a useful app about now, when he fell.

His feet caught on something, maybe a root, maybe a fallen branch, he didn't know, but he crashed down hard, losing his phone as he threw his hands out in front of him to break his fall.

"Fuck me, fuck fuck fuck," he cried as he floundered on the dry ground, the pine needles covering him as he rolled to his back. The fog was all around, the soft, white glow scaring him. The thick fog was impenetrable and he could not see his hands in front of his face.

He pulled himself to his feet as quickly as he could, brushing off the needles and dirt, checking his hands for scrapes.

"Aw hell, where my phone at?" Dwayne muttered, turning around to see if he could find the glow of the flashlight through the fog. "There you are, sucker!" he plunged his hand into the freezing mist and grabbed his cell, the minor victory lifting his spirits. He brushed it off and looked for the reception bars, grimacing as they came up blank.

Dwayne looked up and nearly dropped his cell phone again when the flash hit a shape, a moving shape, in the fog. He took a step backwards, unsure, frightened, as he tried to find the figure again with his light.

"Fred?" His vice was low, almost a whisper, fear tightening his throat. "Is that you, man?"

The light caught the figure again, and he breathed a sigh of relief. "Fred, man, you scared the shit outta me. Where you been at, man?"

Fred didn't move, he just stood there, his head hanging down, his cap missing. "Man, Robert gon' bust yo ass if you los' yo cap! He be talkin' 'bout how dese things cost like eighty bucks each and he has to 'splain why he need to order more an', um, Fred? Freddy?" Dwayne slowed as he drew closer to his colleague, a feeling of dread spreading through his bones.

"Dude, you okay?" Dwayne stepped closer and reached out to touch Fred, his hand falling just short. "Man? Dude?"

Fred lifted his head and Dwayne stumbled backwards, his arms flailing as he tried to keep his balance, shocked at the sight of Fred's eyeless sockets. The flashlight had highlighted the blood dripping down his face and the mangled gums as Fred opened his mouth in a torturous parody of a smile.

Dwayne turned and ran, he ran as fast as he could away from the ragged body of his workmate, dodging trees and trying to keep clear of anything that would make him trip. He couldn't think, couldn't make sense of what he saw, and his panic didn't give him time to ponder it. He just ran. He ran as if his life depended on it, as if the thing that used to be Freddy was in hot pursuit. He didn't see the edge of the woods, he couldn't see any light from the parking lot, but he didn't care right now, he just ran.

In front of him, he didn't know how, a figure stood, and he stopped, grabbing the trunk of a tree to stop his momentum. He blinked, just once, trying to clear his mind, trying to clear his vision, and he realized that somehow Fred had gotten in front of him, had cut him off. Though what was left of the man stood there, still, not heaving for breath after running at breakneck speed as Dwayne was. Not wanting to stare at the mess of Fred any longer he turned to run, but there was something else in front of him, something tall.

So very tall.

And thin, it was thinner than any man should be, and so much taller than any living man Dwayne had ever laid eyes on. It had two very long arms, waving, bony arms, and they reached for Dwayne. Dwayne shuffled backwards until he hit a tree, and as he turned to run, he was confronted with Fred's eyeless face, the blood standing out in stark contrast to the deathly pale skin. He tried to turn the other way, but the thing's arms were there, not just one, or two, but so many arms, waving like snakes, writhing and weaving in every direction.

Dwayne turned back to Fred and shoved him as hard as he could, dropping the man into the fog. He ran then, dodging tree trunks, running fast, his heart slamming an erratic beat of exertion, fear, and blind panic.

He didn't get far before a long arm circled his waist and lifted him high, so high, he could see the canopy of the trees. The grip of the thing was like a vice, cutting off his air, cutting off his ability to breathe, to scream, to move or struggle. Black spots danced before his eyes and his mouth hung open, attempting to gulp at air as it moved soundlessly. Mercifully, the dark spots in his eyes joined together, and he knew no more.

Robert looked at his watch as he crushed out his cigarette and yawned. The sun was completely up now, and he was getting more and more irritated as the minutes passed. His hopes of finishing early enough to grab a quick meal on company time were fading; if the guys took too long getting back to him, they wouldn't have the time for anything but cutting the trees and driving back to Crosspine. He tapped his foot, then decided to take a minute and look for the guys. If he could get their asses back, like now, he may still be able to grab a greasy bag of takeout.

He looked at his cell one more time, he had full bars, but every time he tried ringing Fred or Dwayne, he got the *cell phone is out of range* message.

With a grunt of dissatisfaction Robert headed towards the trees. The cold fog was an uncomfortable inconvenience, his feet were frozen, and he wished he'd worn his wool socks that morning. He hadn't banked on being this cold at the start of summer and hadn't put a jacket in the car.

The woods were very dark, so he couldn't see too far in, and he wondered if his subordinates had just lost their way in the dark. He sniffed and closed his brightly colored safety vest, then stopped, unsure, confused, and a little frightened.

Fred stood there, just inside the woods, the fog whisping and folding about him like a fairytale cloak. Robert noted Fred's cap was missing, and where normally this would be enough for his anger to explode, he also noticed that the front of Fred's shirt was covered with something dark, something that was dripping, something that looked an awful lot like blood.

"Fred?" Robert took a step forward, not sure if he should render assistance or run. "Fred, did something attack you? Are there bears in there, man?"

Fred lifted his head, his empty black sockets such a shock that Robert fainted, hitting his head heavily on the gravel surface.

CHAPTER THIRTY-FOUR

Wallis pulled in the drive, smiling at Lisa, who stood on the front porch holding two cups of coffee. He gave her a kiss on the cheek as he accepted a coffee, noting the dark circles under her eyes. He didn't comment, he was sure he looked a lot worse than her.

"Anyone up yet?"

"Just the boys, I think I heard Simon as I came outside. Harry is still asleep, I just checked on her. I'll get her up soon." Lisa followed the Sheriff into the house.

Alex and Ayden were at the table, both men looking at the same laptop, their hair still damp from showering. They both nodded a greeting to Wallis as he walked in.

"Any breakthrough on the web search?"

"Nah, nothing useful," Alex told him. "Nothing that really adds anything to what Uncle Simon told us last night, anyway. What about you? Anything happen, any ideas?"

Wallis filled them in the night's highlights as his brother joined them, everyone listening quietly, their faces thoughtful, as he told them about the man in the cells.

"Not much happened here. We actually got some sleep, well, some of us did," Ayden looked at his mom. "I don't think Mom went to bed at all."

Lisa smiled at him, but any answer was cut off when Wallis' cell rang. He listened more than spoke before hanging up. "That was Peter O'Grady. He says his nephew was possessed last night by the spirit of an ancient warrior, and that he thinks he can help stop the monster. We should get there as soon as possible. We need to wake Harry."

Lisa nodded and hurried upstairs as Alex, Ayden and Simon grabbed their jackets.

"Did he say what the name of the warrior was, Sam?" Simon asked.

Wallis shook his head. "He did say it was the brother of the girl that the curse was written for, so it's a safe bet it's Harry's ghost's brother."

"I'm thinking he may not've been the one that called the monster back, then," Alex spoke as he was tying his shoelaces. "He wouldn't be telling us that he can stop the thing if he was the one that called it up."

"Maybe. I'm not convinced, though," Sam sighed. "He may just be panicking because a lot of innocent people are dying, not the timber guys they would have been planning on getting rid of."

His phone rang again, and he frowned when he looked at the number. "It's the station, I'm guessing something is going on there."

He answered it as he walked into the kitchen and refilled his mug, carrying it back into the dining room and sitting at the table to wait for the girls, the cell phone held to his ear with his shoulder.

Lisa came down the stairs, her coat in her hands. "What's happening?"

Wallis hung up the phone and shook his head. "Another two guys from the timber company went missing, third one in hospital with head injuries. Looks like he fell and cracked his skull. He hasn't woken, but Shirl thinks it's all related. The day's barely started and we've already got casualties. Time we got this thing ended. Simon, make sure you bring the necklace thing, okay?"

Simon nodded and tapped his chest. "I got it on, tucked safely under my shirt. I got the journal too, in my jacket. Just in case."

Sam gave his brother a reassuring smile. He worried about him, more than he let on. His mental state was fragile, so fragile, it wasn't so long ago he was the town's resident lunatic, the madman everyone made fun of. The object of his obsession had gone, for a while at least, and he seemed better, but Sam worried that he never talked about the loss of his only son, or his estranged wife. These things shouldn't be ignored, but he didn't want to press him.

He also didn't know if Simon had discussed anything with his therapist, but he did know the weekly visits he booked for his brother were continuing, as much as Simon resisted them, and he did seem to be benefitting from the therapy. He worried that this reemergence of the creature would be enough to send Simon over the edge of sanity that he teetered on, but there was nothing he could do. The creature needed to be stopped, and he needed his brother there to help stop it.

"Ready!" Harriet bounced down the stairs, looking far brighter and cheerier than anyone else in the room.

"Good morning pumpkin," Sam stood and gave her a kiss on the top of her head. "You look awfully happy."

Harriet shrugged. "I feel happy. It's completely weird, you know, but I have this feeling that we're going to win this, that we're going to find a way to end the K'aas, and for good, this time."

"Is that something your resident spirit told you?" Wallis asked her as he held out her coat.

"No, Dad, it's just a feeling. It'll probably fade as the day goes on, but you know, I'm taking it, for now." Harriet put on her coat and looked around the room. "We're going to have to take two cars, aren't we?"

"I brought the minivan from the station, we can all fit in together," Wallis told her. "I'm driving, too."

He led the group to the car, Lisa taking a back seat to allow Simon to sit in the front with his brother. "How's the arm going, Simon?" Wallis asked. "With everything that's going on, I forgot to ask."

Simon put on his seat belt and looked at his brother. "To be honest, so did I, most of the time. It's only when I try to use it and it's stiff, that I think about it."

Starting the car, Wallis backed out carefully, and stopped with the car halfway out onto the street.

"That's not good," he said and pointed back to the house. Everyone in the back seats strained forward to see what he was indicating, and there were a couple of gasps when they saw what had caught the Sheriff's attention.

Surrounding the house and flowing out onto the street was a very low, light cover of mist. While it was a more flimsy, airy flow, it was still unnatural, and they all knew what it was from.

"Just drive, Sam, there's nothing we can do about it here," Lisa told him.

"Why is it coming now?" Alex asked, a hint of panic in his voice.

"I think it's a good sign," Simon said. "I think it means Harry is right, we have a chance to beat this thing today."

"I hope you're right, brother," Sam sighed as he continued to back the car out.

They were silent on the way to the O'Grady Ranch, no one saying anything until they reached the tall wooden gate at the start of the long, winding road up the hill. There were multiple 'keep out' and 'private property, no trespassing' signs on and around the gate, and Simon started to unbuckle his seatbelt. "I'll get the gate," he said.

"No need, there's a buzzer here, and a speaker," Sam told him as he opened his window. There was a small blue button that he pushed, but nothing happened. He pushed it again, and a voice cracked over the speaker.

"*Who is it?*"

"Sheriff Wallis, to see Peter O'Grady."

The gate started to open, and Wallis closed his window and drove through, seeing the gate close behind him through the rear-view mirror.

"Have you ever been here before?" Lisa asked.

"Yeah, we came up here as kids, we were maybe five, or six?"

"I think no older than six, because, well, you know."

"Yeah," Sam reached over and patted his brother's knee, not wanting to bring up the death of their parents by the creature when they were six years old. "Our parents were friends with Peter's parents, and we visited a couple of times. I haven't been back since, but Shirl had to take one of their kids home after he busted him for graffitiing in town."

"It's really huge!" Harry leaned forward, her arms folded on the back of the front seat. "It takes up all the hills here! Look at the horses, oh my gosh, I've always wanted a horse!"

Harry squealed in delight as the herd of horses galloped up to the minivan and followed it to the next gate. It opened without any buzzers, though Sam noted there was a security camera mounted on a pole beside it.

The horses didn't try to follow, a large cattle grid prevented them access through the gateway, and Harry turned to watch them gallop off as they drove away, but grew excited again when a herd of mares and their foals cantered alongside the path, the baby horses bucking and frolicking in the early morning sunshine.

"I wish I lived in a place like this! You could ride every day, how wonderful!" Harry pulled out her cell and snapped pictures of the horses as they drove.

"I'm sure you'd get sick of them if you saw them every day," Alex teased. "Besides, isn't it a bit cliché for you, all girls like horses, and all that?"

"I don't care! I've always wanted a horse, haven't I Mom?"

"Yes, you have, but I'm terrified of them, so I decided we weren't getting a horse."

"Buzzkill, Mom," Harry complained as she took another snap of the foals.

They slowed at a third gate, and this too, opened without buzzing.

They were at the top of the hill now, and they drove through another field, this one seeming empty. A fourth gate opened in front of them and they drove down from this hill, then onto the next, finally coming to the fence that surrounded the main house.

The road wound around an elaborate, park-like garden, with many beautiful trees and garden beds arranged throughout the expansive yards, and as they drew closer to the house they could see a tennis court to one side, to the other a large swimming pool, and off to the distance was a riding arena, stables, and multiple sheds and barns.

Ayden whistled as they drove up to the house, a grand, old-style ranch house, with a white picket fence that seemed to surround the entire house, long, covered verandahs, and huge bay windows which covered the front of the building.

A man stood near the front gate, and he waved them around to the side, along a white gravel path, to the rear of the large house. There were other cars parked around the back, and Wallis pulled the minivan in beside them.

"So this is how the other half lives," Alex remarked.

"Sucks to be a millionaire, huh," Ayden agreed.

"Enough of that, boys, let's just get inside." Wallis turned off the car. "We're here for one reason only, so zip it, okay?"

"Chill, Dad, we're cool," Alex laughed. "It's not like we're snotty teenagers anymore."

"You'll always be snotty teenagers to me, boy," Sam answered, but he smiled, trying to relieve some of the tension he felt gnawing at his insides. "Sorry, I guess I'm a little tense."

Lisa took his hand and squeezed it as they walked to the gate in the picket fence, the aroma of roses warming in the sun flowing over them like a gentle perfume.

The man had walked around the verandah and stood waiting for them at the large glass doors, a smile on his face, but it was a grim, forced smile, pasted there out of politeness only.

"I'm Peter O'Grady, please, come inside," he held out his hand to shake the Sheriff's as he welcomed him.

"I'm Sam Wallis, this is my brother, Simon, my partner Lisa, her boy Ayden and my boy Alex." Peter shook each hand as they were introduced.

"And this one is my daughter, Harriet."

Harry smiled, holding out her hand. "Please, call me Harry. I only get called Harriet if I'm in trouble, or they're doing roll-call at school."

Peter shook her hand warmly and led them all inside. "I won't introduce you to everybody, but these are all the people that stayed last night, and my nephew, Mateo, the boy I told you about."

Harriet stopped in front of Mat, and tipped her head to one side, in that strange effect that the spirit used.

Mat reached out and touched her face, and a tear found its way down his cheek.

"My sister," he spoke softly. "Forever and an age I have wanted for you."

"My Hagen, my savior, I have missed your guidance and care for all these seasons."

"What's happening? What are they talking about?" Stephen's mom jumped to her feet. "Why are they staring at each other like that?"

"If I may, ma'am, this is something that's none of our business." Peter looked both angry and tired, and more than a little fed up. "If you'll please go to the dining room, you'll find the cook has prepared a meal for all of you." He turned to a rather large, stony-faced man standing near the fireplace. "I am taking the Sheriff and his party into my office, and I do not wish to be disturbed. Running Wolf, would you please ensure these people are fed, and keep them away from the front wing of the house?"

"Yes, sir, of course," the stony-faced man replied, and Peter gestured for the Sheriff and the others to follow him, ignoring the other people in the room.

Mat and Harry did not move, so Simon put his hands on their shoulders and guided them, neither taking their eyes off the other as they walked.

The house was indeed huge; they walked along a lengthy hallway and turned several corners before finally coming to an ornate door, which required Peter to unlock it before they could pass through. The door opened onto another hallway, Peter taking them to a door at the end, passing many other doors that looked exactly the same.

He unlocked the door and let them into a very large, very informal office. The walls were lined with bookshelves that were stuffed with books, both old and new. Where there were gaps between the shelves, a print of a soft geometric patterned wallpaper decorated the walls. The large bay windows looked out onto the beautiful front gardens, and further, beyond the hills, the azure sky provided a scenic and breathtaking backdrop. A huge desk was placed near one wall, facing the view, and there were several sofas and large, overstuffed armchairs, all arranged around a double bed sized coffee table.

Peter took a seat on one of the armchairs and indicated everyone to sit, watching Simon as he left Harry and Mat standing, their gaze still only for each other. "I will order coffee for everyone soon, after I give my staff a chance to cater for the crowd of people I have surprised them with. Not a situation that happens often, here, let me assure you."

"What's going on with them?" Lisa asked as she looked at Harry and Mat, her face lined with concern.

"Sit, Lisa, let whatever is going to happen, happen. I think things are kinda out of our control," Sam placed a hand on Lisa's lower back and guided her to a sofa.

"He told me to bring *the one*, that's what he called her. He said I had to bring the one, or everyone in Campbelltown would die." Peter ran a hand through his hair, and Sam noticed how tired he looked. It seemed that he and Lisa were not the only ones that didn't get any sleep the night before.

"When did he start speaking as the spirit?" Sam asked.

"Sometime after midnight," Peter answered. "Everyone was asleep, and he just walked in, like he was sleep walking, and started to spill his story. Said his name is Hagen, and he is a twin, his brother will appear in Mateo's twin brother, Luca. I've tried to tell him that isn't possible, though."

"I know Luca, I tended to him when he had stayed in hospital the winter past with the flu," Lisa said, and turned to the others. "Luca has cerebral palsy and is nonverbal, as well as being confined to a wheelchair. He has no use at all of his limbs."

"That's right, so the brother will have to just sit there and listen," Peter continued, and explained all that Mat/Hagen had talked of the night before. "Mateo's brother is a vegetable, he has no thoughts, no movements, nothing above the level of a newborn baby."

"You think Harry is this *one* that he talked about?" Sam asked.

"Your daughter is the one, she is the only one that my sister, Ix iLa'al, has been able to join with. Your daughter is strong, she is able to listen while Ix iLa'al speaks, she is able to be present," Mat/Hagen said, stepping forward to the middle of the group. "The boy, he does not accept me as the girl accepts my sister. He is not always aware. He mostly slumbers as we speak."

"Are you hurting him?" Peter stood up, concerned.

"He is safe, just as the girl is. We will never harm him. We will never allow them to be harmed. The same as this one's brother, he is safe, and unharmed. He is curious and accepting of my brother Tadeas and enjoying his voice."

"This is all very amusing, but I need to know what we do now," Peter sat down, but was agitated. "We need to stop the K'aas, and you need to tell us how we find who started it up this time."

"We thought it might be you, or one of your family," Wallis frowned at Peter. "I don't know anyone else it could be, anyone that has strong ties to the land, or to the bloodlines of these, um, forefathers? I don't know what to call them, I can't figure out how to take them, possessing the kids like that."

"We are aware it is disconcerting, and we apologize," Harry/Ix iLa'al moved beside Mat. "We will endeavor to stay away unless we are needed. We will only come to you if you call us, will that make it easier to interact with us?"

"Yes, absolutely, but don't go just yet, we're here to figure out an end to this, and we need your help." Wallis looked around at everyone in the room, noting his brother was hunkered back in his chair, looking very uncomfortable and awkward. "Can you give us any idea how to pinpoint who called your monster back? Any clues or hints? Some sort of criteria?"

Alex had his notebook out, ready to take down anything that might be helpful.

"We cannot tell you much more than you already know. The person would have to be a descendant of my father, or at least of my people. They would have to be at least a little proficient in the ways and traditions from our time, as they did not perform the curse correctly, or the K'aas would not be killing indiscriminately." Harry looked at Mat for confirmation.

"Yes, that is correct," he answered. "But to call it they have a great deal of knowledge and must be following our traditions. There cannot be too many that would do this, one would think?"

"Hold up a second there," Ayden interjected. "You say that they didn't perform the curse correctly as the thing, what did you call it, K'aas? You said it's killing indiscriminately, but that's what happened before. It killed anyone and everyone it wanted, anyone that went into the woods in summer was marked. Does that mean you guys didn't do the curse properly either?"

"That was the fault of myself," Harry sounded distressed. "When I was trying to end the curse, before I died, I was able to only stop part of it, the part that bound it to the soldiers that it was written for. I died before I could finish, I died before there was a chance for it to end."

"Why did it kill so many of my family," Simon spoke quietly, shyly, his eyes unable to meet anyone's other than Harry's.

"You know the answer to this, mostly," Mat answered. "When the first of your family touched the stone with their blood, they bound the creature to his bloodline, though not entirely, for he did not know the words to say, and did not perform any rituals. So, the K'aas sought out your bloodlines, but it was also free to seek out anyone that would come in contact with the place that it lives."

"The woods? That's what you mean, right?" Alex asked.

"Yes, that is right," Harry looked at him with the eyes of his sister, but the voice of another. "We do not know why the woods became the home of the K'aas, or why they grew. We could guess, but we do not know. It is perhaps due to my death while I was trying to break the curse, but we cannot be certain."

The phone on Peter's desk rang, and he jumped up to answer it. He spoke briefly before returning to the others, his expression grim. "That was my brother. He got my message, and he's on his way home from Crosspine with his wife and kids, and my mother. He didn't say much else, but he believed me. Normally he scoffs at this sort of thing or any talk of the creature in the woods, but he believes me, this time."

"That is excellent news!" Harry exclaimed. "I long to speak to my brother again!"

Peter made a face at this but didn't comment.

"There is so much I want to ask you both that isn't tied to the problem we're having right now," Lisa said. "But now isn't the time. So much about the afterlife, and what's happening, but maybe I can talk to you after this is over?"

Mat sighed. "We do not know if our spirits will linger once the K'aas is defeated. We are sorry, it is something we cannot predict."

"Peter, do you know of anyone from your tribe that might still practice the old ways?" the Sheriff asked.

"Apart from my mother? My grandmother is still alive, she was right into it all, she would be the one to ask. If she could talk, that is. She had a stroke about five years ago, can't talk anymore. Barely walks."

"What about any of her contacts, people she knows? Friends? Maybe she worshipped with others, or something?" Ayden suggested.

"Son, my grandmother is one hundred and three years old," Peter sneered. "Anyone she knew is dead. And my tribe doesn't have a tribal church, that's not how it works."

"Oh, sure, sorry." Ayden blushed, sitting back on the sofa like he was trying to hide.

"Your mother, she still follows the old ways?" Wallis asked.

Peter nodded. "A bit, probably more than she likes to admit. She maintains the sigils on the doors and windows that keep this place safe."

"You have a way to make the place safe?" Simon was shocked. "We could have been safe all these years, our parents could have been safe, survived? My son, my wife?"

Peter turned to Simon. "I don't know, maybe, I guess. I don't know if the sigils only work because we are on tribal land or not. I'm sorry, I really don't know."

Simon inched forward a little. "Would your mother know?"

"Simon, not now, okay?" Wallis gave him a stern look. "This isn't helping, and it's not like you can change the past. Let it go."

Simon opened his mouth to speak, but the look on his brother's face silenced him.

"How long until your brother arrives?" Lisa asked.

"He called me from a gas stop on the ninety-five, so maybe another half hour?" Peter looked at the teenagers standing in the middle of the room. "We should find out everything we can from these two before the others get here."

"Can you show us how to do the sigils?" Simon asked.

Wallis shot him another look and dismissed the question with a wave of his hand. He turned back to the teenagers. "What else can you tell us? What are we looking for when we find the person that renewed the curse? You said we need to break the figures up, will they be like the ones that you made? Like little stick figures?"

Harry shook her head. "I made those from my hair, and the threads on my garments, and from branches and twigs I found on the ground. They are made to break the curse, not to catch it. I had nothing else to work with. I do not know what was used to make the curse, but I can help you break it."

"My brother and I made the curse, we are the ones that started it," Mat said. "We made sacrifices of fine bred animals, and we slit the throat of a soldier to drain his blood."

"We won't be slitting any throats, that's not happening," Wallis stood and began to pace. "There has to be something else we can do to stop this."

"You do not understand. You do not need to kill anyone to stop the curse, that is what we did to create it."

"Wait, are you guys saying that whoever started the curse this time had to kill somebody?" Alex asked. "Is that right? They sacrificed animals and killed somebody?"

Mat shook his head. "The curse was already created. They merely had to awaken the K'aas."

"Well, that's a relief," Wallis said. "So, did they need to sacrifice any animals?"

"They would make a blood offering, an animal that was precious to them is the most effective. They would need to make a representation of what they wished to curse, and this is what you need to find. They must be destroyed, and if you wish the curse to end, do not make any further figures to bind it to. We will give you the words to say, and you will say them when you face the K'aas, and it will end."

"We need to find someone that practices the old ways, someone that recently offed their favorite cat, and then force them to give us their little pottery figures?" Wallis asked. "Sounds easy. Not like we're looking for a needle in a haystack."

Mat and Harry both tipped their heads to one side at the same time, and they both smiled.

"It wasn't meant to be funny," Wallis growled.

"He is here," Harry replied.

"Who? The K'aas?" Simon jumped to his feet.

"No, my brother is here," Peter answered as he looked out of the window. "You can see his car coming up over the rise."

CHAPTER THIRTY-FIVE

"They don't want to stay in the conference room anymore, Mike," Harmen leaned over the Sheriff's desk where Mike was sitting. "They want to go to the O'Grady's ranch and confront them and take their boys home."

"Tell them they can leave, the risk is on them, not us, but warn them to stay away from the ranch," Mike said.

"Hang on, I'll talk to them, set them straight, okay?" Shirl ran a hand through his hair, hoping to control his mess of slept-in curls. Mike threw him a cap and he tucked that on, shuffling the rest of the unruly hair behind his ears. "I'll make sure they don't go near the ranch."

"How're you gonna do that? They want their kids. You can't tell them to stay away from their kids."

"I'll think of something, Mike, trust me," Shirl looked at Joan, standing near the CCTV monitors. She was watching the stationary man in the cell block, yawning into the back of her hand as she watched. "Hey, Joan. Come with me to talk to the parents, okay? Soften the blow a little?"

Joan glanced back at the monitors before looking at Shirl and nodding. "Sure, why not. I'm too freaked out to go home, even though it's daytime. Michelle will be in soon; do you want to unlock the front doors?"

"I'll do that when she buzzes," Mike answered.

"Good luck in there, guys. Those parents are vipers. Seriously, I feared for my life!" Harmen winked at them and moved to answer the phone ringing on the Sheriff's desk.

238

Shirl knocked on the conference room door but opened it without waiting for a response. Everyone turned to face him; they all looked tired, disheveled, and more than a little pissed. Two fathers were facing each other, and one had a handful of the other's shirt. From what Shirl could tell, they looked like they were in the middle of a bust up.

"Thanks for your patience, people," Shirl tried to fake his most reassuring smile. "Mike says you are ready to go home?"

"Not all of us are," the man holding the other man's shirt replied. He let go of his handful and turned to the deputy. "I don't think we'll be safe. One of the families that died five years ago lived right next to me. Right next door! I'm not willing to risk my life, or my wife's, for the sake of a shower and a change of clothes. Your Sheriff says he'll take care of things and I believe him. I do."

"Well, not all of us do, sonny boy," the other father pushed him aside and walked up to the deputy. "Shirl, is it? Well, Shirl, I want to go home. But first, I want to go get my son, and take him home. And not you, or anybody else has any right to stop me."

"You want to go to the ranch, is that right, to collect your son?"

The father nodded at the deputy.

"Not us," another piped up. "We want to go to the ranch and stay there like they invited us. They said it was safe, so we want to go there."

"After we call past home to get a change of clothes and some things," his wife added, holding his arm.

"So, not everybody is in agreement, am I right?" Shirl asked.

A lot of heads nodding answered him. Shirl looked thoughtful, then nodded as well. "Okay, here's what we'll do. I'll contact the Sheriff, see if it's okay for those that want to go up there to get their kids, or stay, or both. He's there at the moment. The ones that want to go home, you can do that, but we hold no responsibility for your safety if you do so."

Joan stepped forward. "For those of you that don't know me, my name's Joan, I work on reception at nights, and sometimes on the weekends. I'm not easily frightened. I've worked here for over fifteen years, and I've seen pretty much everything, all kinds of mayhem and crime. I knock off in about an hour, but let me tell you, I'm not going home. I'm not going anywhere, not until the Sheriff tells me that he's taken care of things, and we are safe. So, you can all do what you want, like Shirl says, none of you are under arrest. But if you want my advice, or even if you don't, staying here is the safest thing you can do."

"What about the ranch? Is that safe?" one parent asked.

"Could be, but I'm not going to take the risk and drive there, who says the drive is safe?" Shirl told them. "Take your risk if that's what you want to do, but like I said, I can't guarantee your safety, and I can't guarantee you're still welcome at the ranch. I'm happy to try and contact the Sheriff to check, it's up to you."

No one spoke.

"Okay, what if I give you a little time to think about things? I'm going to turn the security cameras in the room back on, anyone not behaving themselves will be dealt with accordingly," he paused and looked at the men who had been about to fight as he entered. "For those staying, I'll send in someone to take breakfast orders, the station will pay, and you are welcome to use the showers and change rooms, I'm sure you found them last night. Those that want to leave, I'll open the doors for you upon request."

With that he turned and opened the door, allowing Joan to exit first. As he was about to leave one of the fathers called out.

"Shirl, be honest with me. What are the chances that the Sheriff will kill this thing for good?"

Shirl sighed. "To me, I'd say better than not doing anything would be. A chance is a chance, and we've got to try what we can." With that he closed the door, following Joan down the hallway to the main office.

"Can you turn the cameras on in there, Joan? I don't want anyone killing each other in the police station."

"Sure thing, Shirl. I think maybe you should talk to the parents in Sam's office, too."

Shirl grimaced. "Shit, I forgot about them. Okay, thanks, Joan, I'll get right onto it."

"No need," Mike informed him. "I've already been in there, they're happy to stay put. They are terrified, and not going anywhere until they have some good news. How'd it go with the others?"

"Lots of tension, but hopefully I've calmed them down. They'll come out if they want to leave, I've told them they can go if they want. I don't think they will, though. Shit, I'm not going anywhere, and I'm willing to bet you aren't, either!"

"You got that right, buddy. I guess all we can do is hunker down and wait. I'm starving though, let's get Aaron to grab some breakfast orders and the boss can write it off on petty cash."

The front door buzzer sounded, and everyone looked towards the security TV monitors.

"You guys should come and look at this," Joan called to them.

Shirl and Mike walked over, Aaron, Jacob, Orville and Harmen all following. The monitors were all feeding vision from the CCTV cameras on different angles of the building, and on three of them they could see people standing.

Not just people.

The kids from last night, standing at each corner of the front of the building, their heads tilted towards the roof, their eyeless sockets facing the cameras.

"What the fuck?" gasped Mike. "They're out there in broad daylight!"

"It's a quarter past six, people are going to be out and about real soon," Orville looked at Shirl. "What're we gonna do?"

"I don't know. Jeez, this is, well, I don't know what this is!" Shirl moaned. The backdoor alert buzzed, and they all jumped.

"Oh my god, it's Michelle!" Joan exclaimed. "She's at the back door, oh god, what if one of those things gets her?"

Shirl and Mike looked at each other, then turned and ran towards the hallway, with Jacob and Harmen hot on their heels. They skidded around the corner, racing towards the back door, skidding the second corner and both hitting the wall beside the door at the same time.

"Hurry!" Joan called. "They're moving!"

Jacob and Harmen hit the wall as Mike slapped the green door opening button. Shirl reached out and grabbed Michelle by the arm. He dragged her off her feet and into the building, giving her no time to speak or protest as they fell to the floor in a heap, before Mike slammed the door behind them.

"What the hell was that for?" Michelle screamed. "Have you gone completely mad?"

242

"Just in time," Mike tapped the monitor that showed the view from the backdoor cameras. Shirl stood and helped Michelle to her feet. They stepped up to the monitor to see the three teens, their jerky, strange walk unnatural, their arms stiff at their sides as they drew up to the back door. One of the boys reached up and pressed the buzzer, and even though they knew the noise was coming, they all jumped at the sound.

"Is it locked? Is the door locked?" Michelle asked, her voice panicked.

"There's no handle on that side, and yes, the locks are engaged, both electronic and manual," Jacob assured her. "And we've been safe all night, not one of them has been able to get inside."

"Not one of them? How many are there?" Michelle ran a shaky hand down her clothes to smooth them.

"We've seen four, on and off," Mike took Michelle's bag, and everyone turned to walk back to the main office. "Even got one in the cells."

"Not anymore," Aaron greeted them at the end of the hall. "He's disappeared."

"What do you mean, disappeared?" Mike looked even more astounded. "What happened?"

"We don't know," Joan called to him as they walked towards the bank of monitors. "He was there before you guys ran, and next thing he wasn't. I didn't see him go; I didn't see anything. I was too busy watching the other three, I didn't think I'd have to keep an eye on him."

"This is great. This is just great. I thought we were safe in here," Shirl shook his head.

"What do you mean?" Orville's voice was high-pitched, frightened, and his face had turned a shade of white.

"If one of them can get out of a triple, quadruple, actually, set of doors, then we have no way to make sure we're safe in here."

No one spoke, the expressions on everyone's faces were the same - fear, confusion, and a tinge of panic.

"I ordered breakfast. It should be here any minute," Aaron gasped.

On cue, the front door buzzed, and everyone turned to look at the monitors. Two men stood there, each holding a good-sized carton containing their breakfast orders. There were no eyeless people in any of the camera views, only the delivery men, their vehicle at the curb behind them.

"Let them in," Shirl spoke quietly, and Mike opened the swinging doors to the foyer, then the doors to the front. By the time he was opening the main doors three of the day shift deputies, Joel, Russell and Luke, had arrived, confusion reflected on their faces when they saw Mike, Shirl, Aaron and Jacob.

"What're you guys doing here? Aren't you nine to fivers?"

"Things have happened, guys. Come in and we'll explain," Mike turned to Shirl. "Pay the diner guys, will you. I'll bring the morning staff up to speed."

"Should I lock the doors?" Aaron asked, and Shirl nodded.

"Yes, leave the doors closed. If anyone needs to enter, they can buzz. Michelle, can you go with Mike and the morning shift, he can fill you in as well. Jacob, you and Aaron distribute the food, and Orville and Harmen can help me figure out what to do next."

"This day is ridiculous," Joan took Michelle by the arm and walked with her through the swinging doors.

Shirl followed them and stood at the monitors, not wanting to join in with Mike's explanation to the deputies now sitting around Wallis' desk. He had managed an hour or so of sleep, but it wasn't enough. Shirl was tired, bone tired, and the stress of the supernatural happenings were taking a further toll on his stamina. He didn't think he'd be able to sleep now, though he desperately needed it.

"Who else is due in?" Harmen asked as he leaned against the wall beside him.

"No one. Normally Mike and me at nine, Aaron and Jacob would be in at ten, then Alex and Ayden at four, and you two at ten this evening. Those three," he nodded towards the deputies at Wallis' desk. "They leave at two-thirty, normally. Oh, there's Lila, the afternoon receptionist, she comes in at two, but we've got a little while before we worry about her. Michelle's early, she doesn't start till eight, normally."

"I asked her to come in early," Joan explained. "I was going to leave early; I had a dentist appointment. Guess I'll be rescheduling that one."

"This day is going to be a crazy, all hands-on deck situation," Shirl turned and leaned against the wall. "I just don't know how long the boss is going to take to get things done."

"Or even if he can," Orville looked grim. "Anyway, we've got breakfast, let's all go to the staff room and eat, the new guys can keep an eye on things for now."

Mike stood and the three deputies sat for a moment longer, looking at each other with shocked expressions. Shirl walked over to them, trying to keep his face as professional as possible and mask the tiredness he felt. "You guys wanna ask us anything?"

"Um, yeah, I guess," the deputy looked at his companions. "Luke, Russell and me, well, we got young families at home. We're kinda spinning out about their safety."

"I get that, Joel, I do, but they're probably a lot safer at home than we all are in here, truth be told. If you want, you can go home, we won't hold that against you, but think about it. Once you've been here, you could be taking whatever this thing is back home, it could follow you right there."

"He's right," Russell stood up. "We signed on to be deputies to help people, not to run and hide when the scary shit comes down. I'm staying."

"Yep, me too," Luke stood.

"Sorry, guys, I can't, my baby is six weeks old. I need to go home; I need to look after them." Joel stood and looked at his friends. "I'm sorry."

"Dude, just call your missus, get her to go to her mother's. She could use the visit, and she'll be safe, her mom lives in Crosspine, doesn't she?" Russell suggested. "My wife's mom lives there too, I'm gonna call her now and send her there with the kids. She can even pick your wife up, if you like?"

"Okay, yeah, good idea, I don't know why I didn't think of it. I'll call her now."

"What are you going to do, Luke?" Shirl asked.

"I must be psychic, guys," Luke smiled. "My lot are in Metro city till next Tuesday. I sent them up because I pulled a triple shift, need the dollars."

"Good. We'll be in the break room, you guys take care of things, cool?"

They nodded and Shirl walked off to join the others, pulling his cell out. He needed to let Wallis know about their eyeless visitors, and prompt him to hurry and find a way to end the creature.

CHAPTER THIRTY-SIX

Peter had left the room to greet his brother as the car pulled into the garage, access to which was available from inside the house. Everyone sat quietly for a few minutes, feeling strange, awkward, not knowing how to address the spirits that inhabited the teenagers.

Lisa cleared her throat, looking at Harry. "Um, Ix iLa'al, can you tell me what it's like where you are? I mean, when you're not inside my daughter?"

Harry opened her mouth to speak but they were interrupted by the door opening, Running Bear helping the kitchen staff bring in coffees and pastries, smiling as they set them out on the large table. When the door closed behind them, Harry walked to her mother and squatted down in front of her.

"You have lost someone, yes?" she asked in a soft voice. Lisa nodded.

"You want to know if they are safe, or happy, or if you can speak with them?"

Lisa nodded again, her lips tight.

The door opened again and Peter entered, followed by a girl about Harry's age, then a man who looked exactly like Peter, and his wife, who was pushing a wheelchair.

The boy in the wheelchair looked very similar to Mat, but there were subtle differences. His teeth were not as straight, and his hair was shorter. His face was thinner, and less mature. His eyes were bright, eager and excited, and Sam found it hard to believe there was no intelligence behind them.

"These are the people you told me about?" Peter's brother turned to everyone and gave them a tight smile. "My name is Ben, I'm Peter's brother, as you can tell. My wife Elyse, my mother Miriam, our daughter Zoey, and our son, Mateo's twin, Luca."

Miriam and Elyse nodded at everyone as Sam introduced them, then they turned to Luca.

"Hello," he said, his voice dry, croaky, as if it had not been used in some time.

"I don't understand, I thought you said he was nonverbal?" Sam glanced at Lisa.

"He is, or, I don't know, was?" Elyse looked at Mateo, expecting him to react to his brother's sudden ability to speak. "He started talking last night. He sat up on his own, or tried to, then spoke, very quietly, but the things he said, well..."

"Well, he said he was some dead boy from centuries ago named Tadeas," Ben finished.

"He's never talked before," Zoey smiled at her brother. "We thought he couldn't talk, that he didn't know anything, really, but, now, oh my god, Matty, he can talk!"

"It is not your brother who speaks," Mat tilted his head in that strange affectation both he and Harry used. "It is our brother, and he has given your brother the words so that we can help you."

"Mat?" Elyse looked frightened.

"I told you on the phone about this, Elyse," Peter took her hand and led her to the chair, sitting her down gently. "The girl is possessed, too, all three kids are. They needed twins to come to us, and a girl of single birth."

"Why didn't you choose me, then?" Zoey asked. "I'm not a twin, you could have chosen me!"

"It's not a competition," Alex said. "Seriously, I don't know why they chose my sister, I don't think they really understand it, either. They tried for a long time to find a way to talk to the living, and this is the only time that it worked. Me and Ayden think it's because one of our forefathers mixed his blood with the medallion, the talisman, by accident, and that meant we were involved now."

"Not me, really, I'm not related," Ayden said. "But my sister is. So, it had to be your blood, and her blood. She has both the forefather's blood and your blood, from way back, so that gives her a double whammy."

"Anyway, that's our theory, for what it's worth," Alex finished.

"You have a valid theory," Lisa noted. "It sounds right, based on what Harry, or, um, Ix iLa'al told us. So, we're all here now, all of us, and we can get down to working things out."

"Yes, we can do that, we will help you. We thank you for letting us work with you to bring the K'aas to an end," Mat said.

"Why do you need to do that?" Miriam spoke for the first time. "Why would you want to end it?"

"Because it's killing people!" Simon exploded, jumping to his feet. "Clearly you've never lost anyone you love to that thing or you wouldn't even have to ask that question!"

Sam grabbed Simon and held him in a bear hug for a second before pushing him back, his hands on both of Simon's arms. "This isn't helpful, Simon. We can talk about all of this later, when it's all over, okay? Right now, I need you to sit back down, and be quiet, while we work this out. I want you to be quiet unless you have something to say that actually helps, can you do that?"

Simon stared into Sam's eyes for a moment before he nodded and sat back on the sofa beside Alex. His nephew placed a comforting hand on his knee and squeezed just a little to reassure him.

"The K'aas will never die, grandmother of this boy. It cannot die," Mat said. "We seek only to end the curse we created. Its time is over, its purpose fulfilled. That is why it does not work the way it should, killing only those that it was made to destroy, but kills everyone, *will* kill everyone, even those in this house."

"It can't get in here, not this house," Ben said. "It can't even get past the house yard. All the fences surrounding the house, all the gates, they're protected, they have the ancient symbols on them. I checked them myself before we left for Crosspine."

"They're not working, Ben," Peter told him. "Last night the fog came all the way up to the verandah. And not just the fog, there were other, um, things, too."

"That's not possible!" Elyse exclaimed. "Nothing can get through the yard!"

"The house still seems safe, for now," Peter gestured towards the window. "Nothing came over the verandah. I waited the whole night; it didn't come over the verandah at all."

A knock on the window startled all of them, Lisa crying out with surprise. Everyone looked over and Elyse screamed, triggering everyone to jump to their feet.

At the window was a man, a short, slightly chubby man, wearing a safety vest and work clothes. His head was hanging low, and the front of his clothes were covered with blood.

"That can't be," Peter stepped in front of his sister-in-law. "It's on the verandah!"

The man knocked again, and Sam, Alex and Ayden stepped forward, walking slowly to the window, guns in hand. The man raised his head and seemed to look at them with his eyeless sockets. He opened his mouth, and blood fell in a huge glob, obscuring part of the name tag on his chest, covering the sawmill name, leaving only *Fred* and the tree logo visible.

Sam drew closer, his gun pointed at the head of the man, not sure if that would do anything to stop it should it break through the multi-paned floor to ceiling window. It knocked again, then dropped its hand to its side as fog lapped all around it.

"The sigils are still working for now, but they will soon lose their power," Mat informed them. "Your family's lives, and the lives of everyone in this building, will not be safe. There will be nowhere you can hide."

"I don't understand, we're protected!" Miriam clutched at the medallion around her neck. "We all wear these! We've all got these around our necks!"

"They will fail, also, as the sigils are failing," Harry was facing Miriam. "Even you will be vulnerable. Even you will fall to the K'aas as its power grows. For now, it cannot enter the house, so we still have time to take action."

"Why are you looking at me? I don't know how to stop it!" Miriam cried.

"Did you call the K'aas back?" Peter asked her. "Was it you, Mom?"

"No, it wasn't me! Why would I do that? For the sake of the gods, son, that's the last thing I'd ever do! You know that thing killed my boyfriend in college, you know how that made me feel! I've told you that story over and over!"

"Who was it, then? Who could do this?" Ben asked.

"There's more coming!" Sam called out as figures appeared in the fog, heads hanging low as they jerkily walked towards the house. "If they all start knocking, they could break the glass!"

"Miriam, excuse me, sorry, but I need to ask," Simon got up from the sofa, and he walked closer to the expensively dressed woman. "If it wasn't you, I mean, if you didn't call the K'aas back, then, maybe, you might know who did? Or not who did, but maybe, who could? Maybe who has the knowledge?"

"Mom?" Ben turned to his mother. "Do you know anyone? Any of your friends, or anyone you can think of?"

Miriam glanced at the window and her hands flew to her mouth. "Oh lord, oh my lord!" she cried.

Ben glanced at the window and saw the people standing there, people that were no more than walking corpses, all standing at the window, looking in with eyeless stares.

"MOM!" Peter grabbed his mother's arm and shook her a little. "Mom, don't look at them, don't think about them. Is there someone you know that can make the curse?"

Miriam didn't look at her son, she couldn't take her focus away from the window.

"MOM!" Peter took both her shoulders and gave her another shake, turning her away from the window. "Do you know anyone, Mom? Think, is there anyone that could do this?"

She looked at her son, her lower lip quivering, and nodded her head.

"Who is it? Mrs. O'Grady, who do you know?" Lisa asked, her voice soft, hoping she made it calming, soothing. "Can you tell us who it is?"

She nodded, her lips still quivering.

"Who is it, Mrs. O'Grady?" Lisa pleaded. "Please, tell me who it is, can you do that?"

Miriam nodded, tears starting to flow.

Someone knocked at the office door and opened it. Running Bear poked his head around, one hand up in apology. "Sorry to interrupt, but the people here are scared, they want to know what to do, and if you'd noticed the fog right up against the windows?"

Miriam pointed at Running Bear, the tears falling freely down her face.

"Sir?" Running Bear looked at Ben, waiting for a reply.

"Is it him, Mom?" Peter asked.

Miriam nodded, still pointing at Running Bear.

CHAPTER THIRTY-SEVEN

"There's fog out there," Joan hadn't moved from the bank of monitors, she now had a chair to sit on, and a mug of coffee in her hands. "It's everywhere out the back. And it's getting higher."

"Any word from the boss?" Luke asked Shirl.

"Nope, but let's take that as a good sign. Maybe he's just busy getting it done." Shirl was sitting at the Sheriff's desk, Mike beside him. "If he wasn't busy, he'd call or text."

"Let's hope," Michelle sat mugs of coffee on the desk for the deputies.

"You don't have to do that, you're not our waitress," Mike told her.

"I know, I know, I just don't have anything else to do. It's really weird, normally the phones are fairly busy, but there hasn't been a call for ages. It's after nine, and no one has walked in, no one has called." Michelle turned back to the coffee machine and filled more mugs.

"Just a thought," Russell took one of the coffees Michelle offered. "Have you checked the phone lines?"

"I hadn't thought to do that, no," Michelle handed out the rest of the coffees as Shirl picked up the phone on his desk.

He listened for a moment, pressed some buttons, then put it down. "This one's dead."

Russell and Luke checked the other desk phones, all putting them back down, shaking their heads.

"I got no cell reception, either," Aaron held his cell up towards the ceiling, trying to get a signal. "Me neither," Jacob put his phone back in his pocket. "I'll check the phone at the front desk, it has a main line, not power reliant, not internet dependent."

He pushed through the swinging doors, and Joan stood up. "Fog's around the front, now. Shirl, check the city cams, see if it's through the town."

Mike moved the mouse to wake up the computer and Shirl typed in the password.

"Um, excuse me? Hello?" One of the parents stepped into the main room, a couple of others behind him. "We've got no cell service, and the phone in the conference room is dead."

"Same here," Veronika's father called from the Sheriff's office.

"We know, but we just found out," Jacob told them. "We're not exactly sure what's happening, not yet."

"Internet's down," Shirl scrubbed a hand over his face. "Jesus, Mary and Joseph, what the fuck is happening?"

"You're scaring the general public dude," Mike spoke quietly, not wanting the parents to hear him.

"They're not the only ones scared, dude. I'm freaked out right now." Shirl stood and looked at the parents. "We don't know what's happening, we don't know how to stop it. You guys can stay in the conference room or walk around. Just don't touch anything you shouldn't."

"You sure, Shirl?" Harmen stood up from his desk. "That's a lot of people to be wandering around the station."

"They're in this as much as we are. Maybe they can help if something goes down. I'd much rather they were informed than panicked if we need to move quickly, or whatever."

"We'll go back and explain, and see what they all want to do," the parents turned and moved off back down the hallway.

"The fog's getting thicker, I can't see anything else now," Joan told them. "It's like some scary movie out there."

"Any walking corpses?" Joel asked.

"Not that I can see," Joan pulled her chair closer to the monitors. "The fog is too thick to see anything except white."

"Just a thought, guys," Russell looked around and shrugged. "Well, just another thought, I guess. What if the power goes out? Those front doors are only locked electronically. The others all have manual locks, but not those at the very front."

"He's right," Mike stood, his expression worried. "If the phones are out there's no guarantee the power won't go out, too. Any ideas how to lock them?"

"Safety grill." Shirl got up and walked over to the monitors. "There's a panic button here, see? Slams down the grill at the front, it's on a roller, like garage doors, just inside the roof. We can activate it if we need to, it comes down in, like, two seconds."

A scream startled them all, sounding like someone was right out the front. Joan stood up, startled, and checked all the monitors. "I can't see anything still, just fog."

Another scream and everyone were on their feet, Shirl and Mike going out through the swinging doors to the foyer.

"See anything?" a voice behind them asked. Turning, Shirl saw it was one of the parents. He turned back to the glass doors, looking out to the anteroom and the very front glass doors there. "I can see as much as you can, sir."

"Well, I think I can see something," Jacob moved past them and put his face up to the glass, his hands shielding his face from the overhead lights. "Yeah, there's something out there, sort of dark shapes, I guess, but I can't tell what they are."

Something crashed against the front glass and everyone jumped. Jacob fell back on his butt. "What the fuck?"

It was a cow, beef bred, large, brown and white, and with long horns on its head. It moved again, crashing once more into the glass, leaving a smear of blood as it moved.

Like the teenagers earlier, it had no eyes, and blood was frothing from its nose and mouth. Another cow drew closer and crashed into the first one, before they both turned and stumbled back into the fog.

"Fuck me!" Mike grabbed Jacob's arm and helped him up.

"Time to activate that safety grid, Shirl," Orville held the swinging door for everyone to file through. "If those cattle break through the windows we're done for."

On cue another bovine hit the glass, and Shirl nodded to Joan. She hit the panic button and the screens slammed down, not just on the front, but they could hear them at the back, closing off the open loading bay.

The power went out then, plunging the station into darkness for a moment before the emergency lights came on. They could hear a few squeals of surprise as parents reacted to the sudden darkness. The conference room had no windows, and only one emergency light. Before long the parents filed out into the main office, too shaken to stay in the dark room by themselves.

"We need guns," a parent said, moving up to Shirl. "We can help defend the station."

"And our families!" added another.

"I'm not handing out police weapons to civilians, sir, you'll be safe inside the station without them." Shirl gestured at the deputies, all circled around him. "There's enough trained personnel to defend the station right here. And we have two badass receptionists if we need back up."

"Damn right!" Michelle called out from her place at the monitors, standing beside Joan in her chair. The monitors were still going, the emergency generator now powering them and the lights. The computers were still on, but without any internet they were useless.

An occasional crash against the glass from the cattle would make everyone jump, but nothing could be seen on the monitors other than dark shadows in the fog.

"Well, what do we do now?" Mike asked.

"We can check every window is shuttered correctly; the shutters would have closed each one when the safety grill was activated. Better know now than find out the hard way." Shirl nodded to the deputies. "Take a dad each with you and check each room, each window, make sure everything is secure and locked down. No room for errors here. And grab the chairs and the sofa from the conference room so we've got seats for everyone."

It didn't take long before they all were done, gathering back in the main room. The chairs were arranged about under the emergency lights, no one wanting to sit in the dark. A couple of people pulled chairs up with Michelle and Joan at the monitors, their only eyes onto the world outside the station.

"So, what now?" Harmen asked.

"I guess we wait. We can't do anything else." Mike sat at Wallis' desk and Shirl joined him. "Let's get some coffees and whatever snacks we can find and hand them out. The key to the snack machine is in the top drawer of the desk in the boss' office."

"I'm up for that," the father who'd asked for a gun put his hand up. "Anyone want to help?"

A few of the other fathers moved to him, and they went off to make the coffee and raid the vending machine.

"Keeps them busy," Mike noted. "Good thinking."

"Well, they'll be busy for a little while." Shirl ducked as another scream split the air. "They sound awfully damn close still."

"There's nothing other than the cattle on the screens, Shirl," Joan told him. "Occasionally a horse bumps into the glass. I suppose they don't see very well without their eyes."

"That's weird, right? I mean, weirder than before," Mike said.

"Before? You've seen this before?" One of the mothers pulled her chair up to the Sheriff's desk.

"Yeah, kinda," Shirl answered. "We've seen people with no eyes, but never any other animal. Never heard of any cattle mutilations or anything, either."

"What about dogs?" Michelle pointed to the monitor in front of her. "There's a dog licking the glass. It's got no eyes, either."

"I don't understand it. I hope it's escalating because the boss is onto something and it's fighting back." Mike looked at Shirl. "What do you think?"

"I'm not thinking right now, Mike," he took a coffee that one of the dads offered. "I'm surviving on caffeine and whatever was in that breakfast burrito I ate earlier. I have no rational thoughts beyond that."

CHAPTER THIRTY-EIGHT

Running Bear was sitting on a chair in front of Peter's desk, everyone surrounding him. He was a mountain of a man - muscular, tall, so tall that sitting down his head was at the same level as the other standing men in the room. He was dressed in jeans and a plaid shirt, his long black braids falling over his shoulders. He seemed shocked, looking from one face to the other, avoiding the gaze of the three possessed teens.

"We need to know now, Running Bear, it's beyond urgent!" Elyse pointed at the window. "Can't you see the zombies out there? The fog? God knows what else is out there, all waiting to get in and kill us!"

Running Bear's eyes were wide, his expression fearful.

"It was not him," Luca spoke softly, barely above a whisper. "He was not the one that called the K'aas."

"How do you know? You can't know that. You can't be sure!" Zoey turned to her brother, his wheelchair pushed in front of everyone. "He's the only one that knows how to call that thing!"

"No, I am not," Running Bear told her. "I do know the words, I know how to summon the K'aas, but I only know this because my mother showed me, she taught me, she is the one that keeps the old ways." He pulled a medallion that matched the ones worn by the O'Grady's from his shirt. "She knows how to make these things, she's probably the only one left that knows."

"Where is your mother, Running Bear?" Ben asked him.

"She's in our rooms, I think, or if not, she might be in the kitchen, helping out," he told them. "I'll go find her for you."

"No, you wait here, I'll go," Peter said. "I don't want you to panic and take off or anything."

Running Bear looked offended but didn't reply.

"How did you know he wasn't the one?" Simon asked Luca.

"We will feel a connection when we are close to the one that summoned the K'aas from its slumber," Luca answered. "It will be subtle, but unmistakable for us."

"Should we get ready with the words, the spell, or incantation, whatever it is?" Simon asked.

"We will see if the mother of this warrior is the one we seek," Harriet answered.

"Why do you call me a warrior? I'm a pacifist, I don't hurt anybody."

"Your heart is brave and strong; it is the heart of a warrior. You are one to be revered and respected," Mat answered.

"Whatever you guys are going to do, try and hurry!" Sam called over his shoulder. He was standing a few feet back from the window, the deputies at his side, all with guns drawn. "These things are right on us. Looks like everyone that's been missing."

The door opened and Peter entered, an elderly woman on his arm. She was a stark contrast to her robust son - she was tiny, smaller than Harry, and looked very frail. Her long silver hair hung in braids over each shoulder, and her skin was pale and wrinkled.

"Mama," Running Bear stood and offered her his chair. "These people need to talk to you, and it's very important that you tell them the truth, okay Mama?"

"I only ever speak the truth, son of mine," her voice bore the heavy indigenous accent of her people. "Have you ever known otherwise?"

"I'm sorry, Mama, of course I haven't."

"These children, they feel different," the old woman looked at the three teenagers. "You are not Mateo and Luca anymore, are you? And you, I don't know you, but I can feel the power coming from you."

"We are the blood of your forebears, we are your past, your history," Luca whispered.

"You are the one that we have been seeking," Harry smiled at the woman. "What is your name?"

"Young girl, I am She Who Seeks, my friends call me Seeka. You are welcome to do the same."

"My name is Ix iLa'al, my brothers are Hagen and Tadeas, and we welcome you. We also need to ask you where you called the curse, as the creature is now beyond anyone's control, and soon shall enter this house, killing anyone who resides here."

Seeka folded her arms. "I'm not scared. I am old, I have lived many years. I'm ready to die."

"Mama! I'm not ready," Running Bear knelt beside her. "What about these children? You love them like your own, you don't want them to die, do you?"

Seeka waved off his words. "They are protected, they will be safe."

"No, Seeka, we won't," Zoey stepped forward. "Tell them, Ix iLa'al, tell them what you told us about the medallions."

Harry nodded. "They soon will lose the power to hold off the K'aas, and it will take them, it will take all of them. No one will survive, not here in the house, nor in the town. Not the old, nor the young. Not the babies, not the parents. All will be taken, and the K'aas will not stop there. It will continue to kill, it will grow in power, until it's too powerful for anyone to stop it."

Seeka looked at the faces staring at her, seeing the fear, and seeing her son's pleading eyes.

"You are sure of this?" she asked Harry.

"Of this we are certain. If you try, you can feel it too. Can you not feel it?"

Seeka looked at the three teenagers with her brow furrowed, her eyes narrowed as she studied them. "You are right, I can feel it. And I can feel it coming, it's on its way here. You can feel that too, can't you?"

Harry nodded.

"Okay, yes, I'll help you. Yes, it was me that called the K'aas."

"Why, Mama, why would you do that?"

"They were cutting down the woods, my son! Those woods are part of our history, our tradition, and they were going to cut them down!"

"That's not worth killing people, Seeka!" Ben ran both hands through his black hair. "We went to Crosspine and slapped an injunction on them! They won't be cutting any trees down, not without a court case, and that could take years."

"They are not part of your tradition," Harriet said.

"What? What do you mean?" Elyse asked.

"When I was brought here from my lands, there were only one or two trees, there was no forest. The forest grew from the curse, from evil magic. It only grew because my blood spilled here, my blood spilled on the twigs and seeds of the small pine tree. You are fighting to save something that is evil, that stands only to keep the K'aas protected." Harry turned to Mat, who nodded.

"This forest, these woods, would be better cut down, they would be better destroyed for all time," he said. "Plant trees if you like, but make them not pines, make them not the same. They should be burned down if you do not cut them down, they are a scourge on the land."

"Do you not see that no creature lives there, no deer walk there, no hawk flies there?" Luca whispered. "They are not for your people, they are only for evil, and they should go."

"But if they're cut down, the wood will be used to make houses and furniture and stuff," Simon frowned. "Wouldn't those things be cursed, if they use the cursed woods?"

Harry shook her head, her blonde curls bouncing in the light. "The curse will be broken today, and the evil removed. Is that not right, She Who Seeks?"

Seeka nodded. "Yes, yes I believe it will. What do you need me to do?"

"We need you to take us to the curse, where you said the words, where you made the sacrifice. We need to break the figures, we need to say the words, and we need to summon the K'aas."

"Wait, what?' Simon moved so he could see Harry better. "Why do we have to summon that thing?"

"You must confront it, as you did last time. You need to present the talisman to it, you need to fire it as you did last time," Mat said.

"I… I don't know how I did that. I, ah, jeez," Simon looked around for his brother, panic burning in his belly. "I didn't know what I did back then, I don't know if I can do it again!"

"You can do it, uncle of this girl," Harry's face smiled at him. "You are also a warrior, of strong blood, and strong heart. If you trust in yourself, you will prevail."

"So where are we going, Mama?" Running Bear asked.

"I made the curse in my room, but I did not say the words there." She looked at her son and reached out to stroke his face. "I spoke the words when you were in town, my son. I took my pony, my dear old pony, and I rode him to the edge of the woods. I cut his throat there and said the words. I took his blood and sealed the curse."

"The woods? How're we going to get to the woods?" Peter threw his hands in the air. "There's no way we're getting past those things!"

"Where are the clay figures, She Who Seeks?" Luca asked.

"They are in my room. I didn't know how to make them myself, my hands," she lifted her hands, so frail, her knuckles twisted and gnarled, her fingers bent. "I bought the figures from the gift shop in town, they are made by local artists, and some from the kids at the high school. I thought they would do, they're clay, and they're hand made."

"It makes sense now," Lisa gasped. "That's why it's attacking the town, you used clay figures made by other people!"

"Okay, let's get to your room, we need to get there now," Ben said. "C'mon, everyone, I'll help Luca."

"We must make haste," Mat said. "The K'aas is advancing, it will arrive here soon."

"What about my brother?" Simon's voice was high-pitched, panicky. "I can't do anything without my brother!"

"Yes, he should come. The *Kimen* cannot yet enter," Harry told them. "We all need to come, there may be need of anyone here."

"Are you sure?" Sam called over his shoulder.

"We are sure," Luca whispered, and Alex, Ayden and Sam followed the others out of the office. The hallway led them to another hallway, and Running Bear opened the door to his wing. Everyone filtered in behind him, with Ben pushing Luca's chair. Running Bear locked the door behind them. They were standing in a warm, brightly decorated living room, indigenous paintings on the wall, and throw rugs and weavings on the sofas in bright colors of red and yellow, bright blues and soft browns.

"Follow me," Seeka turned and led them down a short hall, the door to her room was open. Her room was decorated in the same style as the living room, the bed covered in a deer skin, and a chair with the weavings was in the corner. Seeka walked to the window, and pulled the curtains open, falling backwards as she did, a cry of alarm on her lips.

The eyeless people stood at the window, their heads no longer hanging low, they looked as if they were watching Seeka, moving their heads to track her movements. Sam pointed his gun at them, "Get back!" he ordered.

"The figures, the clay figures, they are on the sill," Seeka gasped.

Running Bear didn't hesitate, he stepped over and scooped up the little figures, carrying them back into the living room. He placed them on a dining table that was against a wall at the side of the room. Zoey picked one up, and her face scrunched with confusion.

"These are the figures you used?" Elyse picked up a small clay figure in the shape of a clown. "They're cartoon creatures, horses, and cow people, and a dog, a fat man, these are what made the thing chase everyone?"

"I knew they had to be clay figures, there was nothing in the tradition to say what they had to look like," Seeka said. "They worked; the creature came back."

"They did not work the way you wanted," Mat told her. "The curse was not performed correctly, and many people have died for this error."

Seeka looked shocked. "All I did was call it back, I didn't want to kill anyone, I wanted to scare them, to frighten them off. That's why I used comic characters, not real people. I thought it would stop the K'aas from killing anybody."

"Seriously, lady?" Sam snorted. "You thought recalling a killing supernatural creature wouldn't turn out to be another murder spree?"

"Well, I did not plan it to kill, but I did not really care," Seeka shrugged. "These white people are tearing down our traditional forest, and no, I didn't care."

"Mama, we are going to have a serious talk when all this is over." Running Bear looked at Mat. "So, we need to break these things up? Is that right?"

"Yes, but not you. They need to be broken by this girl, this Harriet. I will take a step back, now, and let her do it."

Harry closed her eyes, then they snapped open again, and she gulped a huge breath before looking around at everyone. "Oh my gosh, you have no idea how crazy that is! Like, she was in my head, and she was me, but she wasn't me!" Harry gushed. "I was like, woah, and then, wow!"

"Um, Harry, I don't think we really have time for this right now," Ayden pointed to the table. "You need to smash those things up, so we can get this curse out of the way."

"Yeah, I know, I could hear everything." Harry picked up the little clay dog and tried to break it with her hands. "Argh, I can't break it, it's too hard!"

"Here," Seeka handed her a large chunk of basalt. "This rock is from a fire pit, it's many centuries old. I think it's appropriate to use it."

"Cool!" Harry accepted the rock and brought it down on the first figure, smashing it to pieces. She quickly broke through all of the figures, then sat the rock down. "I guess that's it for me, guys. I'll see you on the other side."

Lisa hugged her daughter. "I love you spud."

"Be careful, pumpkin," Sam whispered.

"I will ensure she is safe," Harry said, but she was no longer Harry.

"You can't really do that, though, can you?" Lisa smiled grimly.

"I will do everything that is possible to ensure she is safe," Harry smiled reassuringly at Lisa.

"What now?" Simon asked.

"We need to summon the K'aas," Luca said. "We can do this for you. When the K'aas is here, the uncle of the girl will face it with the talisman as the girl and her father recite the words that ends the curse. Then it is done. It will be over."

"And you, what happens to you three?" Zoey asked. "Will you be leaving my brothers, and her?"

"We do not know," Harry looked at Mat and Luca. "We have not the lore to tell us this."

"We need to summon the K'aas from the outside of this building," Luca whispered.

"Why?" Peter looked shocked. "It's not safe out there, the fog is right up to the windows!"

"The house is still protected by the sigils. The K'aas can not enter."

"How can we go outside safely?" Simon asked.

"The people that wear the medallions. They can form a guard around us, they can keep us safe."

"Take the medallions from our necks, we will not need them for now," Luca whispered.

"Give them to Alex and Ayden," Sam said. "Keep them safe while they hold back the walking corpses."

"Take mine as well," Seeka said. "I can't keep anyone safe, I'm too old. I'll wait inside with this lady." She took Lisa's arm. "We can watch from the inside."

"Let's go. We have no time to waste." Peter led them back down the hallway to his office.

"The windows here are actually French doors, they open out onto the verandah. Will that do?"

"As long as we are on the ground, we will be able to summon the K'aas," Mat said.

"Wait, hang on, what about the words? I need to know what to say," Sam looked worried.

"When it is time, we will help you with the words. Do not be worried," Harry told him.

"Are we ready?" Ben looked around, noting the deputies tucking the medallions under their shirts.

"Ready as we'll ever be," Sam said. "You okay, Simon?"

Simon had the larger talisman around his neck, the stone glinting and softly shining in the daylight. He kept reaching up to touch it, then pulling his hand away as if it were hot.

"Simon?" Sam repeated. "Are you with me?"

"What? Oh, yes, I'm here, I mean, I'm ready, yeah."

"Let's go," Ben pushed the doors open, the fog rolled and drew back, and as Ben and Peter walked out, the fog pulled away, parting to let them through. Ayden and Alex went next, then Sam and Simon, the fog opening, swirling around them, but not touching them. Running Bear walked through the doors, taking his place at the front.

The three teens moved out next, Mat pushing Luca's chair into the circle the others made, and Sam turned back to Lisa. "Shut the doors, don't open them till this is done, okay?"

Lisa nodded and pulled the doors closed. Elyse and Zoey were to one side of her, Seeka on the other, and they stood there, watching as the others stepped off the verandah.

The fog opened as they walked, but closed behind them, swirling at about waist height. The teens were in the middle, and Elyse gasped.

"Luca is standing up!" Zoey exclaimed. "How is he doing that, Mom?"

"I... I don't know. It must be the spirit inside him."

Running Bear moved the chair back and the teens stood together, holding hands, eyes closed. Their mouths were moving, but Lisa couldn't hear anything. They stood like that for a few minutes, then threw their heads back, chanting into the sky.

"Look!" cried Seeka, pointing behind the group on the lawn.

The fog was higher behind the group, reaching above the surrounding trees and obscuring everything.

Everything except the tall shape, the thin shape, gradually moving closer, its long arms waving as it approached the group. Lisa felt herself take a step back inadvertently, her heart pounding in her chest. She never thought she would face this horror again, never thought her daughter would be forced to face the creature one more time.

The teenagers dropped hands and turned to Simon.

"It is time for you to act, uncle of this girl," Harry said. "I shall step back now and let this girl work to say the words. You are at the end, now. You are going to finish this, and you will be restored."

Simon looked at Harry, confusion darkening his face. "Restored? What do you mean?"

"It's getting closer!" Ben looked at Simon. "Whatever you're going to do, you better do it now!"

"Those other things are getting closer, too," Running Bear looked around at the figures approaching.

"The fog isn't staying back the same way, either," Alex was holding his medallion as he sat down on the grass.

Ayden swayed and fell, rolling into a sitting position.

"It's happening again," Alex looked at his father. "I'm feeling weak, drained by that thing. I can't stand up."

The fog lapped at him, touching him and swirling around him, doing the same to Ayden.

"Dad?"

"It's okay, Alex, just sit there, this shouldn't take too long now."

Simon took a deep breath, the talisman in his hands, the crunchy chain around his neck. The K'aas came closer, the fog parting to allow everyone a clearer look at the thing they were facing.

"Get behind me!" Simon shouted, holding the talisman out in front of him, pulling it tight on the chain. Nothing was happening, no glow, no light beam, no electric power. The K'aas was closer, and it began to grow, it was towering over the group now, the rough black body a thing borne of nightmares.

"That thing has no face," Peter gasped. "It's just plain white, no eyes, nothing."

"Look at its back, it's growing more arms!" Ben moved back behind Simon.

The K'aas had sprouted more arms, many more arms, they waved like great snakes from its back. It had not

271

stopped growing, the thing looked thirty or more feet high, and it started to reach out for Simon.

"The medallion's not working!" Simon cried.

"Take your hands off it, Simon! Let it sit on your heart!" Sam called.

Simon let go of the talisman, letting it fall back onto his chest, and immediately he felt the power from the thing. A surge of pure energy passed through his body, more powerful than he remembered, more powerful than he thought he could bear. Finally, mercifully, it started to glow.

A bright beam shot forth from the stone and hit the creature in the chest, a white, pure, blinding light that burned into the K'aas.

"It is time," Harry turned to her father. "I will step back now and allow you to say the words, to end the curse."

Harry closed her eyes, shrugged off her spirit visitor, and turned to look at the creature. She stumbled backwards, her feet tangling, and she fell, her rear hitting the ground hard. Sam leapt forward and grabbed her, helping her to her feet.

"Oh my god, I feel so weak, so drained."

"It's the thing, the monster," Alex gasped. "It's doing it again, we are getting weaker, like last time."

"We need to say the words, Dad, we need to do it now." Harry was hanging onto Sam to keep herself upright.

"I don't know the words. I don't know what to say!" Sam looked at the creature. "They never told me!"

"We will help you, father of this girl," Luca stepped closer to Sam, his body stiff, his arms bent. "I will whisper them into your ear, and you will say them aloud, with your daughter."

"Look at the K'aas! It's turning white!" Peter pointed at the monster, and he was right, the rough black body was draining of color and it was shrinking, dramatically dropping in height.

"Now, Daddy!" Harry started to speak, the tongue foreign, a language Sam couldn't understand. In his ear, Lucas whispered the words he had to say, the language was the same as Harry was speaking, but the words were different. Sam repeated each word, yelling them at the creature, hoping he was saying them right, praying it would work, praying the creature would fall.

Simon seemed to be glowing himself, he was surrounded with multicolored lights, and the air hissed and popped with static electricity. His hair was standing on end, and he stretched his arms wide, electric currents seemed to dance along his arms, snapping and crackling around his fingers. The monster was now only seven or eight feet tall, the extra arms had withdrawn, and it slumped forward, the faceless head cocked to one side, the two remaining arms hanging by its side. The white fog was withdrawing, then stopped flowing backwards and started to disappear.

Harry stopped speaking, and Luca stepped back, no more words were whispered into Sam's ear. The talisman continued to glow, sending the brilliant beam into the K'aas. The creature shrunk even more, diminishing, it was now smaller than Simon and it continued to shrink. The fog had completely faded; there was no sign of the glowing white mist at all. Simon leaned forward as the creature shrunk down into the grass, the beam still firing at it.

Mat walked forward and stood beside the shrinking K'aas, waiting, looking at the thing that was the object of everyone's fear. The beam from the talisman started to darken, from bright white to blue, then gray, then it stopped altogether.

Mat reached down and picked something up, holding it in his closed hand. Simon, drained and dizzy, fell to one knee and felt the strong grip of his brother as he tried to help him to his feet. He looked up at his brother's face, a face so like his own, and he smiled. "I don't feel restored," he said, and he blacked out, Sam catching him as he fell.

"What do you have there, Mat?" Peter asked, and Mat opened his hand to reveal a stone. It was very similar to the one on the front of the talisman, but this one had black flecks and streaks running through it which seemed to swirl and move when you looked at it.

"Simon, my god, Simon, he's not breathing!" Sam laid his brother on the grass, all else forgotten as he focused on his brother.

Alex ran forward and felt for a pulse, shaking his head when he found none. Sam started chest compressions, worry lining his face as he pumped Simon's chest.

"Still no pulse," Alex said, with Sam continuing to pump. Lisa opened the doors and ran out, kneeling beside the men on the ground. She lifted Simon's eyelids and she, too, felt for a pulse.

"What do I do?" Sam gasped between compressions. "What do I do? He's not breathing! This isn't working!"

Lisa placed a hand on Sam's arm to stop him. "He's gone, Sam."

Sam rocked back on his feet, falling to his rear, his face in shock. "It can't be, it can't be…"

Mat walked forward and touched Sam, waiting for the man to look at him before speaking.

"He will be restored, as we promised." Harry and Luca joined him, and they all kneeled around the prone figure on the ground. The three teens closed their eyes and began to chant in the language used before, their soft voices the only sound in the garden.

Mat opened his eyes and lifted the talisman, centering it onto the middle of Simon's chest, the stone face down. The kids continued to chant while he did this, their voices as one, slowly gaining in volume, becoming louder and louder, and static electricity prickled the kin of all those who watched. Mat placed the K'aas stone on the back of the talisman with an audible click as it set itself into the gold medallion. Mat removed his hand and the stone flashed and glowed, a crack of electricity splitting the air like lightning.

Sam grabbed Lisa's arm and scuttled backwards, Alex doing the same on the other side. The stone fired bright blue fingers of electricity into the sky, and Simon's body shuddered and rocked with the power coursing through it, the electricity sparking from his fingers, his hair standing on end, his feet drumming an irregular rhythm on the grass.

The teenagers joined hands and slowly rose, a smooth movement, perfectly in time with one another, their hands over the vibrating body. Their chanting was now as loud as they could speak, their heads thrown back, the electricity surrounding them, sparking and crackling with a primal power.

A sudden clap of lightning from the sky hit the talisman, and the teens dropped hands, their voices silent, their faces flushed. The talisman was now quiet, all power had left the air, and Simon lay still. The scent of ozone hung heavily around him, a reminder of the power that had just coursed through him. The children stumbled a little, seeming confused, and then they fell to the grass. Elyse raced to her fallen sons as everyone crept in a little closer, not sure if it was safe, not sure what to do.

Simon groaned and Sam grabbed him, cradling his head in his lap.

"Let me go, brother," Simon struggled to sit up. "What're you doing? Here, help me to my feet, will you?"

"Oh my god, Simon," Sam grabbed his brother and hugged him, sobbing into his shoulder.

"I'm okay, Sam, I just passed out. Got a little lightheaded, is all."

Sam laughed and helped his brother to his feet, wiping his eyes as he looked him up and down. "You feel okay? You sure you're alright?"

"Stop fussin' like a momma hen, I'm fine!"

Harry and Mat stood up, and Lisa grabbed her daughter, checking her for any burns or marks left from the electricity bursts. "I'm fine, Mom, and I'm me, too," Harry told her.

Mat waved his father off as he tried to check him but gave Harry a lopsided grin. "I'm me, too, I guess. I kinda heard most of what was going on, but it was weird, like a dream."

"More like a movie," Luca said, and Elyse burst into tears. She was sitting on the lawn with his head on her lap, and he struggled to sit up. Mat dropped to his knees and helped him, Luca giving his brother a crooked smile, his eyes bright and happy. "Hello brother."

Mat started to cry as well and wrapped his arms around his frail brother in a hug. "I've waited so long to hear your voice, bro."

Luca pushed him back, his movements jerky and not very well controlled, but his face was jubilant. "I know, Mat, you told me so many times. I can't tell you how much I tried to answer you. But I heard everything you said."

Zoey squealed and grabbed her brother, kissing him all over his head.

"We did it, didn't we? We stopped the K'aas?" Running Bear looked at everyone, his voice shaky with emotion.

"Yessir, I think we did!" Alex was standing, Ayden beside him. From the side of the house they were joined by the people from inside, Mat's friends and the parents that had spent the night.

"We definitely stopped it," Harry said. "That last bit wasn't just restoring Uncle Simon, it was binding the K'aas back into the medallion. This is like one of those happy endings in a movie," Harry looked at her dad. "It doesn't seem real. I'm like, waiting for the music to start and the end credits to roll."

"Let's just take the win for now, pumpkin, and be happy for a moment. Don't forget there's a heap of people missing, including your school friends. There's no happy ending for any of them." Sam's cell began to buzz in his pocket as it delivered multiple messages which had been blocked from being received earlier.

As he pulled it out of his pocket it rang and he answered it. "Shirl, are you all okay there?"

CHAPTER THIRTY-NINE

The fog followed the music as the sun set and the town was now blanketed in white. This time the mist didn't stay low to the ground, it covered the houses and buildings along the street. The music had faded as the fog had grown, the town was now eerily silent, and the fog was so thick that Paul couldn't see more than a foot or two beyond the windows of the jailhouse. The deputies left for their own homes a few hours ago after nothing more than the fog had arrived, and Paul was in the jailhouse alone. He stoked the fire that he built when the fog first rolled in. Even though it was in the middle of summer the strange white mist had brought a chill with it that was dry and bone deep. Paul shivered as he threw another log into the potbelly stove and shut the door, standing up to rub his hands above it. He was alarmed by the music and the mist, even more so once his adopted son reacted with such terror to it. Was he right? Was the boy correct?

He knew the child was different all these years. All the times Paul thought he was silently mourning his family, was he really communicating with the thing in the woods? Was he somehow attuned to it? And why did he feel connected to it, apart from the fact that it had taken his family, he never had any contact with the thing. And God knew he had never been back into the woods. Paul was sure of that. Without a doubt. So why was the kid so certain they were all doomed? And where was Hank? Why had Hank wandered off like he was hypnotized? And then to just disappear? And the screams, oh lord, the screams. It sounded like every pain and fear and sorrow was bundled up and projected into those terrifying calls. Paul feared he would go mad if he had to listen to those calls every night.

A tap on the window startled him and he looked over to see who it was but could not make out the shape by the window. The figure tapped again, and Paul walked to the door. He checked his handgun before he unlocked and opened the heavy wooden door and gasped when he saw Hank standing there.

"God, man, where have you been? We searched for you for hours." He threw the door wide and smiled at his friend. "Where did you go? What happened?"

Hank was facing the window, head hanging down as he started to turn towards Paul's voice. He turned slowly, his movements jerky and stiff. His hat was missing and his hair disheveled. His shirt had one sleeve rolled up and his guns were gone, though his gun belt was still in place.

"Hank, are you okay?" Paul stepped out onto the boardwalk. Hank's head still hung low, looking at the ground and Paul saw that his deputy was missing his boots. "Where are your boots, Hank?"

Hank took a step towards him, still jerky, still moving strangely. "Hank...what is it? Did you hit your head?"

Paul felt his stomach lurch when Hank finally looked up.

His eyes were gone. There were only the reddened sockets, no eyelids, no eyeballs, just the empty holes and cheeks splashed with blood. Paul took a shaky step backwards. "Hank, what happened to you? Come inside, I'll get Doc Farley..."

The deputy opened his mouth in an eerie grin. All his teeth were gone. His bloodied gums were a stark contrast to his pale skin and Paul took another step back and stumbled, falling heavily onto the boards. He tried to move backwards, his boots failing to gain purchase as he scrambled to get away from the mutilated creature that had been his friend.

Hank grinned wider and lunged at Paul as he attempted to scramble away.

The sheriff's scream was loud and long but went unattended. The town just thought it was another of the screams that haunted them like on the previous night. The phone rang, giving everyone a fright. Some cried out, and someone crashed to the floor as they fell back in their chair. The lights blinked on and the air conditioner purred to life.

"Something's happening," Shirl stood up, placing his coffee on the desk as he stood.

"I'm thinking it's something good," Mike replied.

Orville answered the phone, and Michelle hurried out to the reception desk as more lines lit up. "Looks like we have life back, at least."

"*Guys, you have to come out and see this,*" Michelle's voice called over the intercom.

The deputies pushed through the swinging door, followed by several parents. The grill shutters allowed a small amount of vision through the rungs, and everyone walked to the shutters, finding Michelle already there, peering through. They all found a place along the front, where they could see.

The fog had gone, there was not even a wisp of mist to be seen. What they could see, however, was a street littered with dead cattle, all laying where they fell. Here and there was a dog, a horse, and a few cats, all as dead as the others, all missing their eyes. Opposite the station there was a man standing on the sidewalk, looking up and down the street, shaking his head.

"That guy, see him?" Jacob asked. "He's got eyes, he's a normal person."

"Let's get these doors open. Michelle, answer those phones, Joan, if you can, please help her. Maybe Aaron and Jacob, you guys can grab some calls too. I'm going to call the boss," Shirl looked back at the scene on the street. "I have no idea how we're gonna clean this up, or even what sort of reports we need to write."

"Holy mother of fuck," Mike gasped. "There's dead people out there too. Lots of them!"

Shirl turned back and looked through the grill as the Sheriff answered his cell.

"*Shirl, are you all okay there?*"

"No boss. Not even close," he answered. "You guys need to finish up whatever you did and get back here. There's bodies, and dead cattle, jeez, boss, it's like a bomb went off here."

"*I'll be there as soon as I can, Shirl. Just hang on and do the best you can.*"

The grill started to rise, chugging slowly up to the ceiling, and Mike could see the street more clearly now. It didn't make it any better. The man across the road had walked across to the police station and was waiting for it to open, standing right next to the doors.

"That's Evan Blake, from the motor shop," Harmen ducked under the grill to open the doors.

He let the man into the foyer, and Evan stood there, his back to the street, his face pale, shaken, like he was in shock.

"You okay Mr. Blake?" Harmen asked him.

Evan looked at Harmen, his eyes didn't seem to focus on the deputy, though, and his lips were quivering. "Outside…"

"Yes, sir, there's a lot of dead cattle outside. The Sheriff will be back soon, he can explain everything."

"No, um, not the cattle," Evan waved vaguely, and shook his head. "In my shop, no, *at* my shop, I got a rather long, covered area, you know? Well, under that, maybe stacked two, three feet high, there are bodies. Lots of bodies."

"Cows?" Mike asked, joining the two.

"No sir, not cows." Evan looked at Mike, and he seemed to recognize him. "They are all dead, Mike. Bodies of people, all stacked up under the covered bit, and they're all dead."

"Come out the back, Mr. Blake, we'll get you some coffee, and one of the boys'll grab your statement, okay?" Mike nodded his head, trying to get Evan to copy him. "Evan? Earth to Evan?" Mike clicked his fingers in front of Evan's face, and the man smiled. "Luke? Luke, take Mr. Blake out the back and get him some coffee, would yah?"

Luke took the shocked man by the arm and led him through the swinging doors. Mike looked at the front again, staring at the front door. There were dozens of people there, waiting to get in.

"We better let them in, Mike," Shirl told him. "We can't put this off any longer."

"Hey, our kids have called," one of the parents came through the swinging doors. "Oh shit. Okay, I'll get people on coffee duty, and get the chairs lined up. Let them in when you're ready."

"I don't know if I'm gonna kiss that guy, or deputize him," Shirl said.

Mike shook his head. "How about both?"

EPILOGUE

"Did you see the paper?" Lisa grabbed her purse from the table.

"Yeah, I did. Reporting's fair, for the most part." Sam filled the carry mug with hot coffee and screwed the top on. "I think I look fat and old in the picture, though."

"Well, I think you look very handsome. And they're right, you *are* a hero, saving all those people from the deadly gas leak a month ago," Lisa smiled as Sam grimaced.

"Simon is the real hero. Him and the kids," Sam sighed. "If I was a hero, I would have stopped the K'aas before it killed over a hundred people."

"You all are, honey. Oh, thank you!" Lisa accepted the coffee and a kiss. Sam handed her a brown paper bag, rolled over at the top.

"Cheese salad on rye, an apple, and a twinkie," Sam smiled at her. "You okay to take Simon to his interview?"

"If you're not, I can take a cab," Simon pointed over his shoulder at the living room. "We don't have to put up with that every morning, do we?"

Lisa looked at Harry and Mat, they were on the main sofa in the living room, making out. "Hey, you two, take a breath! Mat, you sure you're okay to drop Harry at the diner on your way to your summer job?"

"Yeah, sure Mom, it's why he comes over so early!" Harry said, jumping up.

"I'm happy to drive her, Mrs., um, Harry's mom," Mat blushed, the red cheeks complimenting his copper-colored skin.

"Please call me Lisa, I've told you that before. You know I don't mind you coming over before work now and then, let's just not make it every day, okay?"

Mat glanced at Harry but nodded. "Sure. I can make it every second day."

"Don't forget, Mom, I'm going to Mat's after work to ride horses," Harry said. "I'll stay for dinner, too. Mat can bring me home."

"I'm not sure I'm one hundred percent on board with my daughter having a boyfriend yet," grumbled Sam. "But at least he's driving her around, saves me leaving for work too early."

"If I get the job today, I could be the one driving," Simon stood and let his brother straighten his tie.

"They were right, weren't they?" Harry tilted her head, reminiscent of the spirit that possessed her. "You *are* restored. You and Luca, you're both normal."

Sam frowned. "He's always been normal."

"And Luca has a long way to go getting his muscles and limbs working right, but he's on the way. Braces on his teeth and all," Mat grabbed Harry's hand, then kissed her on the cheek. "Funny to have him talking, though. It's weird having a twin brother, I mean, a normal one."

"Oh, I don't know," Simon winked at Sam. "It's not all bad."

ACKNOWLEDGEMENTS:

With thanks, as always, to my children. You are my inspiration.

I am so grateful to my publisher and editor Peter Blakey-Novis and his wonderful partner in crime Leanne, without whom this book would never have eventuated.

Thank you to my wonderful friends, Helen, Joan, Alison, Julia, and Vikki. Sorry I killed off some of you, nothing personal.

Thank you to Mary for being my practice reader, your feedback was beyond useful.

Thank you to Todd, for your invaluable support and letting me bounce some plot ideas and possible titles off you.

Thank you to all the wonderful readers who have left a review, you have no idea how special and inspirational they truly are. Please leave a review if you can, if it's not too much trouble and you enjoyed this book. Know always that I am inspired and sustained by them and wouldn't be able to continue without them.

Also from Red Cape Publishing

Anthologies:

Elements of Horror Book One: Earth
Elements of Horror Book Two: Air
Elements of Horror Book Three: Fire
Elements of Horror Book Four: Water
A is for Aliens: A to Z of Horror Book One
B is for Beasts: A to Z of Horror Book Two
C is for Cannibals: A to Z of Horror Book Three
D is for Demons: A to Z of Horror Book Four
E is for Exorcism: A to Z of Horror Book Five

Short Story Collections:

Embrace the Darkness by P.J. Blakey-Novis
Tunnels by P.J. Blakey-Novis
The Artist by P.J. Blakey-Novis
Karma by P.J. Blakey-Novis
The Place Between Worlds by P.J. Blakey-Novis
Short Horror Stories by P.J. Blakey-Novis

Novelettes:

The Ivory Tower by Antoinette Corvo

Novellas:

Four by P.J. Blakey-Novis
Dirges in the Dark by Antoinette Corvo

Novels:

Madman Across the Water by Caroline Angel
The Curse Awakens by Caroline Angel
The Broken Doll by P.J. Blakey-Novis
The Broken Doll: Shattered Pieces by P.J. Blakey-Novis
The Vegas Rift by David F. Gray

Follow Red Cape Publishing

www.redcapepublishing.com
www.facebook.com/redcapepublishing
www.twitter.com/redcapepublish
www.instagram.com/redcapepublishing
www.pinterest.co.uk/redcapepublishing
www.patreon.com/redcapepublishing

Printed in Great Britain
by Amazon

38521938R00159